I0593205

COOL UNDER PRESSURE—UNTIL SHE HITS HIS HOT BUTTON

Knight, iceman head of Sentinel Security. A loner dedicated to the mission. Until he meets Lily, a woman who questions everything he believes. He falls hard and fast for the midwife, but Lily has a stalker. Her ex. Out of fear for her friends and Knight, she runs, leaving Knight angry and betrayed.

Months later, in Africa, terrorists kidnap Lily and Sentinel executes a daring rescue. Home in England, both realise falling in love may not be a choice. But Lily has a secret. A secret that puts Knight on the run. Before they can move forward, Lily's past threatens to destroy their future.

SENSITIVE CONTENT WARNING

Before Lily reaches her happy ending with Knight, her story contains scenes of coercive control preceding domestic abuse. This may be difficult and possibly triggering for some readers, so please take care of your personal safety and emotional well-being and seek support if you need it.

SAVIOUR

SENTINEL SECURITY BOOK 2

ELIZA RENTON

CHAPTER ONE
LONDON, ENGLAND, UK

Knight raised the remote and watched the tv screen fade to black, the same way it had done for the past three weeks. Two a.m. He hadn't slept much since he got back from Africa this last time.

Knight raised his half-empty beer glass at Mike. Twelve long months after he stepped on the IUD that tore him apart, his mate's ghost sat opposite, silently repeating the jackpot question. Why was Seckou still breathing?

Good fucking question. Not for lack of trying on Sentinel's part. This last trip, he could have sworn they had him. But fuck him if the aircraft engine wasn't still hot when the intel reached them. Seckou, the terrorist bastard, had done it again, slithered across the Sahel into Mali without a trace, no opportunity for vengeance.

Knight tipped his glass at his friend and glanced at his watch. Too late to visit Maeve. Most times after a mission, she calmed his adrenaline rush, took the edge off his rage. They had a perfect understanding, but lately not even her talents shifted his black mood.

The empty glass fell from his hand as his eyes drifted shut. When he opened them, Mike had gone, and the fucking pigeons had taken over the trees outside his windows and were creating a racket.

By the time he showered, changed, and made quick work of two pots of coffee, the morning had disappeared. The prospect of showing up late for Kate's birthday lunch only compounded his shit attitude.

"Fucking rain," He cursed, the heel of his hand thumping the steering wheel. Hail, the size of golf balls, swept across the Thames, and pounded vehicles butted three-deep to the curb.

Kate Gibson, Mike's sister, rated as one of a few people he'd bother trying to navigate this bollocks.

Growing up with religious zealots for parents, any celebration was a stretch. A test. Birthdays and Christmas were the devil's work. At school, it sucked. Other kids never invited him to their parties because weirdo never reciprocated. *Yep.* Kate had better appreciate his bloody sacrifice and have a beer waiting.

Come to think of it, the last party he'd attended was Kate and Doc's engagement. There had been this stunning blonde, slim, shy, long eyelashes, pouty lips. Damned if he remembered her name.

A horn blared as he slid into a miracle park close to Kate's. "Yeah, yeah. Working on it." The impatient sod on his tail returned his one-finger salute

Legs stiff, Knight extricated himself from the front seat of his MGB and cursed. *I hate fucking rain.* He shrugged, lifted his collar closer to his chin, and ran the short distance to Doc's house.

Inside, people stood wall to wall. Given his lack of sleep, he had a bit of catching up to do. Right now, their voices were a decibel or two above comfortable. Knight shook the hail from his clothes, stamped his feet on the mat and looked around for that beer.

"Over here," Crystal yelled. Spanner's lady waved him over to join her and the others. Kate, Doc, and Snake, their Comms man. Sentinel's Alpha team.

"You made it. I was about to send out a search party." Kate pecked him on the cheek. "Great to see you. Where's your plus one?"

"Just me." Knight tapped the tip of her nose, mainly because it irritated the fiery redhead. It was fun seeing her bristle.

"Leave the boss alone, sweetheart." Doc's possessive arm wrapped possessively around his wife's waist.

"Not likely. I need his opinion."

"On what?" Doc asked, nibbling the side of Kate's neck.

"Never you mind. Come on, Knight, keep me company while I wait for Lily." Kate tugged his arm and dragged him to the door.

Spanner snatched a beer from the table next to him as they passed. "Here. You may need this."

"Thanks. Totally fucked." Knight raised the bottle at Doc and followed Kate.

Couples surrounded him. First, Crystal and Spanner, now Kate and Doc. Wedding bells before too long, if he had to guess, leaving him and Snake the sorry stags tossing back post-mission shots. "If I didn't know better, I'd say you were trying to set me up, Ms Gibson."

"You should be so lucky. Why don't you try it Knight? A relationship." Kate laughed.

How many times had they had this conversation, his answer the same? He loved all women. He couldn't settle on one. "I'll leave it to you lovebirds." Still single at thirty-six, thanks very much, and no matter how hard Kate flogged marriage, he liked it that way. Maeve understood him. No promises, no finger rock.

"Trust me. There's a woman out there for you. When you least expect it, she'll waltz round the corner and knock you for six." Kate grinned.

Knight crossed his arms over his chest. "Me and one woman. Never going to happen, sunshine. It's enough that you and Crystal have my men twisted around your pretty little fingers."

The significant difference between the two women and his mother? They would never be slaves to domestic duties. Alone for months, the CWA bake sale the highlight of his mother's year.

"You talk big. I'll tell your bride you said that, just before she glides down the aisle." Kate teased.

He couldn't resist a snort. "You happy standing in the rain? Surely Lily can find your door."

"Yes. She shouldn't be much longer, I…" Her voice trailed away.

Odd she rarely looked unsure, but something had her frowning this afternoon. "You worried she won't show?" he teased. "One less present for the table by the door."

Kate punched his upper arm. "A little. She's been through hell lately. I hope she hasn't got cold feet."

Didn't sound good. His curiosity piqued, but he needed to sleep more than a date. "Sorry, Kate, I can't stay, but I didn't want you to think I'd forgotten you." Knight reached in his pocket for the small present, cutting her off before she protested. Thank God Crystal rescued him and shopped for him. He had no clue what she'd bought. "Happy Birthday."

Distracted, Kate took the gift and thumped his arm. "Thanks."

Guess he was that bloody miserable running before he finished his beer. Good job his black moods didn't faze Maeve.

"There she is. You have me. Maybe you can cheer each other up."

Following the direction of Kate's waving finger, he watched Lily draw closer. Now he remembered. Despite the fucking rain, his afternoon just improved.

A blue dress, neckline low enough to tease, clung to her slim body. Six degrees, and she wore no coat! Strands of natural blonde hair whipped across her face. His fingers itched to play in the sea of sunshine.

"Hi, Kate. Sorry, I'm late." She tilted her umbrella. "There'll be a rainbow if we're lucky. I can't remember how it happens, but isn't it magic when it does?"

Their gazes met and the only thing supernatural were her blue eyes. They swept him away with the strength of a stormy sea. Rain raindrops kissing her creamy skin were damn lucky.

"Kate. Emergency. Help." Doc yelled from the doorway. "Hi Lily. Glad you made it. Sorry, sweetheart. Spanner can't find the meat."

"Try the big white fridge." Kate rolled her eyes. "Boys. I'd better rescue him. You two are on your own. Play nice, Knight." She rushed off, grinning.

"Lily, right? We met last year, briefly. You were helping Kate and Luke move here."

"Yes. I remember. Nice to see you again." She held out her hand.

Her shy smile, he remembered, peeking over packing boxes, crossed her lips, and she shivered.

"Lose your coat?" Glib even for him. Tentatively, he stepped forward, intending to rub the thin sleeves covering her arms, keep her warm. Something made him stop. He had no problem taking the lead, but he hardly knew her. Instead, he slipped off his jacket and draped it over her shoulders. "It's freezing out here." He cleared his throat. "Let's go inside." *Curiosity was a curse.*

"Perfect idea," she agreed.

Pretty the way her smile blossomed in two words. A light in the darkness. *Shit.* His brain scrambled to find words. Awkward, unsure, her head swivelled towards the door. Perhaps he wasn't the only one debating whether to make a run for it.

"Lily. There you are." A man's voice boomed over Knight's shoulder.

Fantastic. The whole fucking party attracted to them.

"Pete," Lily whispered. "What are you doing here?"

The hairs on the back of his neck bristled. Lily's flinch, hard to miss, but the stranger ignored it. Her unease sealed it. He would hang in a little longer.

"Holsworthy, Peter Holsworthy. I work with Lily's father. And you are?"

"Knight." He cringed at the man's limp handshake. Nose in the air, the slight inflexion in Pete's voice, reminded him of the snot-green officers straight out of Sandhurst, piss-wet behind their arrogant ears.

Experience told him his height could intimidate, so he angled his body, more for Lily's benefit than Pete's, opening the gap between them to give her space.

"Thanks for the coat." Lily slipped it from her shoulders and tugged on the end of her thin sleeves.

He should take her not-so-subtle hint as his cue to leave, but when Arseworthy snatched Lily's forearm hard enough to make her cry out in pain. Knight gripped Pete's shoulder. Added pressure until the dick released her.

Pete's nostrils flared. Lily's chin fell to her chest. Fear, like a fucking halo, hung over her shoulders and he wanted to deck Pete for daring to lay his hand on her.

"Please, Pete." Why was he here threatening to ruin Kate's party? She never bored her or Crystal with the sordid details of her relationship with Pete, but they knew enough, she was sure they would never invite him.

Angry at the two of them, Lily pressed her lips together. She couldn't go anywhere without Pete turning up. Add Knight to the mix and the testosterone levels were through the roof. Frustrated, she tugged at her mother's locket. A present for her tenth birthday. Pete's arms snaked around her waist, preventing her from taking a full breath.

"Why did you wear the blue dress, Lily? You look better in the red one I bought you. It's more flattering, shows less of your..." He jiggled under her ribs and her cheeks flushed.

If it were possible to die of embarrassment, she willed it to happen now. "Pete, you're hurting me." He loved to point out her rounded tummy, no matter how hard she worked at her weight.

"Sorry, babe. Your friend said you were chilly. Just warming you up."

"Thanks, Pete. Have you seen where they set up the bar? I'd love a drink." Hell, she would scull arsenic if it got her away from Pete. This time, the steely gaze from Knight's hooded eyes made her tremble. Humiliated, she smoothed the front of her dress and willed the floor to swallow her whole.

"Now you're talking, babe. A shot to warm that heart of hers, ay, Knight?" He pinched her cheek.

Knight didn't answer, and Pete's smile collapsed. *Damn.*

"Here, miss, over here." Pete pointed his finger at the tray of drinks Crystal carried. "Fizzy stuff for you, babe?"

Crystal spun around and glared at them.

"Thanks," Lily stuttered. If she refused, Pete could get mean. More humiliated by the second, she racked her brain thinking of ways to make him leave without a fuss.

"Where's the hard stuff, sweet stuff?" Pete cackled. "Knight, what's your poison?"

"Sorry, sir, wine, beer, and soft drinks. Spirits are available in the kitchen." Crystal's face remained deadpan as she kept walking. Pete trailed after her.

Lily sighed. "He's not always like this." She shouldn't make excuses for him, but she couldn't risk him losing it, not here. "He's not good in crowds."

"Your husband?"

The jagged scar, etched into Knight's jaw, drew her attention to his full, perfectly sculpted, unsmiling lips. Streaks of grey threaded through his short hair. His eyes, the colour of forged steel, sent a shudder down her spine.

"No. We're not married. Lived together for a while, but I left him three months ago." She laughed nervously. "Not that I'm counting." Lily wiped a non-existent speck from her dress. "My idea. He's not handling it well."

Her hands clenched. Why was she telling him? He didn't want to hear this. She needed air. Fresh air away from everyone's stare. She rubbed her forehead. "Sorry, excuse me for a sec."

"Come with me." Knight placed a finger on her elbow and nodded towards the French windows leading to the garden.

They were halfway there when Pete, a drink balanced in one hand, grabbed her other elbow. A favourite move. The clamp on her ulna nerve guaranteed to make her squirm.

"Hey, enough." Knight thrust between them, breaking Pete's hold. Every pair of eyes focussed on them. What a bloody mess.

"What's it to you, tough guy?" Pete leered at her.

"Pete, please, not here," she pleaded. When Pete drank, there was no reasoning with him.

"Yes, Lily, right fucking here."

She gasped as Pete struck out at Knight. Faster than she could blink, he caught Pete's fist before he made contact. Lips locked in a tight line, he twisted until Pete cried out and buckled at the waist.

"What the hell's going on?" Doc came from nowhere. Spanner by his side.

"Damn." Pete supported his wrist in his other hand. "He broke my wrist. That's assault, shithead. I'll fucking finish you."

"Doubt it," Doc mumbled. "I'm a doctor. Let me look."

"Lily, are you okay?" Kate appeared through the crowd gathered around them. All eyes fixed on them.

"Kate, I'm sorry. I…" *Leave, leave now.* All morning, she told herself, coming to the party was a bad idea. Pete had found her–he always did. She bit her bottom lip and pushed her way between two people. "Please, let me through."

"Lily, wait. Knight, stop her, don't let her leave alone." Kate's words followed her.

"Hey, wait up." He caught her at the gate, held his jacket over her head, sheltering her from the rain.

Teeth chattering, she welcomed the warmth flowing from his broad chest.

"Easy." His breath blew against her cheek, calm against the chaos.

Placing her palm against his chest, she gently pushed, grateful when he budged. He didn't deserve to get mixed up with her and Pete.

"You hungry?" he asked.

She didn't want to be alone. Should she say yes?

"I asked if you were hungry, Lily. Do you like Spanish? Tapas?"

"Not fussed." She glanced over Knight's shoulder, expecting to see Pete charging after them, and sighed with relief when he didn't appear.

"Don't worry. He won't follow us." Knight bent lower, forcing her to meet his gaze.

"How can you be sure?"

"Trust me."

CHAPTER TWO

Thank Christ the hail had eased. The driving, bitter wind pinched and reddened Lily's pale cheeks as they escaped Doc's house. Not usually one for romantic sentiment, but the glow suited her.

"C'mon, not much further," Knight said, drawing Lily further under his coat.

The smell of oranges mellowed by a hint of jasmine teased his nostrils. Lily's scent, must be her shampoo, lingered between them as they bolted the last hundred yards to the restaurant.

He leaned in, tempted to hook an arm around her waist, draw her slim body closer. Only the flash of warning in her blue eyes stopped him.

Lily laughed. Shrill. Nervous. Comical didn't figure in his skill set. A half-hour ago, he had been within a breath of decking her ex. He put it down to adrenaline. The rush could do strange things to a person.

"*Lo siento, señor,* we close now. Dinner is at six. Do you wish to make a reservation?" The waiter guarding the restaurant's doorway shook his head and hooked a thumb into the apron tied around his narrow hips. Ready to do battle, his pointy shoe hammered the concrete.

Nice try. A focussed out-breath would send the numpty tumbling faster than the leaves swirling in the gale. Knight inhaled, prepared to bribe him to stay open if it meant spending another hour with Lily.

"It's okay. I'm not that hungry." Lily stepped onto the street before he could wedge his foot in the door and prove he didn't have to throw a punch to get his point across.

"Hey Lily, slow down. I didn't get any of Kate's cake. I could eat a grizzly bear." He laughed, a lame attempt to lighten the mood. Make her smile.

And Lily didn't disappoint. His cock led the rest of him, twitching in appreciation at the time it took to carve dimples into her cheeks. Perfect hollows for the stroke of his tongue. Making her do it again became a mission. Knight stroked his chin, puzzled by his fascination with the woman. *Call Maeve. Straight forward, Maeve.*

"Funny. You don't look as though you're starving, I'd say the opposite." Lily's perfectly shaped eyebrows crowned her eyes, hinting at appreciation for the time he spent in the gym.

Hell, all that sweat. There had to be perks. Rough and tumble with Lily? Tempting if he was in spit of her league. Delightful. Vulnerable. Too fragile for the carnal pleasures he had in mind.

"Man needs meat." He beat his chest to prove his point.

"I bet. If you are honestly hungry, there's a small restaurant round the corner. I've not eaten there, and the food might be terrible, but it's open twenty-four hours. You game?"

Oh, Lily. Game? The rougher, the better.

The drizzle fell heavier as they walked, and despite the jacket draped over her shoulders, Lily shivered. A gentle tug on her arm and finally her head hit his chest. Score one for the big guy. He pulled her under the shelter of a large oak. "Wait here while I fetch the car."

"No, it's okay. The place isn't far. We won't melt. Grab my hand. Let's run for it."

Home. His fingers, entwined with Lily's, agreed. His mind

searched for an anchor. A reason not to feel as though he just jumped out of a plane without a fucking parachute.

Five minutes later, they stood in front of a hole in the wall. *Abra-Kebabra*, the neon joke, flashed above a half-open door.

"You do eat kebabs? According to Crystal's boyfriend, this place has the best for miles."

Spanner, gourmet extraordinaire, the man who couldn't find the meat. He should have guessed. "Are you kidding? Let me at it." He hadn't eaten a kebab since Doc and Spanner found domestic bliss and pub crawls fell off the team's post-mission agenda. But watching the rain drip off Lily's cute button nose, she could ask him for the moon, and he would search the galaxy to bring it to her.

Lily tilted her head, exposing the long, graceful curve of her neck, and checked the menu above them. Drawn to her like dots to a football, Knight braced against the counter to stop from stepping closer.

"They have wine. Care for a glass? My treat!" Her eyes sparkled and dimmed in the space of a single breath. He hated that.

"Sure. Where's the list?"

"Red or white, small, medium or large?" Lily grinned.

His turn to be embarrassed. Bluer than the Mediterranean, on a summer's day, her eyes searched for a place to rest. They settled for the spot between his nose and mouth. Lids lowered. Guarded. One hand stroked the stubble on his chin. Did Lily prefer clean-shaven men? "Red. Large."

"Well done. Two glasses, please. A large for my friend and a small for me."

"No problem, pretty lady," said the man, sporting the shit-eating grin. Smitten too.

"Cheesy chips?" Lily asked. Her enthusiasm for fat-filled potatoes catching.

"Are there any other kind?"

Her soft laugh brightened the dingy décor of the cheap café as she added the heart stoppers to their order. He had no problem with a woman who liked to eat.

"Have a seat, and I'll bring your food when it's ready," said kebab man.

"Thanks," Lily fumbled for something in her pocket.

When she offered, Knight debated letting her pay, but there were only so many out of character moves a man made in one day. He shook his head, paid, and nodded to a table by the window. Lily tensed when he reached for her seat.

"I can do it." Lily assured him.

"I'm sure you can but allow me." He drew out her chair. Every woman commanded basic manners. Surprised Lily didn't take the fact for granted, he vowed to make sure she did while she was with him.

"Thanks."

He could get used to her pale pink tongue sweeping across her bottom lip. A lethal combination—sexy and sweet.

He considered taking her hand and apologising for his earlier behaviour, but his massive palm would swamp her slim fingers. Yep, fragile top of the growing list of reasons not to go any further with Lily. Share a meal. Make sure she got home safely. End of story.

Their food and two enormous glasses of wine arrived. With the agility of a pro, the waiter shuffled plates and glasses to make room on the small table. When he picked up the candle, Lily's hand shot from her lap. "Leave it, thanks."

"No problem." He grinned. "Want me to light it?"

"Please."

Knight leaned back, amazed how the glimmer of a 50p tea light magically relaxed the tension around her eyes. Earlier he'd noticed the dark smudges beneath them, suspected more than lack of sleep dulled their sparkle. He raised his glass, a barrier between Lily and the temptation to dive across the table and kiss away those shadows. "Cheers."

"Cheers. Hope it's not vinegar." The glow from the candle highlighted her cheek bones.

Beneath the table, their knees touched. Lily immediately pulled away.

"Um… Knight? I'm sorry about before, at Doc and Kate's."

"It's Daniel, and *you* do not need to apologise."

"Daniel." His name rolled off her lips as though she were practising. That she meant to do it often. The best sound he had heard for a long time.

No one called him Daniel, not since his mother's death. A sharp gust of wind drove the rain into the window. Goose pimples raised the hairs on his arm.

"I'm not sure how I'll make it up to Kate. It's a mystery why, but Pete still thinks we should be together," she mumbled.

Knight's blood boiled. The gorgeous woman sitting opposite didn't need to explain or excuse Arseworthy's behaviour.

"Forget Pete. Men, our egos are a curse. They bruise too easily. He'll get over it." *If he knows what's good for him.* Two fingers lightly resting on the rim of the bowl, Knight shoved it across the centre line. "Have a chip."

Lily's eyes sparkled. "Mmm, thanks, they are excellent. Try one."

Knight shook his head at the greasy veg in his hand, moving to his mouth, making Lily happy. *Get it together.*

"Kate mentioned you were joining the team at *Afrique Santé.* When do you leave for Burkina? The clinic in Dori, right?" He knew the clinic too well. Despite their horrific experiences last year, Kate and Crystal refused to give up their work with young African mothers wanting to escape illegal teenage marriages.

"If all goes well in two months. Plenty to do before I go. Since Crystal moved in with Spanner, I've been staying at her bedsit, but I need to find my own flat. I moved around a lot as a child, teenager, then I went to university. I don't have much stuff, but it deserves a home."

"Army brat?" he asked.

"No. My father travelled for business. Mother and I went with him everywhere until we lost her in a car crash."

Lily rolled her lips. It baffled him how in any language, and he knew a few, some words were hard to say. Death, for example. People didn't get lost in car crashes. His mother died when he was a kid. He didn't misplace her, and nothing filled the emptiness caused by her death. Add a nomadic childhood, and he had more in common with Lily than he found comfortable. "How old were you when…"

"My mother passed? Nine." Lily cut off his question with another bloody euphemism.

He rubbed his thumb over the top of her hand, but she curled her fingers into a fist and pulled away. Served him right for pushing. Knight stretched his legs and regretted causing the awkward moment. "What kind of business does your father own?"

"He's a steel manufacturer. That's where I met Pete. He works for him. The son my father never had. I disappointed dad when I showed no interest in joining the family corporation and studied nursing. He didn't think I had the brains for university or, if I did, why I wasted them on people. Making money offered more. Over the years, my favourite doll broke her arm a thousand times as I tried to make him proud." A nervous giggle bubbled in her chest.

Knight shifted uncomfortably in his seat, doing his best to avert his eyes from Lily's perfect breasts. Small and round, they rolled against the v-line of her dress every time she leaned forward and sneaked a chip. His mind skipped to planning their next date. *Trouble.*

"What about you, Knight?"

He raised an eyebrow.

"Sorry, Daniel."

Hell, he loved the way his name shaped her mouth. "Nothing to tell. Only child. Third generation military."

Used to putting her foot in it, Lily tried not to choke on her chip. She said something dumb. Or why had Daniel gone silent? Distracted, bored, a thinker for sure, she couldn't work out the emotion behind his stormy eyes, the tight line of his mouth. Daniel Knight may be present in the flesh, but his... What? His soul had fled the scene. "I'm sorry, I didn't mean to..."

"Pry? You didn't."

Perfect choice of words. She gave her locket a twist and concentrated on his lips. Locked on the rim of his glass, she wondered how they'd taste if she kissed him. A peck on the cheek. She didn't want him to get the wrong idea.

Lily snatched another chip and slid her hand towards her wine. Taking a long, slow swallow, she squeezed her legs together and prayed the heat between her thighs didn't reach her cheeks.

She was not looking for a date. It might take a lifetime to get over Pete. Trust a man again. Lily had no problem with her own company. Living at Crystal's for the last three months, she had got back to reading, listening to music, going for long walks over the Heath. Little but important things enjoyed long before she met Pete.

"Anything else, friends? Coffee, dessert?" Kebab man asked. Lily sighed, grateful for his interruption.

Daniel flicked his hand palm to the ceiling, encouraging her to order.

"Er, no, not for me, thanks, I'm full, but you go ahead." She grabbed one last chip from the plate.

"No takers, mate. Thanks." He pushed back his chair and stood. "Ready to go?"

More than ready, she sprang to her feet and bolted for the exit. Outside, she plucked up the courage to face him. "Thanks for the meal. I'm sorry things got awkward. The station's just around the corner. I'll walk from here."

Lily shivered. Daniel must think her mad not wearing a coat, her silk dress ideal for Kate's party, not the best in the rain. The night she fled Pete's, she'd only packed the essentials, meaning to go back for the rest later. Until he texted her photos of rubbish bags lined up on the street. The bin men were long gone by the time she got to his flat.

"It's getting dark. I'll take you home." Daniel's palm grazed her lower back.

"Okay. If you're sure, that would be great. Thanks."

"I'm sure."

When they reached the car, he ducked his head until his eyes were level with her face. She had no choice but to look into his eyes.

"What's your address? And to be clear, Lily. You've done nothing wrong. It's me who should apologise."

CHAPTER THREE

Cursing his burning quads, Knight drove his upper body into the bitter winter wind sweeping over Parliament Hill. Keeping his eyes fixed on George, he commanded his feet to keep pace with the mutt's galloping paws. Tongue hanging out, the cocky shit barked, waited for him to catch up. "Yeah, I hear you, steak for breakfast."

Close to where he lived, the Hill was the ball-breaking finale to the ten-mile run Sentinel team tackled every day they were home. There were steeper climbs. This pile of dirt a doddle compared to the SAS training crags in the Brecon Beacons. It spawned an average gradient of almost eleven percent. Yep, he noticed shit like that. He and others who swore the gods created the green demon to spite their thighs.

This morning, Lily, the woman with the right balance of muscle definition and soft curves, distracted him from the lactic acid burn. Wind howled and nipped the back of his neck. It had been hard as hell saying goodbye outside Crystal's manky bedsit.

Knight looked up at the threatening clouds. Thank Christ, Lily had the sense to fix her eyes on her feet and send him on his way before he did something dumb and asked her on that date.

"For fuck's sake." In worse shape than him, Doc coughed up the words. Juggling his position at the hospital with his Sentinel duties meant he inevitably missed a few runs.

"Come on, old man. Race you to the top." Spanner jogged in a circle around him, then sprinted ahead and left the poor bastard trailing his heels.

On a better day, he might have taken after them. Beat both their sorry arses. Not today. Alone in his head, happy to hang with Lily, he kept on plodding. His curiosity wasn't the only thing she aroused, but he sensed an avalanche of complications came with the delightful package.

Neither his job nor his lifestyle fitted with a permanent relationship. No wife, certainly no children. Marriage was for the other guy. Maeve took care of his sexual itch, and he paid her well for it.

"You're quiet this morning, Boss. What's up?" Snake, George's official handler, came back to join him, jogged level with his shoulder.

"Nothing. Thought I'd let the kids have this one." Knight slowed his pace, fell back further.

"Fair enough. See you at the top. C'mon, boy." Snake brushed his hand over George's ears and sprinted after the other two.

After they survived three tours in Afghanistan together, formed Sentinel Security, the team respected each other's boundaries. Verbal or silent, they honoured personal space. Knight sniffed. His eyes watered from the sudden icy rush burning behind his eyeballs. Back to Lily and self-torture.

How she ended up with dickhead Pete remained a fucking mystery. Adept at interrogation, prying secrets from the enemy, he counted the ways he could coax her fears into the open.

Over a greasy kebab, he almost shared stuff not even his Sentinel team knew. His upbringing and past were a no-go zone. A man who got the job done, who had his teammates' backs anytime, anywhere. All they needed to know.

As a kid, he had set his sights on joining the SAS, hadn't been out of school more than a day before he signed up for the parachute regiment. Most important goal—achieve more than his father. At seventeen and a half, he escaped basic training at the army foundation college in Harrogate by a month. Graduated top of his group from the PARA Combat Infantry course at Catterick.

After progressing from Lead Scout to Section Commander, he applied for SAS training and met Spanner, Doc and Mike. Snake joined them later, just before Mike's death. More than friends, he considered them brothers.

Jeez. His heart pounded in his chest. He should take Crystal up on her offer to buy him a juice maker. *Nah.* He still couldn't figure out why he felt the need to clam up, used silence to punish Lily. Simple questions—hard answers. She deserved an apology. Unlikely, as he made no plans to see her again.

"Who's the old man, now?" Doc stood at the summit with his fists punching the air.

Two seconds later, he collapsed on his arse and cradled his head in his hands. Knight bowled in beside him.

"I'm guessing less rumpy-pumpy, and a ton more sleep. Ay, Doc?" Spanner threw his arm around Doc's neck.

"Fuck you."

Knight smiled. He couldn't be happier for Doc and Kate. With her support, his friend had let go of his guilt over her brother's death. Spanner and Crystal had been together the longest. I couldn't imagine a couple more suited to one another. That left him and Snake.

"C'mon, let's get out of this sodding gale. Briefing, my place." Knight offered his hand to Doc and dragged the medic's sorry arse behind him.

"There, there Boss? Can't let a gentle breeze bother you. It blows the cobwebs from the soul." Spanner tapped his chest.

"Fuck you," everyone replied in unison.

George led, sprinting the entire way. No question, four legs were better than two. Before he closed his door, Spanner dived waist deep into his fridge.

"Got any eggs, Boss? Figure I'll whip up a bunch of pancakes to go with the coffee," Spanner hollered.

"Can you cook while we talk?" Knight didn't need to ask. For all his kidding around, Spanner was a trained multi-tasker and cooking focused his mind.

"Sure, Boss. Any blueberries?"

"Yeah, next to the truffles." *Fuck's sake.* "Only what's there, Spanner. Caffeine is the priority."

"Roger that."

"Snake, you ready?"

"Sure thing, Boss." Comms powered up his laptop. "Okay, gentlemen. Purpose of this briefing is to bring everyone up to speed on recent Seckou intel."

"Anything further on our potential leak?" Spanner asked.

"No, Oumar's on it in Burkina, but nothing yet." Knight had confidence in their African contact. His feelers spread wide and deep. "We're still waiting on local government sanction for this latest mission, but it should happen in the next couple of weeks. Whoever's up needs to be ready to go at short notice. Snake?" He nodded for him to keep going.

Snake tossed several copies of a dossier onto the table and continued his run down.

Despite the freezing weather, his living room smelled of male sweat, strong coffee, and fucking pancakes. Knight opened the window and reached for his copy. The sooner they got this done, the sooner he could shower.

Doc scanned the brief and steepled his fingers. "Count me in. I will organise time off from the hospital."

He knew why. Kate and Crystal would be in Burkina. Doc respected the hell out of his woman and would never ask her to stay home, but this mission gave his over-protective arse a perfect excuse to keep her close without breathing down her neck.

Knight speared a rasher of bacon from the plate Spanner held in front of him. "Coffee?"

"Easy, Boss. One pair of soddin' hands," Spanner said, flashing him the doe-eyed apology that worked better on Crystal.

Knight rolled his eyes. "Anyone else want to volunteer?"

"Yeah, me." Spanner reached for the percolator.

Alpha hero number two. No surprise. Lily would be in Africa too. With no dedicated protector. He shook his head. Not his problem. Besides, Spanner and Doc wouldn't let anything happen to her. "Okay, Snake. That leaves you and me covering base."

Snake shrugged. "Suits me."

"Now that we have all been thoroughly obliging, I need a favour, Boss." Spanner took a bite of pancake, closed his eyes, and groaned. "Not bad, considering what I had to work with."

"Favour?" Knight braced, hoping his mate didn't to want to borrow the MG. Last time he drove it, it ended up spinning its wheels in a ditch. "If you're after the…"

"No, Boss. Don't get excited. Car's safe. It's more a request from Crys. She and Kate have organised a movie night. We've said yes." He eyeballed Doc, who offered a half-hearted shrug. A *fait accompli* where his missus was concerned. "Lily's coming and Crys wants you and Snake to join us. A sort of good luck get-together before they head for Africa."

Knight understood, given the clusterfuck that occurred last time they were there, but seeing Lily again? No, not on his agenda. "Can't promise, Spanner. There are still a few holes to plug before we finalise plans for this mission."

"Come on, Boss, you haven't asked when. Don't be shy. Lily doesn't bite." Spanner wiggled his eyebrows.

"And how the hell do you know?" For the first time in the last fifteen minutes, Snake raised his nose from his laptop screen.

Snake and Lily? It shouldn't matter. But. "On one condition. Tell Crystal, no chick flick," Knight said.

"Will do, Boss. I'll confirm time and place. You too, Snake."

Spanner beamed and poured him his coffee as if he deserved a reward.

"Done. Okay, eat, drink, and get the fuck out of my flat. You all need a shower. My flat smells like the inside of a taxi driver's jock strap."

George barked. "Yeah, you too, you mangy mutt."

CHAPTER FOUR

Cold, Lily scrunched together the edges of her cardigan. There were no windows in the small clinic office. Office, laugh. More of a cupboard, but it served its purpose even if it trapped any draught whistling through the place. Every time she worked in there, she always slipped on an extra jumper.

She checked the appointment book and blinked hard when she saw the large black cross scored through the rest of the day. "What's this?" She asked Crystal, wedged behind her, cursing the photocopier. Bloody thing jammed whenever they needed anything urgently.

Crystal peered over her shoulder. "What's what, hun? Oh. That is lunch." She beamed.

"Lunch, but Kate's blocked out the entire afternoon." Lily said.

"Yes. Perfect. Right?" The stuck paper released, and Crystal's suddenly free hand smacked her nose. "Ouch."

"What's the occasion?" Most days, they didn't have time for much more than a sandwich.

Lily's cheeks flushed. A missed birthday? Kate's was two weeks ago. The day idiot Pete spoiled the party. She still felt bad about it, but it was also the day she met Daniel. A part of her wished he would call. Totally illogical, given he didn't have her number.

She tapped the top of finger number two. Not Crystal's big day. Lily chuckled. Last year, everyone knew a full week beforehand. Not that Crys expected presents, just celebration. Not a bad thing. It meant there were always chocolates in the cupboard. On the day Spanner arrived at the clinic with a giant fairy cake, a pink candle stuck in the middle. Patients and staff danced around the waiting room.

"Don't frown, you didn't forget anybody. This is an un-special lunch, Kate's reward for us working like slaves for the past six months. I love our pregnant mums, but if I meet another pair of spread legs in the eye, without a break, I'll..." Crystal's eyes widened, then crossed.

Lily laughed. They were midwives. Legs akimbo weren't unusual in their day job.

Crystal straightened her papers and folded her arms. "I, for one, intend to enjoy it. Trust me, Lily, Burkinabe food is delicious, but nothing beats the elegance of London's finest. Call me spoilt."

"Never. You deserve it. Where's Kate booked for your lunch?"

"Not me, hun. Us—You, me, and Kate. Who knows? Kate's in charge. Happy with that, she's a foodie on the quiet, never get her and Spanner talking restaurants. Trust me, she will have studied the *Good Food Guide* for a week."

Lily nodded, pleased they had included her. For over a month, she had eaten nothing but Sainsbury's cheese and onion sandwiches. Lunch at a proper restaurant sounded fantastic. Her heart sank. Pete had called earlier, made her promise to meet when he dropped by the clinic that afternoon. She needed to call him.

"Are you staying here for a few minutes? I need to clean up the treatment room after my last patient." Tiny beads of sweat broke out on her top lip at the thought of asking Pete to reschedule.

"Sure. You go ahead. Annie Chambers cancelled. Gives me time to make a dent in this mammoth pile of copying." Crystal crossed her fingers and pressed the green button. "I should call *Afrique Santé* too, and firm up our travel itinerary for Burkina. Have you had your jabs?"

Lily cringed. She didn't mind needles. In someone else's arm. As a kid, travelling as they did, she had her fair share of inoculation pricks. "Almost. Just the last shot of the rabies vax and I'm done." Her least favourite, but Crystal pointed out, nobody wanted to die from that horrible viral disease. She hurried from the desk, racking her brain for a plausible excuse to stop Pete.

Halfway to the treatment room, she hesitated. It might be easier to stay at the clinic. Crystal wasn't the only one with a ton of paperwork. Instead, she kidded herself she shouldn't worry, shoved her hands into the pockets of her pink scrubs and kept walking.

Pete worked hard, even harder, since he became eligible for a full directorship in her father's company. As a sponsor of *Afrique Santé*, she had met Kate and Crystal at one of their functions. He refused to understand why she accepted their offer of a job. Unfortunately, her father agreed with him. She held her mobile tighter, refusing to allow her mind to descend into a depressing spiral, and braced for argument.

"I'm busy, Lily. What do you want?" Pete asked. His exasperated sigh whistled in her ear.

Lily twiddled her locket and took a deep breath. "Sorry, I'll be quick. Just wanted to let you know I won't be at the clinic this afternoon."

"Lily. Didn't you listen? It's important and I've cancelled a vital meeting with your father to squeeze you into my schedule."

The thought of Pete and her father getting together made her squirm. "Yes. Sorry. Broken tooth. This afternoon is the only time the dentist can offer me an appointment." Given the turmoil in her gut, her voice remained miraculously steady. "Can you make it?" She should have offered to meet him at his office, but she felt safer on home turf.

"No. Forget it. It's best you get your teeth checked. Ask for a clean while you're there. With your mouth, the teeth so close together, it's easy for bits of decaying food to lodge in between them."

She brushed her teeth three times a day. Did she have bad breath? She scraped her tongue across her teeth and swallowed. "Okay, will do. I..." A sharp click. Bingo—off the hook.

"You finished, hun?" Crystal's voice echoed along the corridor.

"Yes, coming. Where is Kate? I haven't seen her this morning."

"Already left. Toss the spray bottle and let's get out of here." Crystal stood at the entrance, flicking off light switches.

"Coming." Lily slipped out of her scrubs into her street clothes and grabbed her thin raincoat from the hook on the break room door. A *Primark* knock-off she had picked up at the weekend. It would have to do until she found something better.

They agreed to take the tube. Madness driving any time in London traffic, and no one with half a brain threw away money taking a taxi in the West End. Forty minutes later, they exited Covent Garden station.

The light drizzle misting the streets took her back to Kate's party and Daniel. Given the places military men deployed, she found it odd rain bothered him so much. Growling about it on and off all afternoon, insisting on sheltering her with his jacket as they ran to the restaurant. Given he was such a grump, she couldn't put her finger on why it was easy to relax in his company. Pity she messed up at the end.

Splashing through puddles, avoiding the crowds, they hurried through the old fruit and vegetable market. Many of London's boutique fashion stores operated under the glass dome of Covent Garden. A favourite place. Her mother took her, one Christmas, to see the *Royal Ballet's Sleeping Beauty* at the Opera House. Along with every other girl watching the matinee, she dreamed of being a ballerina. At five-four, her height fit perfectly. Pity growing boobs determined a different path.

"Come on, hun, stop daydreaming. I promise we can do the shops after lunch." Crystal threaded their arms together and nudged her inside the stained-glass doors of the restaurant.

They waited for the Maître D to seat them, sumptuous smells drifted under her nostrils, tempting her taste buds. Her stomach growled. Forget she hadn't seen the menu. Minor detail. Whatever she chose had to be delicious.

As they followed the man in a suit to their booth, she took a sneaky peek at people's plates. Ridiculously small portions, but the desserts were heavenly. Lily chuckled. She bet Knight preferred this type of restaurant rather than a greasy kebab house. This place devoted an entire menu to wine.

"Where have you been? I'm into my second Chablis," Kate said, waving her glass.

Lily snorted. Hardly two glasses. Here they filled to the quarter mark. Small, ridiculously small. She shuffled to the farthest seat to make room for Crystal.

"Sorry, hun, we…" Crystal's sentence faded into the general hum. Didn't matter, problems with public transport were as boring as a broken telly.

Wow. A list of tea concoctions spread across two pages of the menu. More than wine, she was desperate for a cuppa.

Kate lightly tapped her spoon on the edge of her glass. "Okay, here comes our waiter. Hurry and decide what you want to eat. If we miss him now, I'm not sure when he'll be back."

"Aye, aye, Captain," Crystal said. They both saluted before collapsing into a fit of giggles.

This was what it was like to have friends. Well, technically, they were work colleagues, but Kate and Crystal had made her feel welcome ever since they'd met. Her new life included making more friends.

A couple of hours later, Lily didn't argue when Kate insisted on ordering dessert. She rubbed her tummy. It grumbled when she ate too much, and the chocolate profiterole with the vanilla ice cream and warm chocolate sauce screamed overkill.

Pete refused to eat with her in public, saying he found the grumbling disgusting. Kate and Crystal weren't embarrassed, or they were kind enough not to show it. Lily cradled her cup of fresh mint tea between her palms and inhaled the delicious aroma.

"Lily. It is you." Startled by the vaguely familiar voice booming across the restaurant, Lily's shoulder jumped. Paranoid much. Any raised voice reminded her of Pete.

"Sorry. I didn't mean to interrupt. We met last year at your husband's Christmas dinner at *Petrus*. In fact, I'm meeting him there this evening."

CHAPTER FIVE

Lily bristled. She always did when someone referred to her as Pete's wife. People could accuse her of many stupid moves but marrying Pete hadn't been one of them. Guess this idiot hadn't heard they'd split. Her heart thudded in her chest.

"Er, yes. Um..." Would he mention seeing her to Pete? She scrubbed her forehead. Should she come right out with it and ask him not to tell Pete?

"Pleased to meet you Mr... I'm Kate Gibson, and this is Crystal Starr. We work with Lily." Kate to the rescue.

"Sorry. David. David Pierce," he answered and turned his gaze from her.

Kate shook hands with the tall, skinny man. The tuft of hair combed over his bald patch looked as ridiculous as his bow tie sitting at a weird angle, doing a poor job of hiding the missing button on his shirt.

"Well, I won't keep you, ladies. Nice to see you again, Lily. Enjoy the rest of your afternoon." The woman hanging on his arm wiggled her fingers and turned to the exit.

Relieved he hadn't asked any awkward questions, she forced a smile and waved. Kate and Crystal were staring at her. "How embarrassing. I forgot his name. I didn't want to be rude." She took another gulp of tea.

"You had me worried for a moment, hun. You looked as though you'd seen an axe murderer."

"Crys, don't be such a drama queen," Kate said. "Lily, is everything okay? What happened after you left my party? Did Knight catch up with you?"

The question she dreaded and one she marvelled it took Kate so long to ask. Silly to hope she forgot after she caused such a pathetic mess. "Yes. I'm sorry I spoiled your party."

"Nonsense, Lily. None of it was your fault, but I can't say the same for your ex. Please tell me you didn't invite him?"

"No, of course not. I've been racking my brains trying to figure out how he got there. I must have said something, but…"

"Lily, hun, is Pete a problem?" Crystal caught her hand before she pulled away.

She hated the pitying look on her face.

"Say the word and Spanner…" Crystal glanced at Kate. She nodded.

"What Crys is trying to say is Spanner, Doc, any of the guys would be happy to pay Pete a visit. Make sure he understands what *over* means."

Lily sucked in a breath and gulped her tears. "Thank you, both of you. You're the best, but I can manage Pete. Besides, we'll be in Africa soon. By the time I get back he'll have forgotten about me."

She snatched her hand from Crystal's grasp and swiped at the tear pricking at the corner of her eye. "Please." People were gaping at her. "It's all good. Before we leave, I'm thinking of spending a weekend with Sam, my friend from university. We haven't seen each other in a while and she's perfect company for a whine night."

"Great idea. Sorry to upset you. Just know, we're here for you." Kate said, mercifully putting an end to the conversation.

"Thank you. Now come on, drink up Crystal. Aren't we going shopping?"

"Sure are, hon. You two need to help me choose shoes. Spanner's taking me dancing Friday night, and I intend to glam up and party."

"Lucky you." Lily meant it. How amazing. A man who enjoyed dancing. Even though she never made it to ballerina, she loved to dance. Before she met Pete, she attended ballroom classes at the Y, but they were in the evening, and he expected her to be home when he finished work. She gave them up, but they were on top of her list to start again.

"Lucky? Doubtful Crys will agree at three the next morning when her feet are killing her, and she has a blister the size of a golf ball on her little toe." Kate grinned and curled her finger and thumb into a hole shape.

"Ha, you're just jealous. A waste of time you buying dancing shoes. Doc makes you take them off, so you don't put him on crutches."

Sitting there laughing, the weight lifted from Lily's shoulders. The least she could do was pay for lunch. "This the bill?" She reached for the small tray and fished in her bag for her purse.

"Put your money away. This is a business expense." With an enormous smile on her face, Kate snatched the silver plate from her hand and laid enough cash in the folder to more than cover their meal.

"Come on. Shoes." Arms linked, Crystal led them out of the restaurant and to nearby James Street.

Lily giggled when they came to an abrupt stop. The word *Galleria* blazed across the front of the shop. Ensured fun, maxing out someone else's credit card. Pete had controlled their day-to-day finances, but thanks to her father, a prenup protected her grandmother's trust. It earned interest in a never-touched bank account waiting for... She wasn't sure what. Her salary at the clinic was enough for her needs.

Credit cards weren't much use in the African villages. No ATMs.

Cash only. She shrugged and made a mental note to organise American dollars for her trip.

"Over here." Crystal pointed to a couple of chairs at the edge of a floor littered with shoes and empty boxes.

Shoppers packed the store, focussed on the thin straps, glued together with sparkly bits. A poor excuse for a shoe. Kate flashed Lily a wink, obviously not immune to the Cinderella temptations lining the shelves.

Lily jumped at the sudden loud noise of a car backfiring. Crowds strolled by the window. If Pete was out there, she couldn't see him.

"What do you think of these?" Crystal asked, oblivious. A purple creation dangled from her little finger.

Heaven. If she hadn't morphed into a boring slob over the last year, Crystal would have had to fight her for them. She bit her lip, nodded, and picked up a small glittery bag, looking very lonely on the seat next to her. "They'd go great with this."

"Ah, Ms Temptation. You're not wrong." Crystal piled the shoes into the box and handed them to the hovering salesperson. "I'll take them. Thank you."

As Lily bent to put the bag where she found it, a jolt from behind made her lose her balance and stumble forward.

"Sorry." Lily's breath hitched at the unexpected apology flung over the shoulder of the pretty woman heading for the door.

"That's okay. My fault." Lily's voice trailed after her. A sense of unease washed over her, and her smile rapidly faded. The afternoon's excitement finally catching up with her.

"Are you going to buy it?" Kate asked, eyeing the bag.

"Sure. Why not." Relieved she had an excuse, she snatched it from the seat. "I'm paying for this, then running for the tube. Time to head home before it gets dark."

"Oh no, you can't leave I need you, hun," Crystal pouted.

"When did you need help spending money?" Kate asked, rescuing her from making excuses.

"You'll be fine." Lily smiled. Cheeks aching, she paid for the bag.

Rushing away must seem odd, but ever since they left the clinic, she could swear someone was following her.

"Thanks, for lunch. I'll see you tomorrow." By now, Kate had decided to try on shoes. She brushed past them on her way out of the shop.

"Yes. Oh, Lily, we're going to the movies on Saturday night. You must come," Kate said. Caught in Crystal's enthusiasm, she bent to pick up a pair of shoes.

"Yes," Lily blurted. Her stomach fluttered. Would Daniel be there? She hoped not. With Pete breathing down her neck, couldn't risk spoiling things again. *No, Lily. You deserve some fun.* A perfect way to relax. Sitting in the dark, a bucket of popcorn perched on her knee. "Look forward to it. Thanks for inviting me."

CHAPTER SIX

The train inched into Euston Station. A steamy dungeon during rush hour, the tube rivalled a furnace. An overweight man in an ill-fitting suit, one wrist hooked through the overhead strap, swayed above Lily, his stinky BO threatening to suffocate her. She loosened her scarf, concentrated on breathing through her nose, and focussed on the newspaper headline opposite her.

As soon as the train stopped, she burst through the half-open doors, her feet hardly touching the platform, and bolted to the escalator. Just her luck. None working. Joining the masses, she climbed the narrow spiral staircase to street level and hurried across the station concourse.

Sunlight, faking a smile through the gaps in the clouds, glistened on the black ice. Waiting for the lights on Euston Road to change, a green sports car whizzed by, and she thought of Daniel's MG. No use pretending, she wasn't worried he might show at the movies on Saturday. What would it matter if he did? They talked; he drove her home. End of story.

Chin tucked into her chest, head braced against the sleet, she concentrated on the busy traffic. A miracle she didn't fall arse over tit, hopping over the uneven bitumen. It took skill to dodge in and out of the double-deckers. Crystal swore they loved to travel in pairs.

People of every shape, size, and colour packed the entrance to the hospital. "Hold the lift," Lily yelled at a girl covered in serious tatts, holding onto a pram with one hand. The other clasped a small boy's wrist. "Thanks," she said as she squeezed in beside them and wiggled her backside, so the doors shut behind her.

The toddler, sticky stuff all over his face, nudged her thigh. Tall enough for her finger to graze his mop of tight black curls and hover over the control panel above his head. Second or third floor, she never remembered. Level three seemed worth a punt.

"Bloody shit day," the girl with the tattoos moaned.

Lily nodded and admired her spiky purple hair. A post-Pete haircut was on her list. A fresh look for Africa. At thirty-two, she was past due for something less Catholic schoolgirl than the scrunched ponytail Pete preferred.

The doors opened, and everyone spilt out of the lift. She hurried to Dr Davis' rooms where walls, whiter than snow, blinded a person. Slowly, her eyes adjusted and settled on the scarlet vinyl covering the seats in the waiting room.

"Good morning. Can I help you?" Blue-black hair, twirled in artistic messiness on top of her head, the thin receptionist peered over the counter. Gothic white skin stretched across her cheekbones and highlighted her purple lips.

Lily blinked. "I have an appointment with Dr Davis. Lily."

"I'm sorry, who did you say you were seeing?" The girl squinted at her screen.

"Dr Davis. I'm late. I can change to another time if it's easier," she stuttered. Other patients stared at the perfect entertainment playing out in front of them.

"Oh, yes, there you are. Nine thirty." Her eyes drifted to the clock on the wall. "Please take a seat. The doctor will be with you soon."

Lily chose the chair, separated from its neighbour by a small table graced with a vase brimming with flowers. A quick rub between two fingers confirmed her suspicion. As fake as the masterpieces lining the walls.

Seated opposite, body hunched, an older woman struggled to hide behind a magazine. Lily understood. Blocking people took work. Lily picked at her fraying sleeve, her thoughts returning to Daniel and the movies. If he did show, she would keep her distance. That way, there'd be no chance of another awkward moment.

Footsteps to her right drew everyone's attention. A tall, elegantly dressed woman posed at the reception desk. Dr D.

Lily rolled her eyes. Where she worked, they struggled to pee between patients. Forget reapplying lipstick.

"Liliana Stor..."

"It's Lily. My name is Lily," she interrupted, peeved because she had made that clear when they first met. Bloody sadistic, the way teachers and shrinks insisted on calling people by the name on their birth certificate. Mum never called her Liliana and her father, only to show disappointment.

"Good morning, Lily. Please, follow me." Dr D's smug smile should have cracked her make-up, but the mask stayed firmly in place. Lily took a breath and reminded herself to choose her words. Last appointment she had shared way more than she intended.

Dr D had been in rare form that day, probing and pushing in her clinical monotone, until she confessed the one bloody time she gave in, succumbed to the shadows, popped one too many sleeping pills.

If she had concentrated on her breathing that night, she wouldn't be walking this treadmill to hell. Pete had come home early, found her passed out on the bathroom floor, and never let her forget the slip, dismissing her cry for help as proof she needed him to look after her.

Ashamed, Lily pleaded with him not to tell her father. Pete ignored her and ingratiated himself deeper into Max's debt. Lily snapped to the present and stared at Dr D. Mouth wide open, hovering on a breath, waiting for an answer to a question she hadn't heard.

Was she suicidal now? Far from it, topping herself, the farthest thing from her mind. Murder, possibly? She had considered a thousand ways to kill Pete ever since he wiped her hard drive and destroyed the only photos she had of her mother. Except the one in her locket.

Watching Dr D tap the pages of the leather-bound journal perched on her bony knees, she gave it a rub for luck. The shrink's owl blink, her cue to speak. Shrinks lived for specifics, fed on raw moments that probed the jagged scars of their patient's hearts. Lily considered asking Dr D to imagine her worst nightmare—take a moment to bring it into the room. Not happening.

"I can't help you, Lily, if you won't talk to me." A practised uncross recross of her legs punctuated the shrink's sentence.

"I'm sorry. I'm not sure where to begin today." *Or any day*.

"That's a start."

Oh, God, help me.

"Tell me more about your job. You mentioned you work at a women's clinic in Camden." Dr D. blinked several times. Did she believe the tragic sitting in front of her worked with patients? Maybe she had a point?

"Yes, temporarily." Lily swallowed the tickle in her throat and tore a few tissues from the box on the table. The inside of her wrist itched.

"Temporary? Tell me more."

"I leave for Africa in a few weeks. My colleagues run a program, training midwives for *Afrique Santé*, a government-sponsored health organisation."

"Ah, I see."

Lily doubted it. Not sure why, but she stopped short of sharing the other half of their work at the refuge. Assisting Aunty to provide sanctuary for teenage mothers fleeing from illegal marriages.

"Is the clinic busy?"

Lily nodded. "All the time. Unpaid overtime begins after the doors close, and I write my patient notes." *Do better, Lily.* "It's an NHS clinic. We serve several council estates."

"You're a midwife. How do you feel about children, a family?" Dr D adjusted her glasses. Her eyelashes battered the slightly tinted glass. Fake for sure. They were too thick, too long.

Lily shrugged. The shrink's open question, designed to make her talk, made her wonder how long they'd circle this painful conversation. Family, kids, lots of them, had once been her dream. A dream she believed Pete shared.

"I love children. I couldn't do my job if I didn't." Lily's stomach twisted. "But I wouldn't make a good mother." Lily averted her gaze, exhausted from trying not to say stuff. "I don't enjoy, I mean I'm not very good at sex."

"I see." Dr D repeated.

The scream burning in her throat threatened to break free. *What? What did she see?* That at her age, it didn't matter much. Her chance for having children was rapidly disappearing. Pete, her last hope, but her naïve attempts to please him were pathetic. Not sexy.

Lights off, lying in bed, she often tried to discuss it with him only to have him pat her on the head. Hurtful, not helpful. Lily sighed. She had her work. Being a mother wasn't everything.

"Tell me why having sex makes you uneasy?"

"It doesn't make me uneasy." That's not what she said. Had she? She didn't want to admit she'd only been intimate with two men and neither set off any fireworks. "I didn't know how to please Pete—he never had an erection." Her face burned with embarrassment.

Dr D shuffled her papers. "Did he speak to anyone about his problem?"

Bloody hell. Floor open and swallow me whole. Lily wriggled in her seat. "No." The suggestion laughable. Lily clutched her stomach and stared at her navel.

"Could you consider Pete may be impotent and have his own issues around intimacy that prevented you from reaching mutual satisfaction?"

"Forgive the crude pun, Dr Davis, but that's a bit of a mouthful. Anyway, it's no longer important. We're not together. Could we change the subject?"

"Certainly. We can come back to it," Dr D scribbled in her notebook.

Over my dead body. Lily cringed at her threat. "Thank you." She reached for a tissue. A quick sniff offered a welcome breather.

Time ticked by as Dr D picked an imaginary hair from her lap. "I see on your form that you worked at Nightingale Hospital. Did you like it there?"

Yes. Rather than argue with Pete over the long hours she had left when they moved in together. "I'm sorry, Dr Davis. I'm afraid I…"

"Go on. You're frightened. Of what, Lily?"

What the hell. At a hundred quid for a fifty-minute hour, she better toss Dr D a few crumbs. "I'm not sure why, but when I'm in yoga class. I hate the part when it gets to breathing. With my eyes closed," she added. What that had to do with anything she wasn't sure, except sex with Pete had always stolen her breath and not in a good way.

"When you concentrate on your breathing?"

"Yes, she asks us to inhale, hold our breath, count to four before exhaling." Lily used to take breathing for granted until yoga sprite turned it into an art form.

"She?" Dr D edged the Kleenex closer and glanced at the small clock on the table beside her. They still had fifteen minutes.

"Harmony, the yoga instructor. I swear she has a degree in lung exercise." Her voice shrill, she confessed the unbearable. "I've always had trouble with meditation, yoga. It's mad, but when they ask me to close my eyes, breathe deeply, and relax, tears clog the back of my throat. My nose blocks and I panic." There, she'd said it. Hysterical laughter bubbled in her chest. Thank the gods for the box of tissues. She grabbed one, blew her nose, and dabbed her eyes.

"Are you asthmatic, Lily?"

"What? No. Occasional hay fever, but I have an inhaler."

"And when you're anxious, do you have trouble breathing?"

Lily's stomach clenched. "Not really, unless you count wanting to stop breathing?" The words avalanched out of her mouth. More than anything, she wanted to rewind the moment.

"You're safe here, Lily." For the first time, Lily heard the concern, the kindness in Dr D's flat, clinical voice. Completely irrational, but it irritated her.

"Yes, thank you." The ticking of Dr D's clock pounded in her head. "Oh. Time's up."

"It's okay. Take a second. You're doing well, Lily. It will get easier."

Lily banked on it. Leaving Pete was massive, but not magic. The trip to Africa was a major step in finding herself again. Grudgingly, she admitted seeing Dr D helped.

The soft thud of the shrinks' notebook confirmed they were out of time.

"I'll see you next week. We'll pick this up then, but if you need to talk before your appointment, call me, and we can reschedule," Dr D offered.

"Okay, thank you. That will probably be my last visit before I leave London." She snatched another tissue and mumbled goodbye.

Another cat-and-mouse session with Dr D over, she bypassed the lift, released the bar on the fire exit, and tore down the stairs that led to the car park. The shortcut back to the tube.

Bastard. Dressed in work pants, business shirt and navy jacket, his legs crossed at the ankles, arms folded across his chest, Pete leaned against his car. He had positioned it to block the narrow exit. Despite the wind, not one hair on his head was out of place.

Shoulders back, Lily kept walking, watching out of the corner of her eye for him to move towards her. Determined to get away as fast as possible, she didn't ask what he wanted or how the hell he knew she would be at the hospital.

"Hi, Pete, what do you want?"

"Do I need a reason to see my girl?" He didn't budge.

"I'm not your girl, and I'm in a hurry. I need to get to work."

"Silly Lily. You will always be Pete's girl," he leered.

She shifted sideways but wasn't quick enough to dodge the stroke of his finger on her cheek. When he shifted his weight, she managed to scurry past him. Shaking, her hands gripped the shoulder strap of her bag.

"Off you go, babe. I'll be seeing you."

CHAPTER SEVEN

Lily lifted the edge of the net curtain and squinted at the outside stairs. It was too dark to see anything. No moon, and the streetlights were pathetic at the best of times. Worst of all, the queasiness in her gut said Pete had followed her home.

Too bad, if it was bin night, the rubbish could wait another week. No way was she going back outside tonight. She clenched her phone, flicked to camera mode, and pointed it at the window. Ready to snap Pete if she saw him. Proof he was stalking her if the police took the time to look, listen to her.

If she had Daniel's number, she might text him, make some excuse for him to come over and keep her company. Yes, she'd only known him five minutes, but she could pay him. Protecting people was his job.

Pull yourself together. She hated feeling this way. A pathetic loser peeping from behind curtains. Determined not to allow paranoia to take control, she let the net fall. Nothing lay in wait for her outside except dried leaves, tossed by the wind, swirling around the iron railings.

Wanting to talk to someone, not to be alone, she scrolled through her phone contacts wondering who would be up this late. Sam's number popped up. Great. The least likely person to accuse her of an over-active imagination.

Samantha Brody. After two tours serving in the K9 unit in Afghanistan, her medical discharge brought her to the same college where they had shared a room, bonding over sitcoms and cheap wine. After graduation, she bought a farm close to Oxford, where she trained assistance dogs for veterans living with PTSD.

Pete never liked her, claimed he was allergic to her animals, so she hadn't visited her much over the last year, but they'd kept in touch. Lily hit the green button.

"Hiya, stranger. You must be psychic. I planned to call you tomorrow," Sam answered, dogs barking in the background.

"As usual, I beat you to it. You're up late, how's life on animal farm?" Except for a few select humans. Lily felt honoured to be one of them as Sam preferred her furry friends, often sleeping in the barn with a sick dog. Lily missed her.

"Same old, same old. Up to my teeth in pups and poop. The mongrels have no respect for business hours," she said with a chuckle.

"Are you up for a visitor? Not this weekend, but the next? Can I stay for a few days?" The words rushed from Lily's mouth, giving Sam no chance to refuse.

"Fantastic. Of course. Whenever, I'm dying to see you. It's been too long. Give me a date and I'll make sure I have adequate provisions."

"A case of *Veuve*?" Their favourite reward after finishing exams.

"Done, and just for you, I'll have them add *beaucoup de fromage*," Sam teased.

"For me? You love a good smelly feet cheese as much as I do?" Lily sank into the over-stuffed sofa, listening to her friend laugh, her earlier fear gone. Fun. That's what she needed. "I'm craving country air. It's been full-on these past few weeks getting ready for my trip."

"Ah, yes. I got your email. Africa. Well done, Lily. Your dream job. I hope you haven't told dickhead Pete you're going?"

"No, but..." She hesitated, not wanting to spoil the moment.

"But what?"

"He showed up at Kate's party."

"What the fuck. That arsehole makes my skin crawl." As always, Sam's colourful vocabulary made Lily smile.

"I remember."

"Over and out on his sorry arse. Yes, Lily?"

"Definitely." No longer taking crap from Pete, the new Lily planned to see a lot more of her friend.

A flash of yellow light swept across the dark living room and her good mood hit the floor.

"Lily? You still there?"

"Someone's outside, Sam. I think it's Pete."

"Bastard. Can you see him?" Sam asked.

Her fingers trembled as she lifted the edge of the curtain. "No, There's no one out there. Ignore me. I'm being stupid."

"There's nothing dumb about you, Lily. Look again. Make sure that son of a bitch isn't out there."

"No, it's okay. I'll see you soon. Enjoy the rest of your night and give the puppies a kiss from me."

"Wait, Lily. Call the police, report him."

"Why? A fat lot of good it will do." Her voice hitched. One time, when Pete hit her, she had called them. All they did was wave a finger in his face. Nothing after that, not even a follow-up call.

"Pack a bag, Lily, I'm coming to get you."

She heard Sam's boots marching across the wooden floor, already on her way. "No, need. I'm fine." Her hand shook. "I can handle this. If I see him, I'll call the police. Promise."

"I'm not happy, you're stubborn. You'll dig your heels in if I push. Do me a favour, lock up tight and try to sleep. Ring me tomorrow and let me know you're okay."

"Will do. Thanks, I'll see you soon. Put that *Veuve* on ice." Lily forced a giggle.

"Yeah, I love you too." Sam groaned. "Remember, call me, unless you want me banging down your door tomorrow."

Lily disconnected. Sam's kissy goodbyes rang in her ears. In the morning she'd ask Kate if she could go to Africa earlier, introduce herself to the staff at Yalgado hospital, make sure supplies were in order before they headed out to the rural clinic.

Reluctantly, she untangled herself from the sofa. A mug of cocoa should quieten her nerves, help her sleep. She shovelled three spoons of chocolate powder into a large mug, added hot milk and a heaped teaspoon of sugar for extra comfort. Her aching muscles screamed for her comfy bed, but it was too far from the front door. She needed to be on guard in case Pete paid a visit.

Lily placed her cocoa on the floor and curled up on the sofa. A frying pan within easy reach. As her eyes closed, she recalled the warmth of Daniel's jacket heavy on her shoulders, his soft whisper caressing her ear. *Sleep well.*

CHAPTER EIGHT

Doc and Spanner towered over Kate. Lily admired the way she stood her ground, insisted it was girl's turn to pay for movie tickets.

"Ah, ah. Stand down, soldier." Doc opened his mouth to argue. Stopped when Kate placed the tip of her pinkie on his lips.

"Six, please." Kate swiped her card over the machine and grabbed the tickets before Doc.

Lily shifted nervously. She'd counted five of them in line. There was still a chance Daniel, or Snake, would show.

"Snake sends his apologies. He had trouble finding a sitter for George." Spanner nudged her elbow and she jumped.

Military dogs were smart, independent, quite capable of being alone. Right? Judging from the communal snort, the answer was yes. Out of the corner of her eye, Daniel prowled across the foyer. His eyes fixed on her. She returned his confident smile, pleased he'd come.

"Hello, again, I didn't expect to see you here." She kept her tone friendly, light.

"How have you been, Lily?" Low and deep, his voice wrapped around her.

"Well, thanks. You?"

"Busy."

Mmm. That went well.

"Okay, grab what you need. We're going in." Kate, their tour guide for the evening, waved the tickets above her head and led the way.

Lily hugged her bucket of popcorn. "You don't want anything?" she asked, pointing to the candy bar, hoping to break the tension.

"No. I think you have enough for everyone." A crooked grin twisted the edges of his full lips.

Her cheeks flushed. The family-size was most definitely overkill. "Happy to share." She tilted it in his direction.

"I'd hang on to it if I were you, hun. Sentinel men never refuse food," Crystal interrupted, clutching her own prize.

Proving her point, Spanner pinched a Malteser from her packet.

Lily laughed and turned to Daniel. "Who does that? Pinches a girl's Malteser?"

"Got me," Daniel said, and snagged a piece of her popcorn. "After you." He swept his arm in front of her.

"Thank you." Such a gentleman. Good manners, unusual for Pete, but not Sentinel men. It didn't matter that Daniel only meant to be polite like he had at the restaurant, holding out her chair. That he took the trouble made her feel special.

Inside the cinema, everyone filed along the row of seats behind Kate. They were the last to follow. As the only non-couple, they stood out like a pimple. They were the last to sit. His thigh brushed against hers and her toes tingled. She leaned closer to Crystal.

"Okay, hun?"

"Oh, yes. Sorry." Lily stared at the blank screen and tried to ignore Daniel's gaze boring into her face. An overreaction, she couldn't blame him for thinking her strange. "Er, have some more popcorn."

"No, thanks. All yours," he replied without taking his eyes off her.

Thankfully, the lights dimmed before things got more awkward.

Kate and her damn matchmaking. After seeing Lily safely home from Kate's party, he didn't plan to see her again, not so soon at any rate, but he agreed on the movie, hoping for a chance to apologise for his behaviour at the Kebab house.

Completely captivated by Lily's sighs, he shifted in his narrow seat, trying to adjust the pressure in his jeans. His dick perked to attention any time he got within three feet of Lily. Inappropriate, predictable bloke, wondering what sounds she made during sex. *Jerk.*

Like a love-sick puppy, he turned his head slightly and tried to glimpse her face. *What the hell?* Tears. His arm twitched, itching to give her a reassuring squeeze.

"It's just a movie," he whispered.

"Yes. But it's sad." Lily's hand flapped in the darkness. Popcorn sailed onto the head of the man in front of her.

Two seats over, Spanner snickered. *Fuck you.* Knight mouthed.

"Shh." The man twisted in Knight's direction, met his glare, and quickly returned his attention to the screen.

"People." The woman beside him huffed in solidarity.

Bang 'em up, shoot 'em up. All in a day's work for Knight. Next to him, clearly overwhelmed, Lily gulped for air. Positive he'd never witnessed anyone have such a powerful reaction to a movie, he took a chance and gently touched her forearm. "Are you okay? Do you want to leave?"

"No. This is the good bit."

Knight's jaw went slack. *Say again.* The good bit? "Have you seen this movie before?" Far from a whisper, his voice boomed over the Dolby sound system.

"Shh!" Wanker's woman hissed.

"Yes, I've seen it twice," Lily said. "This part always gets me, but I'm spoiling it for people." Her finger poked at the row in front. "Stay. It's nearly over. I'll meet everyone outside."

No way. She looked a bit wobbly on those gazelle-like legs.

Knight placed her bucket of popcorn on the floor and shuffled past the rest of his team. Their eyes stayed glued to the numpty hero, taking his time bleeding out on the screen.

When he caught up with Lily in the foyer, she was a magnificent shade of purple. Arms wrapped tightly around her waist, she sucked in air. Still unsure what was happening, he kept his distance, but close enough to catch her if she passed out. "Breathe, Lily."

"Not helping," she gasped.

"Okay. Sit for a sec." Baffled by her over the top reaction, he nodded at the nearby chairs.

"No. I'm fine. Hell, I don't have any tissues."

Knight looked around, spotted a couple of serviettes by the ice cream stand, and shoved them into her hand. "Here."

Lily blew her nose and managed a thin laugh. Relieved her cheeks were a healthier shade of pink, his shoulders relaxed. "You sure you're okay."

"Yes, don't worry about me. I love a good cry in a movie, but I get stuffed up and…"

Fucking bizarre. Should he fetch Doc? "Why did you come if you've seen it?" Knight couldn't recall any film worth seeing a second time.

"Oh, I didn't mind, but I'm sorry you left. Do you want to know how it ends? That man, the one with the scar on his cheek. I bet you thought he was dead, well…"

He laughed. "No, don't tell me. He isn't dead?" Knight staggered. "I'm shocked."

"Okay. Smart guy." Lily raised a tiny fist and punched him in the chest. "Oh, sorry. I…"

"No harm done." He grabbed her fingers, but she kept tugging, so he let go of her hand. "Fancy an ice-cream?" He walked towards the thin lad guarding the fridge. Lily hesitated, and for a second his heart sank. "What flavour?" He added quickly, hoping to stop her from running.

Two steps before she answered. "A small one. Single scoop, thanks."

Now they were getting somewhere. Sugar on a stick should perk her up a bit. "Flavour?" he repeated.

She took her time studying the labels. "Um, *Satisfy My Soul*, please." Her eyes closed and her lips rolled together.

Knight gulped. "Sorry?"

"*Satisfy My Soul*." Lily pointed at the fridge. "It's great the cinemas are stocking these Fairtrade flavours. Truth is, I love all of them. How about you? What's your poison?"

"*Clear Content*." The first flavour his gaze settled upon.

Lily's infectious laugh bounced towards him, and his heart leapt after it. The teenager frowned, clearly not getting the joke.

"Glad to see you two enjoying yourselves. That was the worst movie I have seen in a long while." This time Crystal led, the others trailing behind her. "I could murder a hamburger with the lot. Anyone else homicidal?"

"Count me in," Spanner agreed, grinning, as he hooked his arms around Crystal's shoulder and rested his chin on top of her head.

"Try to keep us away." Kate snagged Doc's hand.

Seeing Kate and Crystal with their men made Lily happy and sad at the same time. She could only imagine how good it felt having a partner who loved and respected you. After Pete, she swore to admire men from a safe distance. Until Daniel lent her his coat.

"Coming for a burger?" She didn't want Daniel to leave but struggled not to sound too keen. No matter how tempted she might be to explore more of the soft centre she suspected lay beneath his moody exterior, her curiosity had led her to Pete, and she had no intention of repeating that mistake.

"No. I should get back. Have a shit load of paperwork to finish."

Hands in his pockets, shuffling from one foot to the other, Daniel angled his body to the exit.

"Come on. You have to eat, particularly if you are working late."

Daniel raised an eyebrow. Had she overstepped? Men like him gave orders. They didn't obey them. Sucking in a breath, she opened her mouth, ready to say goodbye when he stepped past her and held out his hand. "That goes for you, too. I'll bet you haven't eaten since…"

"Breakfast," she offered, but didn't take his hand.

They both laughed and Daniel fell in step beside her, shortening his stride, walking at her pace. A small gesture, but one that meant more than he might suspect.

The wind had picked up. Feeling a little chilly, she tugged at the collar of her jumper.

"Here. Take this." For the second time, Knight's soft leather jacket found its way around her shoulders, and she melted into its folds.

Seated at the burger place, Knight reached for the closest menu and handed it to Lily. "Here."

"Thanks."

Wow. What a smile. No flashing white teeth, but the sparkle in her eyes lit up the whole fucking place.

"Mighty Burgers all round?" Spanner asked.

Knight nodded. The triple layer meat on a bun should fill a hole. Lily wriggled beside him.

"Er. The Classic is enough for me, thanks," Lily said.

"Easy, hun. We don't all have bottomless pits for stomachs." Crystal patted her man's belly.

"Okay, but extra chips? Yes?" Spanner asked.

Knight turned and met Lily's grin. Yes sir. Chips, the fat ones, were more than fine with the petite woman beside him. Hollow legs in that department.

"Lily, what are you doing the weekend before we leave for Africa?" Kate lifted her chin towards Crystal. "We thought we might go camping. Do you want to come?"

Lily tensed beside him.

"I'd love to," she answered.

Blatant, fucking lie. Inwardly, he smiled.

"But…"

Thought so. Here it comes. He often sensed a *but* with Lily, the exception, the excuse. He took a sip of the water in front of him and waited.

"I've been very lucky to have your flat to stay, Crystal, and I'm grateful…"

But?

"I need my own place. Somewhere I can choose my own sheets, hang my favourite pictures on the wall. I won't be able to move in until I get back from Burkina, but I should start surfing the internet and chasing real estate agents. Maybe find a home."

Her last word faded to a whisper. Unable to resist, he rubbed his little finger along the edge of her hand, resting between them.

Lily flinched, and once again he scrambled for an apology.

"No problem," Kate said, and slapped her hands on the table. "Knight, didn't you say there's an empty flat where you live?"

He cleared his throat, feeling the noose tighten around his neck. "Yes. Not sure if it's still available."

"But you can ask, right?"

Fucking buts. Experience told him once Kate had the bit between her teeth, she would ride his hide into the ground until she got yes for an answer. Sentinel should hire her as an interrogator.

"Happy to check." Knight circled the tip of his finger around the top of his beer, marvelling at how stupid he'd become in the space of five minutes. Protectiveness and lust a fatal combination, but he recognised fear when he saw it. Everyone deserved to be safe in their home, and the security in his building added an extra layer of protection for a woman living alone.

"That would certainly save time. Where do you live?" she asked.

"Chalk Farm. Near Primrose Hill."

"Up the road from where you are now," Crystal offered. "Around the corner from the tube."

Lily's blue eyes, a deep blue this evening, rose to thank him. In the second it took for her smile to complete its journey, lift her cheeks, light up her eyes, he erected a wall high enough to barricade his soul. He could ensure Lily had a safe place to live. He would do the same for anyone in trouble. But words like home were foreign territory when describing four walls and a door. "I'll check with Bill, the porter, concierge, and call you at the clinic on Monday."

"Great, no more excuses, Lily, you're coming camping." Kate peered over Doc's shoulder. "Where are those burgers?"

Crystal rolled her eyes. "Do you like camping, Lily? I'm not mad about it. Spanner calls me a wimp for wanting to take the portable loo."

"I don't know. I've only been once."

"Boss. You in? Figure we'd get in some climbing. How's the shoulder holding up?" Spanner asked.

He had caught a bullet when they'd rescued Kate from Seckou last year. The wound had healed, but he was still working on gaining full range of motion through the joint. An aching reminder fuck head, Seckou, was still on the loose.

Kate ducked her head. No matter how much he and Doc worked to convince her, she blamed herself for him getting shot. "Shoulder's good, Spanner." He lifted his finger and waved it in Kate's direction. *Don't go there.*

Trooping off in a gang, not usually his thing, but he sensed a spirit of adventure behind the shy glint in Lily's eye and it intrigued him.

"Camping sounds good. Lily you're coming, right?" *What the fuck am I saying?*

"Okay, if I find a home, but I'm not sure I have the right clothes."

"No problem. Sentinel has enough wet weather gear to kit the whole of Russia in a blizzard."

"But, aside from a three-day camp in cabins at boarding school, I know nothing about sleeping under the stars." Lily's laugh was silent, more a stutter of happy breaths that shot his resolve to hell.

"No buts, allow me to be your first." For a chance to see more of her, he'd join Kate's adventure.

"All right, why not?"

Lily settled beside him, enjoying her meal. Unbelievable, the amount of tomato sauce she poured on her chips. Eyes twinkling, she fished deeper into the bowl and offered him one covered in the red stuff.

"All yours. Build your strength. You're going to need it." Knight grinned. Not fully convinced Lily moving into his building was a great idea, but he looked forward to taking her camping.

"You know coffee's bad for you?" Lily beamed, the tip of her cute nose tilting towards the rim of his cup.

"And the benefits of sugar? Tomato sauce is loaded with it." Knight pointed at her half-eaten chip.

Lily caught his finger, held it for a second before she thought better of it. His cock stirred, enjoying this fun side of her. Disappointment rocked him when her confidence faded, and she let go of his hand.

Tempted to reach for it again, he sat back and admired the way her mouth demolished another fat chip, a crumb from the burger bun gracing the crease between her lips. He should offer to swipe it away. Instead, he turned and counted the umbrellas passing by the window.

CHAPTER NINE

Lily jerked upright. The room was dark except for a slither of daylight edging under the door.

One eye open, her hand pawed in a wide arc over the sofa, searching for the buzzing phone.

As promised, Daniel had called confirming the empty flat, and offering to pick her up and take her to meet Bill this morning. But it was early, too early. Something must have happened. Why else would he be calling? "Hello," she croaked.

"Good morning, slut. Is he there with you?"

She shuddered. This had to stop. "Pete. Stop calling me." Suddenly very much awake and angry, her fingers tightened on her mobile. "It is none of your bloody business." She stood. Having her feet on the ground gave her courage.

"Get rid of him. You belong to me, Lily. No one else."

Wide awake now, she grabbed the scissors she kept under the sofa seat. "Leave me alone. Or I will..." Her hands shook so hard she almost dropped the phone.

"Will, what?" he snarled.

She gripped the scissors tighter. Feet wide, she scanned the corners of the room. *Really bright, Lily.* Not even a bloody cockroach could hide there. Hysteria bubbled inside. "I am calling the police."

"Really? You've done that before, remember? Daddy wasn't impressed with darling daughter the last time. Took me less than a minute to convince him you missed me and were just craving attention. Poor baby," he snarled.

How could she forget? Her father had summoned her to his office like a naughty girl. He barely restrained himself from saying she didn't deserve Pete, then sent her back to her loving man. Pathetic.

Pete's cackle assaulted her ear. He hung up before she could beat him to it. Bile rose in her throat. Hand to her mouth, she rushed to the bathroom and threw up in the sink. Hopefully, Panadol would fix her throbbing head. She took two and fell onto the sofa. Snuggled under her duvet, she finally dosed off, comatose, until banging on the door woke her.

Please, no. Pete. She was sick of playing Miss Sorry Sack in the basement with her scissors. It might be funny if deep down she wasn't terrified. Ignoring him wouldn't make him go away. She clutched the crude weapon and crab-walked to the door.

"Lily, it's me, Daniel." His warm baritone rumbled towards her.

Relieved, she dropped the scissors and gulped her tears.

"Lily?"

"What do you want?"

"Bill. Remember? The porter."

Oh frick. The flat. "Sorry, hang on a minute." She fumbled with three locks plus the safety chain and inched open the door. Her nose twitched. The smell of strong coffee wafting from the takeaway cups meant during the night she had died and gone to heaven.

Without thinking, she rose on tip toe and pecked him on the cheek. "For me. You are a bloody lifesaver."

"A kiss for caffeine. What would French toast get me?"

"Hilarious."

Too late. His eyes landed on the scissors by her feet.

"What's this?" He bent to retrieve them.

"Oh. I wondered where they got to." She snatched them from his fingers. "Sorry, I was up late sewing. I overslept. Give me five minutes to shower?"

"No sweat. Here, better take your coffee." He nudged the cup into her hand.

"Thanks. Have a seat."

Daniel didn't say a word as he shuffled her duvet to one end of the sofa.

Several gulps of double espresso energised her enough to shower and dress. Jeans and a soft blue jumper, complete with ankle boots.

Daniel sat, forearms resting on his knees, frowning as he flicked through the pages of *House Beautiful.*

Lily snatched the magazine out of his hands. She only bought the damn thing because the ones in the clinic waiting room needed refreshing. The sudden move threw her off balance and she would have tumbled into Daniel's lap if he hadn't caught her.

"Steady."

They froze for a moment. Wow, if only her life wasn't such a mess, she could get used to staring into his silver eyes.

"You set? We can catch breakfast after we talk to Bill," he said, then let go of her arm.

"Yes. All good." Her stomach churned, objecting to the idea of food this early in the morning. "Thanks again for helping me. I appreciate it.

"No problem, and don't give Bill a second thought. I keep him sweet at Christmas with a cask of port."

They made it halfway up the stairs before her mobile beeped. Pete never missed his daily text. A litany of her faults and threats. Reminders. She belonged with him.

"You want to get that?" Daniel's patient concern only made things worse.

"No. it's not important. I'll check it later. Wow, this is impressive." Daniel had found a park right out front. "Who did you bribe for the magic parking pass?"

"Stick with me, kid."

She loved watching his dimples hollow when he smiled. A welcome tenderness on his normally grumpy face. Lily switched her phone to silent. After they finished this morning, she would take Sam's advice and file a complaint against Pete.

Daniel drove into the sweeping courtyard of his building, got out and swung around the front of the MG. He opened her door and offered his hand. Taking it, she stepped out of the car, stared at the impressive block of flats, and felt her heart sink.

More than a step up from Crystal's basement, the rent would be well out of her pocket. Mentally, Lily kicked herself. What was she thinking? She should have realised it was a no go when Daniel mentioned a concierge. The word oozed expensive.

Dressed in a dark green uniform, complete with a peaked hat, Bill sat in the small booth in the lobby reading the *Daily Mirror*.

"Morning." Daniel tapped the sliding glass.

"Captain Knight. Morning to you, sir." Judging by his stiff half-rise from the chair, the palm supporting his lower back, Bill spent most of his day sitting.

"At ease, man. Meet my friend, Lily…

"Storm." Lily smiled and held out her hand.

"Storm?" Daniel repeated and laughed. "Figures." A full, deep chuckle shook his broad chest. "A rose by any other name, ay?"

Bill winked.

"Lily needs somewhere to live. You mentioned there may be a flat in our building?"

"Yes. Morning, Miss. Nice to meet you. Been looking long?" His handshake was firm but friendly.

"Hello. No, er, just started." She glanced at her feet—no need to bore either of them with the full sad story.

Bill removed his hat and scratched his head. "Well, must be your lucky day. It's not official yet, but the tenant in number eighteen, the floor above the captain, is vacating at the end of this week." He nudged Daniel with his elbow. "Remember the villa in Ibiza Mrs G's always cracking on about? Go figure. Her mother died and left it to her. The real estate agent on the corner looks after it. Charlie Brown. Yep, no joke. Tell him I sent you."

"Nice one. Appreciate it, Bill. Catch you later."

"No problem, Captain. A pleasure to meet you, Miss Storm." Bill tapped the rim of his hat with two fingers.

"Lily, please."

"Okay then. Good luck, Miss Lily."

Ten minutes later, the bell clanged above the real estate agent's door.

"Good morning. We are looking for Mr Brown. Bill sent us from Eton Grove." Daniel flashed the receptionist a delicious grin, the one that made Lily's toes curl.

"I'm sorry, he is out of the office at the moment." She swallowed and shimmied her skirt over her hips.

"Any idea when he'll be back?" Daniel asked.

"Sorry, no. I'm Tracy, can I help?" The tip of her tongue swept her upper lip.

Lily smiled, betting the sparkle in Captain Knight's eye slayed many women. She was a tad jealous that the warmth from his smile didn't radiate over her. "Thanks, Tracy, is there someone else that might help me?"

Sure, she'd turned it to silent earlier, Lily flinched when her phone buzzed in her pocket.

"Just a minute I'll check with Mr Levy. Take a seat." Tracy took her time wiggling past them, her eyes scanning Knight from head to toe before she disappeared.

"Cheers, Tracy, appreciate it." Warm and inviting, Knight's voice rolled after her. How could she fault him for that?

Daniel nodded at her ringing pocket. "Someone wants to talk to you. Why don't you get it while our friend Tracy is checking with her boss?"

"No. It can wait." This time she double-checked, made sure her phone had switched to phone silent. "There, no more interruptions."

Seconds later, the young woman returned with a set of keys dangling from her perfectly manicured hand. She hung on to them a little longer than necessary when Daniel reached for them.

"Mr Levy says you are welcome to view."

Lily rolled her eyes. "Come on, heartbreaker."

The flat was amazing. She never doubted it. One look at the dust reflecting off the beams of light streaming through the Palladian window and fell in love. A spiral staircase led to a mezzanine with ample space for her queen-sized bed. A claw-foot bath and a galley kitchen completed the dream. She didn't care how many days a week she had to eat beans on toast to afford the place.

Thanks to Daniel, she'd found a home. All before breakfast.

The only blip in a perfect morning. The constant vibration of her phone in her pocket.

CHAPTER TEN

Knight slipped his palm into the small of Lily's back. Lily hadn't stopped smiling since she signed the lease, and hell if his chest didn't swell with pride knowing he'd made her day. Home meant nothing to him but helping Lily find hers. Bonus.

He glanced at his screen. Both their phones had been humming and vibrating all fucking morning and Lily's side-long glances checking to see if he noticed her unease hadn't gone unnoticed.

Three messages from Snake explained his annoying beeps, but not Lily's. And no, clutching her pocket and hardening her jaw didn't stop her phone from chirping.

The hairs on the back of his neck stood to attention. Pete, he suspected, had his finger glued to the green button.

Lily hadn't asked for help, but he'd check with Kate, see if she had confided in her. In the meantime, it wouldn't hurt if Snake did a background check on Arseworthy. He may even pay bellend a visit, make sure he understood Lily had friends.

Priority. Get out of the shit rain smashing the pavement. Familiar ghosts emerged from the wet mist. His mother lying in the mud, a hole in her head. Hair matted with blood. Lily's fingers slip from his hand. With a shout, he snatched her out of the path of an oncoming bus.

"Jesus, Lily. Watch it." Her body slammed against him. Startled blue eyes fixed on a spot above his head.

"Stupid. Stupid. Sorry, I should have been looking where I put my feet."

Both her palms pressed against his chest, but he couldn't let go, not yet, not until he was sure she was safe. "It's okay." He blamed himself for not paying attention. "Locals complained when they switched from the double-deckers. You can't miss them when they bale down on you. These new, articulated snakes are deadly." He faked a laugh, hoping she'd relax.

"Yes, yes. Sorry. I thought I saw him." Her head swivelled left and right.

"Who Lily?" *Trust me, let me help you.*

With a single blink, she pulled down the shutters. He couldn't let it rest. "Who was it, Lily?"

"No one. Ignore me. I need more coffee." Her eyes glistened.

"Lily. You're trembling." Knight wrapped his arm around her shoulders, settled his chin on top of her head, and sheltered her from rain. "Is it Pete? Say the word. I'll be more than happy to take care of him."

Outside the tube station, not the best place for this discussion, but he intended to get answers now, before she completely shut him out. Remembering how overwhelmed she got whenever they got too close, he loosened his grip on her arms. "Please, Lily. Talk to me."

"No. I can handle him, and I don't want to be rude, but it's none of your business. Thanks for this morning, I appreciate your help, but I should head for the clinic. I'm working today."

"Dammit, say the word and I will make it my business." He raised her chin, so she had no option but to look at him. Tears filled her eyes. "Lily." He blew gently on her lips, begging permission, wanting nothing more than to kiss her, reassure her.

"Get a room."

Lily jerked. Knight stepped back and his heel landed on something soft. A dog yelped, pissed that he'd trod on its paw. "Sorry, mate." The golden retriever wagged his tail, loving the apologetic scratch behind the ears. "You like that, ay?" A long, wet lick his slobbery reward. His heart swelled when Lily knelt beside him and nuzzled the dog's neck with her nose.

The owner, her dark eyes boring into them, teetered on her high heel boots. With a huff she tugged on her dog's collar. Her blue-spotted umbrella tipped sideways and dumped water on him. Poor mutt yelped.

"You two are old enough to know better. Canoodling in public."

"Canoodling?" Lily giggled.

The woman, plus shaggy dog, took off along the street.

"Her dog liked you," Lily said, still laughing.

It baffled him how she always found the longing in his heart and jerked its ragged edges. As for her smile—it slew him every time.

"I have a soft spot for retrievers. My friend Sam has three. That poor dog was overweight. Nothing a daily run wouldn't fix. Do you like dogs?" she asked, her eyes begging him not to continue his earlier questioning.

Okay, off the hook for now. Tread gently, or Lily would retreat further. "Love 'em. Hate cats. I hear you never cross the path of a black one."

He had a dog when he was a kid and planned on having another when he retired. *What the fuck.* Pets—never going to happen. Chances were high he'd die on a mission long before he pulled a pension.

Knight squeezed the ends of her fingers. "Let's get out of this bloody rain. Give me a sec to grab something from the flat and I'll drive you to work." They ran the rest of the way, reaching his building at record speed. Lily was fit, smart, and sexy as hell.

"How did you go, Captain?" Bill set his paper on the table. The headline on the back page said it all. Arsenal still fucked, didn't matter how much they paid for players.

"Meet your new tenant." Lily offered Bill a wobbly curtsey. Rain dripping from her fringe.

Yeah, he was getting used to that soft glow of happiness creeping over her face.

"Champion, my lady." Bill doffed his hat. "Best you two get dry before you catch pneumonia."

Knight nodded. "Good idea. Come on. You can towel off at mine."

"Perfect. But it will have to be quick. I have patients waiting," Lily said.

Minutes later, she stood in his living room. Minimalist, a polite word for his furnishings. He cleared his throat, suddenly wishing he had a few pictures on the wall. And the rest. Other than somewhere to sleep, his flat served as Sentinel's office.

"Love what you've done with the place." Looking as though she belonged, Lily turned in a slow circle.

"Smart arse. The bathroom's through there. Clean towels in the cupboard. Spare toothbrushes in the drawer. Use whatever you need." He watched as the arse in question wiggled away from him. *Mind in the game, hero.*

Knight flicked through his emails. Aunty had sent him intel from the refugee camp in Africa. They'd get Seckou this time. Mike's ghost offered him the familiar beer. *Too early in the morning.*

He glanced at the pile of books he'd bought for the kids. Schooling was mandatory in Burkina, but kids had to buy their own books and stationery. Kate had offered to take them with her.

A shuffling caught his attention. Lily stood in the bathroom doorway towelling her hair. A thousand different shades, ranging from the pink of the dawn sun to the pale gold of the moon, glistened in the strands escaping over her shoulders. Shit, he was turning into a poet in his old age.

"Why do you hate rain?" Her muffled question took him off guard.

"You get wet." Knight answered, his gaze fixed on her hair.

"Sorry, I..."

He did it again. Pushed her away. Loss of eye contact, the visible desire to disappear inside her skin. He loathed it. Nothing else for it but to jump right in, spewing intel as though he'd spent days under torture. "I thought we were past apologising." Two strides and he caught her fingers before they covered her mouth. "Rain, it reminds me of stuff I'd rather forget."

Lily stared at their joined hands.

"The day she died. I found her. My mother. I had been up late the night before studying. I slept in, took my time getting up the next morning. When she wasn't in the house, I went to her usual retreat. The garden."

"How old were you?"

"Old enough."

"What happened?"

"Short version. My mother used my father's back-up service revolver to blow her brains out."

She raised their clasped hands level with her heart. "And the long version?"

The warm assault of her delicate fingers was too much to bear. He tried but couldn't pull away. "My father was a hard man."

"I understand that one," she said.

Fuck's sake. If Lily kept gnawing at her bottom lip, she could skip breakfast.

"And... Lily squeezed his hand.

"A career soldier, dear dad, often absent. On duty. My mother missed the cold-hearted bastard. Life wasn't any different when he came home. He ignored her. Except for when he verbally abused her for putting too much salt in the soup, a crease in his shirt, mess in the kitchen."

Lily cringed. Pete. A chip off his father's block. "She left a note, said she didn't want to live alone."

"But she had you."

He claimed his hand from hers. A lame arse attempt to free

himself. Not having any of it, Lily captured his cheek in her palm. Ruffled by the towel, her hair was a mess. Fucking. Beautiful.

"Go on."

Damn. Knight stared at Lily's translucent skin and swore he could read every chapter of her soul.

"After she died, I lost it for a while, angry most of the time. I got into fights. School finally gave me an ultimatum. Pull myself together or leave."

"You were grieving. What did they expect? And your dad?"

"Didn't miss a beat. He sent me to live with my aunt."

"Oh, Daniel, that must have been awful."

Christ, he didn't want this, didn't need Lily's pity. "You ready to go?"

"Daniel…"

Knight ignored her sigh.

"Since I signed up, Spanner, Doc, Snake, they're my family. The only family I need."

She glanced at him. "Me and my big mouth. I did it again."

"No, it's okay, I wanted to tell you."

It took a strength he didn't realise he possessed to hold her gaze, allow her to press her body to his in a hug that made his heart implode.

He snaked his arms around her back, and buried his nose between her breasts, soaking up the comfort.

"Thank you for trusting me." She hugged him tighter.

Knight closed his eyes, amazed at Lily's kindness. He didn't deserve it. For years he blamed himself for not saving his mother, dealt out personal punishment for not listening to the voice in his head that warned of her sadness, signalled her suicide. His breath hitched as he let go of her. "No problem. Let's get you to work."

CHAPTER ELEVEN

Surrounded by the rainbow glow from the vanilla candles Crystal bought her last Christmas, Lily watched shadows dancing on the bathroom ceiling. The gentle breath out of her nose skimmed the bath bubbles covering her knees as she sank beneath the water.

Organising her move was exhausting, list after list until, finally, she'd taken care of everything. There was bound to be something she missed, but she'd done her best.

Daniel had been amazing, helping her when he could. Unlike her, he didn't put his foot in his mouth every five seconds, asking too many questions, though judging by the odd raised eyebrow or two, he had a few.

They had known each other for just over a month. Lily ran the nail of her pinkie over the drop of water trickling between her breasts and sighed. Even when he was grumpy, it felt right being with him.

Beneath the warmth water, her fingers found the nub between her thighs. She stroked and caressed it until the gentle burn became intense and she closed her eyes. Tingles ran across the soft flesh beneath her navel. A soft moan escaped her lips.

Dammit.

Her neighbour's dog howled louder than a wolf at the full moon. Harry. The giant schnauzer hated been left alone and his owner worked nights. Chilly air bit into her shoulders as she gripped the sides as she hauled herself out of the bath.

Screeching tyres, raised voices, filtered through the small crack in the window above her head. Heart hammering, Lily reached for a towel.

Usually, Harry took breaks. Not tonight. Curious to find out what put him on edge, she pulled on workout pants and a hoodie and slipped her feet into comfortable shoes. Before heading out, she grabbed her parka, zipped it to her chin and climbed the stairs onto the street.

"Quiet, Harry," she commanded, mimicking the tone she'd heard Sam use with her dogs.

Lily shivered, the calming effect of her warm bath swiftly fading. The frosty night air nipped her toes, flip-flops not the best footwear. She bunched the edges of her parka tightly around her neck.

At the end of the street, a yellow light spun eerily, casting shadows in between the parked cars. Pity the poor driver who must have called for a tow. Not much fun waiting in the cold for the RAC to arrive.

Behind her Harry let out a bone-chilling howl. Combined with black night, she could have been in a horror movie. "It's okay, boy. Your dad will be home soon." She wished she had a key to her neighbour's.

Despite the prospect of freezing to death, it didn't sit right to leave him barking furiously locked inside, so she sat on the doorstep and chatted to him through the crack in the door.

After ten minutes Harry had calmed enough for her to think of heading inside to thaw. Turning quickly, she didn't notice the patch of ice on the step until her feet slid from under her and her backside slammed hard onto the pavement. Cupping her hand around the piercing ache in her left hip, she scrambled to her feet.

"You okay, miss?"

Startled, Lily turned to see the dark shadow of a man towering over her. "Er yes. Thank you. All good. Nothing hurt, but my pride." She winced.

"Bloody 'ooligans. Must be something on at *Lockside*." He waved a fist toward the local nightclub.

"Must be."

"You okay? Need a hand?"

"No thanks. I'm fine, honestly."

"If you're sure?"

Lily nodded.

"Night." He carried on down the street, mumbling under his breath.

Lily scrubbed the back of her neck and glanced at her watch. One a.m. *Blast.* Thankfully, she didn't have to be at work until noon. Plenty of time to catch a few hours' sleep. As if they weren't busy enough, tomorrow they expected a visit from the young mother's group at the community house.

No barks from Harry. At least he slept. She hurried back to her basement. Halfway down the stairs, the hand gripping the railing trembled.

Her door was wide open. Surely, she closed it. Not to worry, she'd only been a few feet away, easily able to spot anyone on her stairs. Tentatively, she gave it a shove and stepped inside her flat. "Hello."

Seriously, Lily? Who did that? Aunty May.

Her numpty aunty had found the door to her home open once and walked in to greet the burglars—got hit on the head for her trouble. Lily grabbed the umbrella by the door. No knocked over chairs, no smashed vases, nothing except the disturbing feeling she had been invaded.

Too much late night tellie. No one lurked behind the curtain or hid in the shower. The cask of wine in her fridge called. She made her way to the kitchen and filled her glass to the brim. *Large for me.* Comforted by Daniel's voice rumbling inside her, she collapsed on the lumpy sofa and parked her legs on the coffee table. The piece of white paper that hadn't been there when she left stood out like chalk on a blackboard. Hands shaking, she unfolded it.

Hello Lily. Miss me?

No. How much more of this could she take? She reached for her phone and called Kate.

———

"What the bloody hell were you thinking, Lily?" Fuming, Knight, in full protector mode, prowled around the living room after her.

Kate had meant it when she said if she didn't call the police, she'd call Knight to check on her. His question was valid. She hadn't been thinking. Not sensibly, at any rate. "Not a brilliant move. What can I say? I got lost in the moment." An Aunty May moment, she wanted to add, but suspected he wouldn't appreciate the joke.

"What fucking moment, Lily? Sudden death?"

"Now you are being a pain. Kate shouldn't have called you. Why don't you leave and let me sleep? I have a full day at the clinic tomorrow and you always have plenty to do."

"Like hell. I'm not going anywhere. Go to bed, I'll take the sofa, we can talk in the morning."

"Fine." Secretly relieved of the reprieve and grateful she didn't have to be alone, she went to the hall cupboard, tossed Daniel a pillow and blanket, and wished him goodnight. It took ages, but finally must have fallen asleep.

Lily whistled out of tune, still learning, hugged her knees to her chest and held tight to dolly's hand.

"Come on, Lily," her father's voice boomed up the ladder of the tree house. "Let's play Monopoly, 'til mum gets here."

Every time they moved mum joked, she would pack the silly game rather than her knickers. Dolly whined and Lily stroked her hair. "It's okay, she'll be home soon." Her tummy ached and only mummy could fix it.

"Come down, Lily, Peggy made dinner," her father shouted.

"I don't care." Lily stared at her legs. Slim, not skinny, mum said.

Dolly's glassy eyes brimmed with disappointment. She should be on her side. Mummy broke her promise.

No more Monopoly, no goodnight kisses.

Dolly screamed. Lily opened her mouth. Air rushed from her lungs.

Knight's hand instinctively searched for the weapon locked in the safe in his office. *Shit.* Elbows resting on his knees, he sat on the edge of the sofa trying to get a bead on what had dragged him from sleep?

Lily had screamed.

Reflexes firing, he ran to her bedroom and flung open the door. A sliver of light bled on to her bed. Tangled in the sheets, fighting with an invisible attacker, her arms and legs punched at empty air.

"Lily." Not wanting to startle her, he stayed in the doorway. When she screamed again, fucked if he could hold back any longer. He sat on the edge of the mattress and tried not to stroke the satiny skin of her slim thighs. Sweat glistened on her brow. "Lily," he called, louder this time.

Unresponsive, her head tossed side to side. "Lily, wake up." The pads of his fingers brushed her hair from her face.

Eyes wide, unseeing, she scuttled to the far side of the bed.

"It's okay. You had a bad dream." Keeping his movements even, he slowly rose to one knee and offered her his hand. She didn't take it, but her breaths evened out. "Just a nightmare, Lily. You're okay. Why don't I make us some tea?"

When she nodded, he slid from the bed and gave her space, but his heart didn't find a normal pulse until she slipped from the bedroom and joined him in the kitchen. "Sit, kettle's almost boiled."

"Thanks. Sorry, about earlier. I was rude. I'm glad you're here."

The simple apology struck him to the core. He swallowed hard and fixed his gaze on her mismatched teacups. If he moved, it would be to scoop her into his arms and kiss every inch of her.

"Knight?"

"Daniel, remember?" he interrupted.

"Yes. Daniel, you are the protection expert. I understand you're busy, but if you have time, maybe you could give me a defence lesson, show me a few moves before I leave for Africa."

He hated the brave effort to shake off her anxiety, the shiver vibrating through her body, despite how tightly she wound her arms around her waist.

"No problem but let me talk to Pete."

"No. It wasn't him." Her muted response didn't hide the lie.

CHAPTER TWELVE

Knight swallowed the unpleasant taste in his mouth, the acid bile, a combination of anger and deep concern for the frustrating woman who refused his help. He could kick himself for losing it with her the other night.

Sure as shit stank, Pete was her intruder. A part of him hoped she was as wise as Doc, that her instincts were sound, and that by refusing to permit a word in the Pete's ear he would walk away. *Not fucking likely.*

It was a risk he couldn't take. Without notice, he might be called away. Unable to protect Lily. In the circumstances, assigning her one of Sentinel's bodyguard team served as his best bet to keep her safe. She could scream at him later.

He called to say he'd be late, stuck checking last-minute details for the Africa trip, making sure Spanner and Doc had everything they needed when they got the green light.

Sentinel, his brothers, trusted him to keep them alive, and he honoured their trust. Everyone watched each other's backs, prepared to die for each other, and he moved heaven and earth to make sure they never did. Mike's death had been a sharp reminder of what happened when he dropped the ball. Never again. A third-generation soldier. No longer in the military but serve and protect were etched with poison into his DNA.

His job description relied on right world order, not the clusterfuck of emotions threatening his sanity. Worrying about Lily took up too much head space. As tempting as it was to take things further, eventually he'd hurt her. A relationship out of the question.

Right now, he looked forward to showing her a few moves to send Arseworthy to his knees if he came near her again. Taking a deep breath, he strode into Ed's, the martial arts dojo. A large, repurposed warehouse.

Grunts and groans reverberated around him. A small group gathered in the centre of the open space, welcomed a break from slamming heavy bags and egged on the pair sparring in the ring.

He didn't expect to see Snake standing by the row of speed bags. Weekends, he usually hung out at Byzantium. A year ago, they'd checked out the private club together. Snake took out a membership. Knight found Maeve. Different paths to the same end. Consensual sex—no strings attached.

Snake laughed, shifted a fraction to reveal Lily. Dressed in workout pants and a tank top, she held court, surrounded by the mixed martial arts team from the local copshop. Enough brawn between the four men to bulldoze a skyscraper.

And no one could accuse Lily of being mean. Her giggle, free as the air he fought hard to access whenever he laid eyes on her, brightened every dusty crevice of the sweat palace. His heart kicked inside his chest. Her laugh warmed his soul. Made him vulnerable. Ever since the day he found his mother's body, he waited for the next unsuspected kick to his gut. Knight exhaled, freed the tension cramping his hands and moved swiftly to her side.

"Daniel." Lily adjusted her ponytail, wielded her smile like a red-hot poker, searing his resolve.

His name hung on her shallow breathing. Her elevated pulse beat at the side of her neck and the nervousness flashing across her face pierced his armour. "Need help with that?" He tucked a strand of honey blonde hair behind her ear.

"Daniel? Is everything okay?" Slim fingers grazed his as she took control of the recalcitrant lock.

Fuck. He shoved his wandering hands in his pocket and backed away from her sweet scent.

More used to hearing him referred to as Knight or Boss, Snake rolled his eyes. Knight held his gaze, daring him to comment.

"What kept you, Boss?" Snake's tap on the shoulder, a fucking lifesaver.

"Work. Someone's got to do it. Don't you need to be somewhere else?"

Keeping his arms bent, palms out, Snake backed away. "Leaving, Boss. Take care, Lily, see you around." He whistled at George. After Mike died, he'd adopted his dog. Officially, the sixth member of the Sentinel Alpha team. He stirred, nonplussed at having his nap disturbed. Teeth bared in a half-hearted snarl, he padded after his handler.

"Okay, grumpy bum. If you still want to show me those moves, let's start before I chicken out." Lily tapped his other shoulder. The kindness, the light in her eyes as she coaxed him away from being a full-blown dick, slew him.

He threw his gym bag in the corner, groping for precious seconds to pull himself together. "Take a sip of water before we begin."

Lily bent at the waist and grabbed her bottle. "Yes, Boss."

When she caught him staring at her long, shapely legs and well-rounded arse, she blushed.

"Let's start with a gentle warm-up," he coaxed, fairly sure his cheeks flushed too.

If he didn't know better, he'd swear he was possessed. Certainly not himself lately.

Lily jogged on the spot. Light on her feet, they barely touched the ground. For the next ten minutes, he admired her fitness as she kept up with him through a cardio sequence. Her breasts, round and perky, bounced along to the rhythm of her tiny toes, tip-tapping the mat, until beads of sweat glistened on his forehead.

"Right. Now, your blood's pumping. Place one foot behind the other. Heel down. A few lunges to stretch the back of the thigh and calf." He jabbered like a newly minted personal trainer, sucking in his breath when Lily did what he asked. As her torso dipped forward, her cleavage deepened. *Fuck.* He rolled his shoulders and ranted about the importance of flexibility in all areas, including the neck. His eyes trailed across the ceiling, down to his shoes.

"How are you feeling? Ready to learn a few moves?"

"Absolutely. You might not believe this, but I've been looking forward to this session."

"Okay. First rule. Run."

"Excuse me." Her head tilted to the side. He chuckled at the disappointment creasing her face. Inside this quiet, shy woman lurked a fighting spirit, and he itched to shine a light on that side of her.

"Run. Do your best, as soon as possible, to put distance between you and your attacker."

To test her reaction, he flicked his towel in front of her nose, unsurprised when she closed her eyes. Normal in beginners, people not used to aggressive confrontation.

"Keep your eyes open, or you'll never see what's coming at you."

Lily squared her shoulders and stood taller.

"That's it, widen your feet. Eyes open," he insisted. "Your size is both a disadvantage and an advantage." He kept his voice even. "A bigger attacker is likely to be stronger, but you are lighter, quicker."

Lily smiled. "Take your best shot."

Knight didn't hesitate. He lunged for her throat. Startled, she stumbled backwards, unmistakable panic catching her breath. He loosened his hold. It hadn't been tight, intended to surprise, not hurt her. He scanned her neck, looking for injury. No marks. Shuffling back, he gave her a second to recover. "Fact number one. Six seconds in a serious assailant's grip..." He clicked his fingers. "That's all it takes before you are unconscious. Try it again. Ready?"

"Yes."

This time, he went slower, deliberately softening his approach. "What's your first instinct. What do you want to do?" he asked, keeping his gaze on her face.

"This." Lily grabbed his forearms and tried to wrench them apart.

"Not going to work. My press inwards is stronger than your pull outwards." He let go of her and retreated. "Your turn, shrimp. This time, you grab me." Knight bent his knees to bring his torso more in line with hers.

"Hey, less of the shrimp."

He relaxed, pleased the fight returned to her voice. As her hands grabbed his thick neck, he took a step back, ducked, and released himself from the circle of her arms.

"How did you do that?"

"Easy. Take it slow. Grab me again." Lily lurched forward. "That's it. Watch. I step back onto my strong foot, duck, break your grip, then run like fucking hell."

Lily laughed. Pleased, he joined her. The last thing he wanted was to scare her so hard she quit. They repeated the sequence a few times until she successfully accomplished the move.

"I did it. I did it." Lily jumped up and down, bursting with excitement.

His blood boiled at the thought of anyone hurting her. Over the next hour they went through a couple more moves, their inevitable closeness the way her body brushed against his, made him hornier than hell. No surprise if the erection pressing painfully against his jocks left a permanent impression.

"Break." Panting, Lily rested her hands on her knees. "Need a drink."

Knight reached for her water and placed it in her hand. "Good job. You're a fast learner. Let's call it quits for today."

"No, I'm okay. Keep going." She tossed her bottle at her bag and faced him, elbows bent, fists raised in a fighting stance.

"Okay, Wonder Woman, half-an-hour. It's one thing to practice individual moves. Let's try a role-play so you can string a few together."

"Sounds good." Lily nodded once and rolled her lips.

Strong, fit and toned, slightly built, and not very tall. For a man his size, easy to hurt with or without training. "We'll keep it simple. You're the last one to leave the clinic. It's dark. The car park is empty except for your vehicle. Out of nowhere you see a stranger."

Frustration and anger at Lily's vulnerability simmered below the surface. Knight curled his hands into fists and sprung towards her. Lily's sharp cry, her rapid breathing, didn't stop him. He kept coming, unrelenting, unapologetic.

"Knight." Lily froze. Fear replaced her earlier excitement, and she closed those damn eyes.

"Open your eyes," he shouted. "Open your fucking eyes."

"Daniel, stop. You're scaring me."

"I should hope so. I'm a man determined to hurt you, Lily, not take you for sodding dinner." He backed off a little and lowered his voice. "Do I have a knife, a gun? Or just my bare hands to get what I want? What are you going to do, Lily?"

"I don't know. Please, Daniel." Her chin dropped—her voice drifted away.

"Think, Lily. Don't stop thinking or you are dead."

"Please."

"Think, Lily. What's your next move?"

With a roar, she raised her foot and aimed for his balls. A little too close for comfort, forcing him to fall back to a less vulnerable position. "That's it. Now what?"

"Run." She struggled for breath. Her skin pale beneath the flush on her cheeks.

Maybe she wasn't as fit as he thought. Unable to handle her distress one fucking second longer, he sucked the violence out of the space between them and lowered his voice. "Now you're thinking, Lily. Breathe, sweetheart. Look at me, please. You have to know I will never hurt you."

He felt like shit, knowing he'd frightened her. The desire to take her in his arms, protect her from any threat for the rest of her life coursed through his veins. "Come to me, Lily." Her eyes brimmed with tears. He wanted to slit his wrists and bleed out on the dojo mat.

"Why did you do that?" She cuffed a tear with the sleeve of her t-shirt.

"I'm sorry, Lily. Defending yourself is never a game. You're smart, but…" He lowered his body until they were eye level, cupped her chin and willed her to look at him. "Women are vulnerable to men, predators, who enjoy hurting them. Bullies like Pete."

Lily cleared her throat, ignoring his deliberate reference to her ex.

"No, it's me who should be sorry. Thanks for being patient. Pete *has* been bothering me. Phone calls, stupid notes."

He curled his hands into fists, biting back the urge to tell her what to do. It took everything in him to stay silent, not to push, simply honour her trust. Lily Storm had torpedoed a path to his heart. The one muscle in his body he'd been happy to let atrophy. Die rather than feel this longing. Emotion that went far beyond wanting to bed her.

Her slim fingers curled around his forearm. "Join me for a quick cup of coffee?"

"You bet." He cleared his throat and hoped she'd talk more about Pete. "Shower, get dressed. I'll meet you at the juice bar in the foyer. No rush." In his head, he had stretched coffee to lunch and…

"I have to pick up the rest of my stuff."

"Stuff?"

"From Pete's."

CHAPTER THIRTEEN

Lily sat beside Knight; her delectable bum parked on her hands. She hadn't said a word on the drive to Pete's. Quiet passengers rarely bothered him. He avoided chatty people, but when Lily slipped into silence, his world switched to dark. A big black hole without the sound of her voice, her laughter.

He had come on strong in their session. The desire to stick by her until Pete no longer figured in her life, knowing he couldn't, rocked his core. Angrier at himself more than Lily for questioning his boundaries.

Keeping his movement slow and even, he reached for her hand, determined to sort this Pete business, say goodbye, until she dug her chin out of her chest and he drowned in her eyes. An inch apart, her gorgeous face was hard to read—a mix of, yes please, a kiss would be perfect, and how fast can I release my seatbelt and leg it?

"Let me, Lily?" Kissing Lily's downturned mouth became number one on his list. He held his breath, ready to back off if she refused. When she didn't, he jumped right in with a slow linger of his lips against hers. His pulse pounding. His dick dancing a jig behind the zipper of his pants.

"Mmm," Lily's soft moan nudged at the smile curving the corners of her mouth.

He agreed but didn't want to push his luck. He turned the damn key and merged into traffic.

As they arrived at Pete's address, a woman in yoga gear, a crying child perched on her hip, emerged from the block of flats, and jerked her head at her four-wheel drive. *Thank fuck!* No need to search for a park. He waited while she secured the infant in the safety seat and rolled into her spot.

Daniel's eyes sparkled, pleased with his prize. Dreamy, her mother said, every time her favourite actor appeared on the screen. He fitted her mother's description perfectly. A sensual man with lips that made Lily's eyelashes curl.

A chill danced through the hairs on her forearms. Things were moving fast. The kiss, the casual peck that sparked every nerve ending in her body, set off a sea of emotion impossible to unpack in her current state of mind.

She'd taken the bus to the dojo, intending to finish her lesson and get her head together on the train to Pete's place. A quick in and out to grab her memory box before taking a taxi home. Nowhere did getting a lift from Daniel figure in her plan.

"Look. I don't have to do this. The items aren't important. Maybe it's best if I forget them and move on," she said, shuffling on her hands.

"When you say *it's* not important, what are we talking, clothes, shoes? A coat? I'm damn sure you could do with a winter coat." He winked.

Lily blushed. He had a point when it came to a coat. Sort of, she enjoyed borrowing his leather jacket. Drained of blood from sitting on them too long, she shifted her numb hands into her lap.

His back resting against the driver's door, Daniel reminded her of a small boy, wide eyed, furrowed brow. "No. Don't need a coat. Thanks for your concern but I bought one last week." She leaned across the console, unable to resist a quick tweak of the stubble on his chin.

Knight rolled his eyes and twirled his finger in the air, gesturing for her to continue with her list or something else?

"I left a box, mainly photos, under the bed. I didn't take it when…" Her hand dropped fell from Daniel's face.

"When what? Bloody hell, Lily, do I have to waterboard you for answers?"

Whatever that meant? Instinctively, her stomach muscles tightened. "Sorry, I…"

Palm up, Daniel offered her his hand. "Waterboard, torture? Doesn't matter, just tell me, Lily. What happened when—"

The softness in his voice, knowing she'd caused the worry clouding his eyes, made her sad. Given he sat there doing a convincing job of being genuinely interested, she owed him an explanation. "I hate moths." She had to start somewhere.

Concerned Daniel might think her as nutty as Pete did, her body tensed. "No real reason for hating moths. As a kid alone in the dark, listening to the poor creatures caught in the folds of the heavy bedroom curtains, batting their wings, searching for the light, I freaked."

He snatched her hand, squeezed his thumb over her fingers. "And."

"Pete loved to accuse me of seeing things that weren't there. I thought it was one of those times."

"Slow down, Lily, you lost me. What times? Where were you? What did you see?" The warm air from his lips blew across her knuckles, calmed her.

Biting her bottom lip, she struggled to pull together a coherent explanation. "At Pete's, before I left him."

"Go on."

"That night I saw a rat. A white rat. I screamed."

"Fuck me."

Lily forced a smile. "Nose twitching, pink unblinking eyes. Silly, but I thought it might attack me, so I rolled to the edge of the bed and screamed again. Ugh." Just thinking of the rodent made her shudder.

"How the hell did a white rat get there, Lily?"

"Yep, I wondered too. Like a laboratory rat. Not vermin. Pete always had a weird sense of humour."

"Are you saying, Pete put it there? Sweetheart, that's not weird, it's sick." Daniel released her hand. "No joke, it's perverse." The muscles in his jaw tightened and twitched.

"I know. Next morning, I waited for him to leave, then left for good. Unfortunately, I forgot my box."

"Yeah, of stuff." Daniel shook his head. "Mementoes too important to forget, to lose."

"Yes." She swallowed hard, gulping her tears. He understood. She dug into her purse for Pete's keys.

"Let me come with you, Lily."

Her shrill laugh, an over-the-top response. Any hope of moving forward depended on her taking control, doing things for herself. "No. It's okay. Wait here. It's Saturday, but Pete usually works in the afternoon. I'll be quick. Unless he's flung it in the rubbish, it won't take me long to grab the box."

"I'm not happy. Get what you need and leave. If you're not out in ten, I'm coming in to find you."

"Thank you." She would not lie. Knowing Daniel waited for her boosted her confidence. If only to see the frown disappear from his face, he deserved the quick peck on his cheek.

"Lily."

She pressed two fingers to his lips and drank in the courage always there in his steel-grey eyes. "Won't be long." If she stayed any longer, another kiss might change her mind.

A fucking rat. Laughable if he didn't recognise the psychotic signs. The cat-and-mouse game with a weaker opponent. Games his father played with his mother until she took her life.

Knight scrubbed his hand over his forehead and watched Lily duck inside the flats. On high alert, he stared at the seatbelt, chaining him to his seat, preventing him from charging after Lily. His fingers itched to release the clip, but if he hoped to keep her trust, he had to respect her request. He slammed the steering wheel with the heel of his hand and zeroed in on the third-floor window. Pete's place. Knight knew it deep in his bones. *One twitch of that drawn blind, just one fucking twitch, mother fucker.*

He reached for his phone and hit Snake's speed dial. Lily was dreaming if she believed Pete had done tormenting her. With any luck, he hadn't left for Byzantium.

"Boss? How's Lily? She kick your arse?" Snake asked. Knight pictured the smirk on his face.

"Haven't got time for this, muppet. Peter Holdsworthy. Anything?"

"Yeah. Ten years ago, they arrested our mate for assaulting a woman. She ended up in hospital with significant facial injuries. Unfortunately, the police hit a brick wall. Rumour said, Piccolo Pecker Pete, paid her not press charges and disappear."

"Interesting. Keep digging." Knight hung up and glanced at his watch. *Seven minutes, Lily.*

Goosebumps pricking the back of her neck, Lily rattled the key, but the door didn't budge. Could Pete have changed the locks? Steadying her hand, she tried harder, let out a sigh of relief when it creaked open.

Lily whirled in panic at the music blaring in the kitchen. He was home. *Leave now. No.* No more cowering in front of Pete. What good were the moves Daniel taught her if she wasn't prepared to use them? She straightened her spine and set her shoulders, counted to three and marched to the kitchen. Eyes open.

"Lily. You're back." Pete peered over his newspaper, fake shock on his face.

Her insides churned. "Yes. I came to drop these off." She waved the keys, tossed them on the table, and cleared her throat. Forget whispering next time she spoke.

She didn't take her eyes off him as he carefully folded the paper, walked to the sink, and filled the kettle. "Tea?"

"No thanks. Can't stay, I'll just grab the last of my stuff and let you get on with your afternoon."

"Disappointing. Now you're back, I thought we might chat." He flicked the switch on the kettle and reached for two cups from the shelf above the counter.

Violence poured off him. Until the pinch between her shoulder blades made her flinch, she hadn't realised how hard her spine pressed against the sharp edge of the cupboard door.

"What have you been up to, Lily? Don't answer. I can guess." His hand stroked his chin. "Bedding any man that winks at you?"

"Pete, please. I…"

The high-pitched whistle drowned the rest of her sentence. Pete was in her face before she could think straight. Eyes fixed on the boiling kettle, she shifted her weight and prepared to knee him in the groin.

He grabbed her wrist. "Why can't you let it go, Lily? I said I'm sorry, give me another chance. We can see someone, a counsellor, like you wanted. You need me. Remember, I look after you, protect you, make sure you don't hurt yourself," he warned.

"Pete, please. I'm not here to fight."

"You could have fooled me." He released her wrist and placed both hands on the wall on either side of her head.

Just as she'd practiced with Daniel, she shifted onto her back foot and ducked under Pete's arm. Without looking back, she hurried to the bedroom, determined to get her damn box and leave.

The room stank of stale cigarettes and alcohol. Stifling a cough, she opened the top drawer of the chest, the one Pete had let her have, and gasped at her shredded underwear. What sick idiot would do this and keep it?

"Something wrong, Lily?" Pete stood in the doorway. "Sure, you don't want to stay and talk?"

"No. I have to work." Aware Daniel might burst in at any moment, she lied. She could buy more undies, but this was her last chance to get her box. Falling on all fours, she reached under the bed and hooked her fingers around the cold lid of the metal tin.

Stuff secured. She scrambled to her feet and stumbled to the door. "Out of my way, Pete, please." Clutching the box in one hand, she shoved the heel of the other into his sternum.

Shocked by the sudden move, he gasped and staggered, creating space for her to escape. Adrenaline hit hard, bolstering her fragile sense of power. "We're done, Pete. Have a nice life," she hollered over her shoulder and ran.

Daniel stood next to his car, staring at the building. Overcome with fear, the image of her shredded underwear, her legs turned to jelly. *Great.* He turned in time to see her vomit into the hedge.

His hand on her elbow held her steady, kept her from crumbling.

"What happened?"

"Nothing. I'm okay. Pete was home."

Daniel took the box from her trembling hands.

"Son of a bitch. Did he touch you? Wait in the car." The man moved fast.

"No. Wait. I took care of it." Lily wiped her hand across her mouth, tried, failed to smile.

Daniel wrapped his arm around her shoulder. "Come on. I've got tissues in the car."

Lily sat in the front seat, drinking the water he gave her, her precious box wedged firmly between her knees. Tears welled in the back of her throat. Fixing her eyes straight ahead, she concentrated on the autumn leaves sticking to the windscreen.

"You sure you're okay? He didn't touch you?" Daniel asked.

She sucked in a breath, determined not to cry. "Yes, just a little shaken. I really didn't expect him to be home."

His fingers rested lightly on her shoulder. "Do me a favour, spend a few days at mine. I, or Kate, can go with you to the police. File a complaint."

"Thanks. You're sweet, but it won't do any good." She sighed.

"Stay with me. At least until you move. If you're worried. I have a spare bedroom. No pressure."

"Thanks. I can't. I have a lot to do."

"Like what?

"Packing. I want to be in my new place before I go to Africa, and Crystal's flat must be cleaned. I'm a messy house guest."

"Hard to believe."

"Believe it. Plus, I promised to catch up with my friend, Sam before Kate's camping trip."

"Okay, but promise me Lily, any sign of Pete and you'll call me."

"Promise." Lily smiled. "I don't have your number."

"Easy fixed. Give me your phone."

Unsure what Pete's next move might be? Lily gladly handed it to him.

CHAPTER FOURTEEN

Lily shuddered. Just thinking of sleeping outdoors made her more than a little nervous, imagining anything from creepy crawlies to axe man entering her tent at night. Why she said yes to the camping trip was a mystery, except that wasn't entirely true. Daniel had been the motivation. A chance to gaze into those grey eyes of his to steal another peck on a cheek. *Argh, you are pathetic.*

Twiddling her locket with her fingers at least gave her some comfort while she finished scheduling her Monday appointments.

The others had left earlier that morning, so with a last check of her bag, she went outside to wait for her lift. Crystal had lent her hiking boots and a moss green scarf, long enough to wind around her body three times. Add the repellent *Gore-Tex* that covered her from neck to mid-calf and she could easily be mistaken for an ad for *Snow and Roc*.

Daniel arrived dead on time. The smug smile on his face as he stared at her luggage would have been annoying if it weren't adorable. He tugged the tassel on her scarf and tilted his chin at her bag. "This it?"

She nodded. Biceps swelling impressively against his denim shirt, he tossed it over his shoulder as if it were no heavier than a snowflake. Given she had no clue what to bring camping, she had stuffed the bloody thing with gear bound to give everyone a laugh.

With one arm around her waist, Daniel led her to the parked four-wheel-drive. A company vehicle, Sentinel Security, painted across the side panels. Her heart sank at the sight of the serious outdoor equipment strapped to its roof rack.

Where the hell were they going? The Arctic? Adventure officially begun. "Er, I thought we were heading for Wales, not the North Pole. I'm not sure Kate really wants me on this trip. I can't climb."

Oblivious to her grumbling, Daniel ushered her around to the passenger seat. "Where's Snake? I thought Crystal said he'd be with us."

"Don't worry about Snake. He called in sick." Daniel rolled his eyes.

"Really?" Lily seconded the eye roll. Kate and her matchmaking again. It was becoming embarrassing.

Daniel opened the door. "Hop in. Do you see the map?"

Lily scanned the dashboard. Nope, no Navman. "Map, what map?"

"The one in front of you."

A paper map, old school, lay on the passenger seat. *Great.* Her sense of direction wasn't the best. "Er, yes."

"Good, you are our navigator." He pointed to a red circle. "Bryn, a mate of mine, has a farm near where we're heading tomorrow. We'll pick up extra gear then meet the others in time for dinner."

"Okay, but I'm not sure I'm up to Snake's map reading skills." She could get lost in *Primark*. Lily doubted any of the Sentinel men took a step without knowing precisely where they were heading.

"No sweat, Lily. You got this."

Seriously hoping she didn't disappoint, she fidgeted with her seat belt. Nervous, yes, but with Daniel it was easy to relax. That he trusted her to get them to Wales was terrific, although she hoped he had a backup plan. Pete didn't think she could take the rubbish out without getting lost.

They had a long way to go, but Lily was exhausted by the time they reached Watford. Her head, too heavy to hold up, banged against the window.

"Use this." Daniel handed her a bunched-up sweater. "For your head."

"Thanks." His tone was soft, caring. Her skin warmed to the tenderness in his touch as she nodded off to sleep.

It was pitch black the next time she opened her eyes, except for the glow of the headlights glistening on the wet dirt. While she slept, they'd left the bitumen. Suddenly cold, she looked over to the driver's side. Daniel wasn't in the car.

The breath whooshed from her chest when a head loomed in the front window. "Jesus, Daniel, you almost gave me a heart attack. Where are we?"

"Sorry. Nearly there. Damn tyre needed changing."

"Can I help?" She knew how to handle a jack.

"No, all good. I'll sling the tools in the boot, and we can get going. It's too late to reach the others tonight. We'll pick up the ropes and a harness at the farm and camp there. I've told Spanner we'll catch up with them at the base of the climb in the morning."

"Dinner?"

"Don't worry, we won't starve." he said, a deep chuckle resonating in his voice. "Cold?" He rubbed his hands together.

"A bit."

"Me too." He smiled and turned up the heater.

The hand brake squeaked, the engine stuttered, and she reached for the map that had fallen between her feet. And weren't the tents in Kate's car?

"Don't worry about the map."

She wasn't. Try sleeping arrangements.

"We're here. Out you get. First rule. Everyone does their share of setting up camp—you do your bit, or you don't eat. I'm starving, bet you are too."

Lily laughed. Of course, there were rules. "Yes."

"Here, you'll need this." Daniel tossed her a torch. "Can you cook?"

"Depends. What do you fancy?" An image of him spearing a rabbit and roasting it on a makeshift spit flashed through her mind.

Pete never rated her cooking, her lack of culinary skills, one of the many things that disappointed him. Boring, but she'd cheerfully exist on beans on toast with a fried egg on top. An apple for afters. Most of the essential food groups covered. Pity she didn't like milk unless it pretended to be ice cream.

"Menu's up to you. Give me a minute to get the fire cracking while you check supplies. Over there." Hands full, Daniel lifted his chin at a large cooler box and rucksack he'd placed by the tree. "Turn on your torch."

"Right. Torch." An owl hooted, and something scurried in the shadows. Lily turned the corners of her mouth into a half-smile. No wood nymph. At night, she preferred to snuggle by the log fire in the local pub.

"It's probably a fox," he said.

Her toes twitched. It wouldn't take much more to send her running for the last village they'd passed.

"Or a bear." He grinned.

Daniel deserved a kiss for the way he lifted his torch across the creepy moor. Miraculously, her courage sparked along with the fire he built, and thanks to Crystal, she found a plastic container of Bolognese sauce. Add a packet of spaghetti and dinner was ready as Daniel finished putting up the tent. One tent.

"I hope you are hungry?" Proud of her first camp meal, Lily scooped a clump of spaghetti from the steaming billy and offered it to him.

"You first." He waved the plate in his left hand, pulling back slightly on the other.

"Crystal made sauce for ten people. There's plenty," she said. After taking a small portion, she spooned a generous amount onto Knight's pasta. "Enough?"

"I'll take *smores* on the same plate, thanks."

Smores? Lily cocked her head to the side. "More information?"

"Were you a Girl Guide? Some. More." He wiggled his eyebrows, the explanation spilling from his laugh. A confident, sexy growl that sent a flush to her cheeks and warmed the end of her cold nose.

She scooped half her helping to the side of her plate.

"Uh, uh. Just kidding. Have at it." Daniel nudged her plate towards her.

Lily grinned. His eyes were the colour of smoke rising from a smouldering fire.

Palm up, he stretched out his hand. "Right, we have the campfire. Now for the stories. Care to share your ghosts, Lily?"

Tempting. She wanted to be more open with people. So, by the crackling fire, stars shining above her, she took a risk. Daniel, a new friend. A fresh beginning.

"You know most of it. After I left university, I got a job at St Mary's, the maternity hospital. All my dreams come true. Then my father introduced me to Pete. We dated. He did and said all the right things. Made me feel special. After a few months, we moved in together. At first, everything went great, but within a year he changed." She scraped her empty plate.

"Did he cheat on you?" Daniel shifted to sit next to her.

His closeness supportive, encouraging. "I'm not sure. He made it clear I didn't measure up." *Why am I telling him this?* Wrapped in his musky scent, their thighs lightly touched.

"That's hard to imagine, Lily." He kept eating but didn't take his eyes off her.

Bloody hell, she could lose herself in those stormy eyes. She shrugged. He was just being friendly. Her stomach and brain somersaulted, running away with possibilities she couldn't handle, not now, maybe never.

"Easy for Pete. I tried to talk to him, suggested we see a counsellor, but he insisted the problems were in my head. After Mr Rat, well, you know the rest."

"When did you leave him?"

"Three months ago."

"He's a fucking idiot, Lily. Understand this. You deserve better."

"I like to think so."

"Fuck, Lily, if you were mine…" His nostrils flared, and he put down his plate.

She waited for him to continue, but he didn't. The crash of his empty metal plate touching the ground made her jump.

"Okay, time for dancing." Daniel slapped his thigh, and his laughter peeled into the silent sky.

"Oh, no. Not me. Time for washing up." Lily reached for the dishes.

"Leave it. Come on, dance with me."

When was the last time anyone asked her to dance? She swallowed hard and wished she paid more attention when they were shopping at Galleria. Not that their sparkly creations would last long here. "There's no music."

"Listen." Daniel tapped her chest, the spot over her heart.

She rolled her lips and cocked her ear. "A little tinny."

"Picky."

"Picky?" Her turn to play. She lightly punched his chest.

Faster than lightening, he grabbed her fist and kissed it before slipping his arm around her waist and drawing her close. Back beside him, her inside thighs tingled. Not unpleasant, but certainly a sensation she hadn't felt in a long time. Elbow bent, palm facing her, he held his arm at shoulder height. "May I have your hand?"

"Crumbs, you are a gentleman, pulling out my seat, opening car doors, a charming dance partner."

"Women deserve nothing less, Lily. Remember. Let no one tell you differently."

Daniel cradled her in his arms. His scent, musky pine blended with pure male, made her shiver. She closed her eyes and savoured his damp breath tickling her ear and wanted to stay there, explore where his tender touch might lead. But the voice in her head grew louder, insisting to start would be to end.

She stumbled, her hiking boot coming down hard on Daniel's foot.

"Easy, Lily," he whispered. "Listen to the music. Walk with me."

Lily's soft curves trembled against him. "I got you, Lily."

Her answering sigh latched onto years of unsaid longing, buoyed by a hope he let die with his kills on the battlefield. "Lily, I..." The pulse in her neck fluttered against the light touch of his lips.

The sharp pinch when her foot landed on his big toe didn't hurt, but the ringing phone blasting through the night killed the moment.

"What's up?" he snarled. "Dancing, here." He squeezed Lily tighter, not liking the unease in her eyes.

"Er. Sure, boss. Bad news." Spanner said.

"Go on."

"Snake called. They found Seckou. Mission is a go. Doc and I headed back to London with the women. You and Lily are on your own."

"Call me when you land in Ouaga." With that, Knight hung up and returned to the beautiful woman in his arms. "Time to call it a night. That was Spanner. Duty calls. The others are going back to London." Daniel led Lily to the fire. "I'll take care of the washing up. You take the tent. We have an early start tomorrow."

"Are we leaving?"

"No. Spanner and Doc have it covered. Why should we waste the weekend?"

"Okay. Thanks for the tent. Will you be okay? Out here?"

"I'm used to it Lily," he said, warmed by her concern even if it was unnecessary. "Goodnight."

He didn't mind sleeping outside. Tents could be claustrophobic. Even during the bitter nights fighting in Afghanistan, he often slept under a tarpaulin. As a kid, his mother gave up returning him to bed every time he snuck out to kip in the fields. Spank, his border collie, kept him company slaying roman gladiators on the plains of England while his mum stroked the gin bottle.

Rock climbing became a passion when the Marines sent him on a course with the Mountain Leader Training Cadre. Fully trained in cliff assault, he kept his hand in whenever he spent time at home.

Lying on his back, hands behind his head, he traced a familiar line in the sky from the furthest stars of the Big Dipper to the North Star. Closer to home, four feet to his left, Lily tossed and turned in the tent.

Knight exhaled. "At ease, Lily." After years of hollering orders, he sounded rougher than intended.

The rustling stopped.

"Got everything you need?" He swallowed hard and softened his tone.

"Yes, I'm fine. Sorry to wake you."

"You warm enough?"

"Yes, thanks, very cosy. I feel bad taking your sleeping bag."

Cosy wasn't the word for his military issue slug. Positive that Lily had more to say, he tossed the blanket from his legs. "But...?" he offered. The quicker he fixed Lily's problem, the sooner he could get to sleep.

"Nothing. Cold feet. I take after my mother. My father used to tease her."

His eyebrows twitched. *Great.* Icicles for toes. Another excellent reason to keep his distance from the nymph in the tent. He must have been out of his fucking mind agreeing to this trip. *You had options.* Yeah, but...

He fished a spare pair of socks from his pack, strolled to the tent, and opened the flap. A small, shiny red nose framed by enormous blue eyes peered over the edge of the slug. Any man could die happy, lost in Lily's lilac-blue gaze.

"Here, put these on, they'll help."

Lily caught the socks in one hand and buried them in her cocoon. "Thanks."

Knight chuckled at the horror creeping over her face. *Got it, milady, you need to open your sleeping bag.* "Where's your torch?"

"Not sure, but it's okay, I can see." She smiled.

Knight raised his eyes and blinked. Since when did the moon shine that bright? He cleared his throat and grabbed the end of the zipper. "On three?"

Lily drew in a breath worthy of a deep-sea dive.

"One, two…"

"Three." She took control, unzipped the slug, and shivered hard enough to make her teeth chatter. The mickey mouse pyjamas were cute. On anyone else, cotton flannel might not look as sexy. If they were home, in his warm bedroom, he'd enjoy taking time undoing the buttons.

"Here, give me the socks." Knight knelt beside her and uncurled her fingers from the wool ball.

At six foot four, he wore size fourteen shoes. Lily's feet were no bigger than a size six. No lie. Her feet were frozen. Conscious of his massive hands, he carefully rubbed her delicate toes. "Better?"

"Yes, thank you."

Wow. Lily's laugh hit the vulnerable part in his chest every time. *Remember, not your type.* He wasn't so sure anymore.

Lily wiggled her toes. "Much better."

Knight followed the path of the slug's zipper as Lily trailed it from her feet, over her flat tummy and perfect breasts to her delicate collar bones. His breath hitched when her fingers hovered below her full lips. Lips he needed to kiss. His tongue swept across the seam of her mouth and when she opened, he didn't hesitate. He plunged in, enjoying her wet, inviting mouth until his brain switched to sensible.

"Sorry. Sleep, we have a hike tomorrow before we reach the climb."

Lily didn't blast him for taking liberties. Instead, she smiled that smile, the one he pretended she saved for him.

"You, too. Sweet dreams," she said, her voice a sexy whisper.

Her teeth chattered again, despite the socks. He lay beside her and moulded the front of his body around the curve of her spine, spooning her to him.

"Daniel?" Rather than pull away, she snuggled closer.

"Shh, it's a tried-and-true technique. Marines do it to keep warm in the desert." Mmm, that hadn't come out quite the way he intended.

"Oh, okay."

Lily fit perfectly against his larger frame. Soft and giving. It didn't take long before her breaths lengthened, and she fell asleep. *You're a goner Danny boy.* Kate may be right, although it killed him to admit it. Commitment had benefits.

CHAPTER FIFTEEN

Knight rolled onto his back, one hand behind his head, and watched the light cast tree shadows on the wall of the tent. His hard-on, more a response to the woman snuggled against his chest than the usual morning testosterone hit.

Lily hadn't stirred. No way of telling if she was faking sleep. Was she still nervous about the climb? Silly question. After last night, he didn't want to send any more mixed signals. Hand pressed firmly against his side, he resisted stroking the unbrushed curls caressing her slender shoulder, preferring to trace the shell of her ear with his breath. "You awake?"

"Mmm, what? Oh, yes." One graceful arm crept from under the slug and flopped over her eyes.

His gaze followed the luscious curve of her small, round breasts. *Stop right there.* He rolled over, undid the tent flap, and pointed towards Pott's Peak. It jutted into the grey mist swirling over the Brecon hills. Clouds gathered, threatening more bloody rain, a storm not out of the question.

"We have a couple of miles to drive, then there is a place where we can abseil." There were easier climbs. It crossed his mind that a low traverse closer to where they parked the car might be better.

His nose hovering close to Lily's ear. So much for a night sleeping wild. She smelled fucking fantastic.

Lily rolled onto her elbows. Wide-eyed, mouth half-open, a hundred questions that didn't make it past her teeth. Perfect teeth. Knight imagined them scraping across the head of his cock before bringing him to completion. Coffee, he needed coffee. "You ready to abseil?"

"Abseil? That's when you hang off the rock face with a rope curled around your waist and drop, correct?" She sat up and reached for her blue jumper. A colour that matched her eyes.

At the loss of her warm body, his erection softened. Shame that. "Uh, huh."

Lily shot from the slug with the speed of a sniper's bullet, wobbled on her tiny feet.

Knight sighed and crawled out of the tent. "Time to pack up camp. Best we get cracking before the weather turns nasty."

"Looks like rain. You're sure you want to go up there?" Lily raised her arms above her head and yawned loudly.

The edge of her pyjama top rose, exposing a thin band of silky skin. *Damn.*

"Yep. Don't worry. It looks worse from this angle." Outside the tent, he poked his head through the flap. "I'll leave the tent 'til last so you can get dressed."

"Okay. Coffee?"

Knight chuckled. "We can brew a pot once we reach the crag."

Packed up and on the road, lines of worry creased Lily's forehead. He pulled in under the shelter of a few trees, hoping by the end of the day she'd share his love of the Brecon Hills.

"We need to walk in from here. Hungry?" Knight reached into his rucksack and pulled out a couple of bananas.

"Not for me, thanks." Lily didn't look at him. Her eyes had stayed glued on the peak ever since they left camp.

They needed a distraction. The handy canteen of water did the trick. "Here, drink. Choose your climbing name."

"Climbing name?" Drops of water trickled from the side of her mouth.

If he hadn't to keep his eye on the winding road, he'd have licked them dry. "Yes. Didn't Kate include it in her briefing notes? Every climber has a nickname." Given the gobsmacked denial written on her face, keeping a straight face wasn't easy.

She stared at the wild sheep grazing on the moor. "How about Pocahontas?"

"Pocahontas? I didn't take you for a princess."

Lily blushed. "No, I'm not. I mean, I chose it because Pocahontas could handle the wild. John Smith's saviour if you believe the stories. A perfect spirit guide."

"Princess gets no argument from me, although your hair needs work." Knight lifted his hand and pushed a strand of her silky blonde hair behind her ear. Glossy, thick, strong. Could take to take a tug or two. A flash of Lily arched over his arm while he devoured her throat enthralled him long enough for her to turn and start over the moor.

"What's your climbing name?" she called over her shoulder.

"Can't tell. Classified."

"That's not fair. Go on, give it up."

When he didn't respond, Lily stubbed a small rock with the toe of her boot. "Okay, double-oh-seven if you won't share. Tell me, how many greens can you see?"

Mission accomplished. Distraction secured. "Green?"

"There are at least a hundred shades hidden in these fields and hills. You've travelled, seen lots of unique landscapes. Every country has its own shade of green, but England's is the most breath taking."

"Er... yeah. S'pose so." He moved in behind her, waited, gave her a chance to pull away. When she didn't, he wrapped his arms around her waist and lost himself in the smell of her. Orange blossom. Breath taking. Add ball breaking. Too involved with the scenery in front of him, he couldn't care less about the colour of grass.

They were miles from London, but all morning Lily expected Pete to pop out of nowhere. At least hanging over the side of the cliff, it wasn't likely.

"Daniel, I can't do this." She hated whining, but her sweaty fingers were losing their stranglehold on the rope.

"You said you'd done this before."

Well done. Could he sound less irritated? "Camping, not climbing, and only once in high school. A trip to the Pennines." At fourteen, a victim of peer pressure. A complete disaster. She squealed as the rope slipped through her fingers.

"Okay, sorry. Just breathe."

An hour had passed since Daniel coaxed her horizontally out from the ledge. Braced against the side of the cliff, her kneecaps ached from keeping them locked. Spots of rain glanced off her forehead and bounced off her lips and nose. "Please, Daniel. Pull me up. You hate rain. Let's get back to the car."

"No way. Trust me, you'll never forgive yourself if you quit."

Wanna bet?

"We're not going anywhere, Princess, until I follow you over this ledge, which better be soon. Fucking rain," he groaned under his breath. "I'm starving."

The man had hollow legs and a courageous stomach. Ever since they left camp, he'd eaten a non-stop flow of fruit and energy bars. "We'll catch pneumonia." A ditch plea to make him surrender.

"Better get a move on then. Trust me. Abseiling is much quicker than walking to the bottom. And safer. Don't look down."

"Just because you give falling off a cliff a fancy name doesn't make it any easier."

Daniel chuckled. "You got this, Lily. Eyes on me."

That part was simple. Even from this distance, the colour of his eyes matched the grey clouds prowling above them. Taking a deep breath, she focussed on his earlier reassurance that the Prusik loop would catch her if she fell. *Trust him, Lily.* Her mother's locket, warm against her skin, gave her courage. A rush of adrenaline ripped through her, and she let the rope slide through her fingers.

"That's it. Use your legs on the wall of the cliff."

His wild whoop echoing off the limestone rock followed her less than elegant bounce to *terra firma*. Seconds later, his boots thudded beside her. One step and he swept her into his arms. "Oh, no. I'm not doing that again." Lily shoved free and undid the harness.

"Saved by the rain, Princess," he said, watching the drops bouncing off his palm.

Relieved, she picked the climbing rope. A sharp pain shot across her lower back.

"Hey, you okay?" Daniel grabbed her elbow and steadied her.

"Yes, my back's stiff from hanging horizontal for an hour. My fault for being such a wimp. Are there any good pubs near here? I'm ready to eat." She elbowed Daniel's ribs and met a solid wall of muscle.

"Now, you're talking. The King's Head is about ten miles that way." Thick sheets of rain sliced across the moor. "Better get a move on, Princess. Bears love the rain."

"Bears. You are joking?"

Daniel winked and sprinted to where they'd parked, leaving her to hobble after him. She stopped suddenly when another sharp cramp gripped her lower back.

Within seconds, he was by her side. "Hey. You want me to carry you?"

Thunder rumbled over with his deep baritone voice. "All good. Race you the rest of the way. Ready, set..." Swallowing hard, she took off along the path.

"Cheat," he hollered. The rain fell harder, mocked them as they kicked up enough mud to bury any bear.

It didn't take long for him to overtake her. She ran regularly, and most days she'd have made sure Daniel worked for the win. Not today. By the time she got to the car, he was propped, one leg crossed over the other, against the vehicle. His cocky grin showed off the smile lines at the corner of his eyes. He reached out his arms. "Come here, Princess."

Folded against him, her back to his front, she appreciated the strength laced through the corded muscles of his forearms. Last night, snuggled against him, she'd felt warm, safe.

On cue, her mobile vibrated in her pocket. A sharp reminder not to drop her guard. She peered anxiously over her shoulder, looking for Pete. He had her number. She meant to change it, but it doubled as a work phone.

"In, in." Daniel ushered her into the car and made a dash for the driver's seat.

Reaching behind her, he produced a towel and a biscuit tin. "Here, dry off. Goodies are courtesy of Kate."

"Ah, her famous ginger nuts." She sniffed. "Thank you."

"Dig in." He squeezed her hand.

She leaned closer, hoping for another kiss, but her phone wouldn't stop vibrating. "Sorry. Could be the clinic. I'd better take it. One of my patients had a tough time delivering last week. She knows I'm away, but I gave her my number just in case she wanted to talk."

A single chin lift. Daniel didn't believe her. Not for a second.

"Enjoying yourself?" Pete's acid tone corroded her ear.

"What do you want?" She flicked her gaze to the back window, half expecting to see him lurking behind a rock.

"You, Lily, where you belong. Want me to come and get you?"

"I'm working." Her voice stayed steady despite the shiver rattling her bones.

"Working? An interesting euphemism. You have a way with words. A knack for twisting them to get what you want. Soon, Lily. Enjoy your day." Pete disconnected, and she dropped the phone.

Head squeezed between her hands, she swallowed several times, doing her damnedest not to vomit.

"Hey, just how bad is your back?" Daniel placed a finger under her chin and turned her face to meet him. His steely gaze bored into her. "You look like you're going to pass out on me?"

"Under control. Don't worry, not the fainting sort, but let's head back to London. Visit the pub another time?" Knowing there'd be no next time, Lily opened the window and savoured the smell of grass and rain.

Daniel drove to the t-intersection and turned right. "Where are we going? London's to the left."

"Trust me. You are out of your mind if you think we are driving two hundred miles with you wincing every time we hit a bump in the road."

Too tired to argue, she closed her eyes and drifted asleep.

"Wake up. We're here."

Lily stirred, surprised to see they had parked outside an old hotel. "Where are we?"

"Greenhaven."

CHAPTER SIXTEEN

"Stay there."

Before she could assure him she didn't need his help, Daniel was at her side, holding out his hand. Unlike Pete, his commands didn't make her panic. Confident if she opened the door, there'd be no backhand.

Knees bent, he stretched out his arms. "Hands round my neck."

"Stop fussing. There is nothing wrong with me that a bag of crisps and a glass of white wine can't fix." Her insistence she was too heavy to heft around car parks earned an eye roll.

"Okay, Princess, these are your options. I can drag you by your hair." He winked. "Or humour me a sec. Believe me, for this gorilla, you are a feather."

Good to know, but a pity. She missed his biceps flexing as he lifted her out of her seat. Her cheek fell into his chest, happy to inhale the scent of black cherry trees buried in his shirt. Same as when they danced by the campfire. Sadly, when they reached the reception, he gently lowered her feet to the plush navy carpet.

Holding her steady with one hand, he flopped his credit card on the shiny white counter. "Two rooms for this evening, please."

The receptionist's gaze flicked over the drenched woman by Daniel's side. The dark mahogany mirror reflected the flakes of the mud smeared over her cheeks and the trail of muddy footprints behind them.

"I'm sorry. The hotel is fully booked this evening. We have no singles available."

"Are you sure?" Daniel leaned on the counter.

Staring into his eyes, Lily was certain she would find anything he needed. The woman's long sigh, slow blink, confirmed it. She had no problem with how windswept Daniel looked or his gruff voice.

"Let me check. Ah, yes, the two-bedroom family suite is available. It's at the back of the hotel and has a lovely view of the mountains. Breakfast included with an option for dinner in the..."

"We'll take it," Daniel interrupted.

"Certainly. Just the one key?"

"Two, please," Daniel answered, no question.

A relief. She'd been prepared to fight for her own key. It was wrong, constantly comparing, anticipating his reaction to Pete's. *Be gentle with yourself, Lily.* Dr D's words came back to her. It would take a while before she could look at a man, and not remember how Pete had fooled her.

The receptionist waved her hand toward a pair of French doors. "Walk straight through there. It's the last room on the right."

Their boots squelching, they trudged along the narrow corridor lined with framed prints of the stunning forests in the area. Later, she'd take another look at them, loose herself in the luscious green of the fern and moss. She sighed.

"Come on. The quicker we're out of these wet clothes, the sooner we can find food. And a large glass of wine." Daniel's grin widened as he ushered her forward.

"Great idea." She sidestepped. Not wanting him to carry her again. Happy to lead the way. Daniel's palm warmed the small of her back, radiated a gentle heat straight to her core.

Standing in the open doorway of the suite, he tossed the key cards on the coffee table. "Get comfortable while I fetch the bags."

Lily closed the door behind him and lifted the edge of her t-shirt. *Ugh.* Her clothes and skin smelled of mildew and sweat. She slipped off her muddy boots and flipped through the room service menu. Her overworked muscles were crying out for somewhere to sit, but the antique sofa and chairs, covered in a pink, striped material, looked too pretty to spoil. *Shower first.*

There were two other doors. Bedrooms, at a guess. She gave the one closest a push and gasped. A large four-poster bed dominated the space, perfect for a mum and dad's escape from kids. A soundproof sanctuary. If she believed the guest information, the hotel was solid, built in the remains of the castle.

Lily ran her fingers over the thick duvet. A sharp click dragged her attention to the main room. Daniel had carried both their bags in one trip. *Of course. Look at him.*

Lily cleared her throat and claimed hers. "Mind if I shower first?" she said, rifling through her things for something less pongy to wear.

"Be my guest. If it's okay with you, I'll order room service. Food to go with our wine. We can relax, maybe watch a movie." He nodded at the tv and picked up the hotel menu.

"Good idea." Her stomach agreed. Embarrassed, she ducked her head and fished out her wash bag.

"Anything special you fancy?"

"A burger, vegetable, if they can manage it." She grabbed her clothes and stumbled to the bathroom.

"They can. Go, get wet," Daniel replied. She loved it when he winked, the way it gentled his craggy face.

In possibly the most amazing shower she'd ever used, jets of steamy water streamed over her face, chest, pelvis, legs until tension found the exit between her toes. But no matter how hard she scrubbed; Pete's voice refused to leave her head. Waves of unbearable sadness stuck between her ribs, making it difficult to breathe. To hold back the tears.

Worried Daniel might hear her crying, she held back the curtain, flushed the loo, and stepped out of the shower. Lily grimaced, prepared for the shock of cold to hit the soles of her feet, but a comforting warmth flooded her aching calves. A heated floor. The same luxury warmed the thick white towels she hugged to her body.

Feeling better, she reached for her clothes. *Damn it.* She shook the pile to make sure. Yep, in her rush, she'd grabbed two pairs of pants, no top. *Brilliant, Lily.*

Tucking the edges of the towel tight between her breasts, she poked her nose around the edge of the half-opened door.

Daniel stood at the window, staring at the mountains. She couldn't resist taking a moment to admire the way his legs and backside filled out his climbing pants. Long legs made her melt, and his were a pair of the finest. She cleared her throat, feeling only slightly guilty for perving. Still dressed in wet clothes, he must be freezing. "Daniel. Do me a favour and pass my bag, please."

A smug grin on his face. He took his time walking to the bags.

"This one? With the pigeons?" He waved it in the air.

"Funny. They're ducks, not pigeons." Expensive *Mandarina Duck.* She chuckled. "Stop mucking around. I'm freezing."

"Can't have that. Can we?"

Stood still, Daniel was impressive. In motion, every toned angle moved in faultless unison. With the grace of a jungle cat, he prowled around the four-poster bed to meet her. His wiggling eyebrows were icing on the cake.

"Cold. How cold?" The tip of his finger peeked over the edge of her towel and stilled. Suddenly shy, she grabbed it, relieved when he didn't push. Despite their obvious attraction, did she want to take things further?

Pete hated her prominent hip bones, complained they dug into him when he held her. She shivered, thinking of the weird moment when he came in his hand, then collapsed on top of her.

"How cold, Lily?" He tugged on the towel, and she let it float to the floor.

Waves of pleasure, unlike any she experienced when Pete touched her, undulated through her body. The early months with him had brimmed with moments of similar physical attraction, unspoken softness filled with promise. How could she be sure?

Enough of the comparison game. She closed her eyes, pressed her lips together and let it happen.

Daniel ducked his head and cupped her chin. As though she was on life support, she breathed in his musky scent. She shivered at the touch of his lips and willed this time to be different.

His stubble brushed her cheek, shooting sparks of electricity through her pelvis.

"Open your eyes, Lily. Are you still cold?"

Eyes the colour of a lake, charmed by evening light, gazed at her, held her steady. *Bloody hell.* How did she stay upright? Daniel's rough, sensuous voice scorched every atom of oxygen from the room, robbing her of any reasonable explanation why he should stop.

With just enough pressure on the back of her neck, he urged her closer. For a second, she resisted, rested her hands on his shoulders, and checked in with her raging heartbeat. Begged fate not to play tricks. That Daniel wanted her as much as she craved him, because from the moment she laid eyes on him, she regretted it whenever he drifted out of sight.

Unsure if she could handle the desire setting every nerve end in her body on fire, she rested one hand on his chest, loving the way his heart beat steadily under her hand. The fleshy lobes of his ears were sexy. She nipped his bottom lip, urged him to kiss her.

He teased and enticed before he slipped his tongue between her lips and swept her mouth with a kiss that threatened to blow her mind.

Their bodies melded together, and her breathing became ragged. *It's okay, it's not the same. This isn't Pete.* She wished time would slow, give her a chance to catch up with the desires raging inside her. Daniel's fingers lightly caressed the sensitive spot at the base of her spine, and her ears popped.

Lily roamed her hands over his broad shoulders. Desperate to play in the smattering of coarse hair, she imagined covered his well-defined chest. Through his t-shirt, she found the outline of his taut nipples, loved it when the scrape of her fingernails made him moan.

"You're wet. Take off your clothes," she whispered in his ear.

"Now that's hot." He grinned. A practiced tug and the t-shirt climbed over his head and joined her towel.

One push and he fell backwards onto the bed. "Keep your eyes open." Proud she remembered something from their session, she clambered on top of him and pinned him between her knees, her eyes devouring every contour of his body. Daniel's gaze fixed on her hands trailing over his ribs, across the arrow of curls disappearing into his pants.

She undid the button, slid open the zipper, traced the crest of his hips with her thumbs, and kept moving to the tops of his thighs. Panting, he tried to raise his head to kiss her, but she pushed him back and circled his navel with her tongue.

"Jesus, Lily. Again."

"This?" Her tongue dove deeper.

"Fuck, yeah."

Before Pete shattered her confidence, she'd dreamed of bringing her man pleasure, showing how much she enjoyed being with him.

Daniel tugged her hair, and she cupped the bulge straining against his pants. "Take them off," he gasped.

He watched as she wrestled them over his thighs and hurled them to join his t-shirt. No underwear. She giggled. *Perfect.* Every inch of him. The cut of his abdominal muscles, his very impressive erection jutting proudly between them. Thick. Like a match to a firework, Lily burned to have him moving inside her.

She fell on his mouth and sucked the air from his lungs. Her gasp, the pause he needed to buck his hips and flip her onto her back. Her body quivered inside and out. Daniel's hard cock pressed against her pubic bone, and she froze.

"You okay, Lily," His grey eyes were the colour of a winter storm.

"Can't. Breathe. Heavy. Too heavy. Get. Off."

CHAPTER SEVENTEEN

Knight eased onto his forearms. One minute, Lily's tongue jived with his, her laugh echoing in his mouth, the next Lily's wide eyes stared at the ceiling, and her breath stuttered.

"Lily, did I hurt you? Talk to me, what's happening?" Carried away by his passion, his need to have her, had he missed her asking him to stop? Rough sex with a willing partner, okay by him, but they had just started. Delicate and petite, Lily wasn't used to his massive frame. What had he done?

"No… no. You are perfect. Let me catch my breath." Her head turned, her half-laugh less than convincing, eyes glistening with tears were the clincher. Tearing at his insides, threatening to break him.

"It's okay if you need more time, Lily." Yes, he enjoyed control in the bedroom, his pleasure heightened by bringing a woman to climax, but he never pushed anyone beyond her limits.

"Hold me a sec." A blink and her eye colour shifted from the blue of the arctic ocean to the rich sapphire of a warm summer sky.

No second invitation needed. "Whatever you want." He drew her into his arms, content to stroke the back of her head until her heartbeat slowed, and her breaths became even.

Needing to check-in with her eyes, to make sure his touch was okay, he eased them apart. The tiny lines creasing her forehead smoothed, then she smiled, tentative, nervous.

"Please, Daniel." The warmth of her palm caressed his cheeks, urged him towards her breasts. "Kiss," she whispered.

"Relax, we'll take it slow. Let me make this good for you."

Until now, exploring unfamiliar territory never fazed him. As head of Sentinel, he headed the line and in bed he enjoyed taking point. His mind blazed with a million ways and more to please Lily. Drawing in a breath, reigning in his wavering control, careful to make no sudden movement, Knight intertwined their fingers, brought their clasped hands to his lips, and blew across her knuckles.

In response, she leaned closer and whispered tiny butterfly kisses over his eyelids until he couldn't keep them open. Hard enough to drill holes in cement, the pleasure pain so intense he just might come at the flick of her tongue on his eyelashes. At first, considering the woman hadn't ventured any further than his face.

He opened his eyes and met a sparkle that threatened to blind him. A dazzling mix of shyness and erotic delight. She arched back, bringing her rosy nipples in line with his lips.

Burning to lick every inch of her, he gasped. "May I?"

"Yes, please."

He placed his free hand on top of her hip where Lily could see it and lathed her left breast with the tip of his tongue. Rewarded with a sigh, he drew the hard nub into his mouth and sucked.

Aroused further by her sighs, the deep moans humming through her body, how much longer he could last?

"You are beautiful." He cringed at the corny line. "You must have heard it a million times."

Her head tilted. "No."

Unbelievable. Some lucky guy would spend the rest of his life proving it to her. "I want to be inside you Lily, but…"

"Shh." Two fingers pressed against his lips. "I want that too. Maybe another position?"

That he could do. "Turn onto your side." When she didn't protest, he drew her back to his front, the way he had in the tent—only this time, they were naked.

His orgasm built, going slow had benefits. He kissed and nibbled along the top of her shoulder to the delicate lobe of her ear. "Okay," he whispered.

She nodded, and he chuckled. "Words, Lily, I need your words."

"Yes. More."

Daniel slipped two fingers between her legs. Lily had never been more ready. For this man. She regretted her earlier reaction, but when his weight had landed on her chest, for a split second, it was Pete sagging on top of her, robbing her of breath, raiding her pleasure.

With Daniel wrapped around her back, she was grateful he didn't see the tear leaking from the corner of her eye. She sank into his warmth, welcomed the stimulating caress of his fingers. Sad, happy, amazed how this powerful man could be so caring.

Nudging her thighs open wider, his cock slid over her throbbing clit. "Mmm." She sucked in a breath. "Feels great." Lifting her head, she buried the tip of her nose against his throat.

"That's what I like to hear. Remember, we can stop, just say the word. I'm going to lift your leg a little higher. Okay?" he rasped and pinched her nipple.

Her breath hitched. "Yes." She relaxed her hip, allowed him to guide her thigh to her chest.

Lucky for her, her arms were long, another gem of info from Harmony's yoga classes. She reached through the gap in her legs until the tip of her index finger traced the sensitive skin at the base of his penis.

"Fuck, Lily. Yes."

Mutual torture. She smiled.

His wicked smile, the glint in his grey eyes as he found her nipple again, sucking as though he wanted to draw the darkness from her. *Hell.* Flashing her another grin, his cock moved back and forth over her clit, pushing her towards climax.

"What is it you want, Lily? Tell me."

"To come." Immediately she regretted admitting it, but it had been too long. She tried to pull away, but he held onto her.

"Easy, Princess."

His breath caressing the side of her neck gave her courage. "I want you inside me."

"Another can do moment. Stay still."

She shivered, cold from the loss of his touch, as he grabbed a condom from his wallet, sheathed himself and settled back behind her.

No more words, only heavy breathing as he took his sweet time entering her. A snug fit. Her breath hitched. "Please, Daniel. Move."

Her grip tightened round his neck, welcoming his kiss, dismissing the idea the universe made this man just for her. Daniel's tongue joined the dance, circling her teeth, lathing the roof of her mouth.

The prickly heat running up and down her inside thighs burned its way to her core. Her hips rocked. Following his lead, she held on for the ride, matched his pace. Faster and faster until she thought she would lose her mind. "More. Harder."

"Fuck, Lily," he groaned. "I'm close."

Daniel lifted her leg higher and pinched her clit. Blood pulsed in her temples. "I'm coming." A naff thing to say, to scream.

"With me." One, two more thrusts and Daniel followed her over the edge. Darkness crept from the sides of her vision, exploding in a shower of stars as she dove into a place she'd imagined, but never dreamed could be this powerful.

Lily lay boneless in his arms, the smile of an angel tugging at the edges of her soft, plush mouth. He'd been right there with her as her hot, tight muscles milked the life out of him. She came hard, and his own release still shuddered through him.

For a man used to frequently staring down danger, he couldn't put his finger on why sex with Lily made him twitch. Deep down, he suspected it was more than their off-the-charts physical attraction. Not that he was complaining. Mind-blowing orgasms were a bonus, and he would spend his life just for the chance to hold her.

Maybe it was because he had behaved like a sex-crazed gorilla? When she trusted him, allowed him to make it good for her, he came apart in her arms, grateful for the calm that washed over him.

It had been a long time since he'd felt this kind of peace. He should head for the shower, dispose of the condom. Not lie there, enjoying their ragged breaths mingling in the slim space between their lips, but he didn't have the will or the strength to shift.

Lily's flat belly, her silky skin, demanded stroking and the sweet smell of her hair commanded serious attention from his nose. Still buried inside her, an unfamiliar tug on his heart, reason crumbled under the sleeping beauty beside him.

"Hey, Lily, come back to me."

"Huh?" Her voice floated in the distance.

Head propped on his palm, he steadied his breathing, watched as if he'd always been waiting for her. "You okay? Did I hurt you?"

"No. You didn't hurt me, Daniel. Don't look so serious."

His gut clenched. Her thumb stroked his cheek and smoothed the spot between his eyebrows with her thumb.

"You have wonderful eyes. The colour of the sea as the last ray of sun disappears into the water."

She smiled and all he wanted to do was pull her inside him, lock her away from more sadness. "Wow. Poetic. Good sex agrees with you." And as soon as he got rid of the bloody condom, he planned to sheath himself again, bring her to many more orgasms, just to watch her fall apart in his arms.

"What do they see when they look at me?" she murmured.

His heart sank at the tear resting in the corner of her eye. Silently pleading for no regrets, he caught it before it fell. "Hey. What's the matter?

"Nothing. Kiss me."

Her sadness was everything. Sweat had long cooled on their skin, but the smell of their lovemaking lingered. *Sex, just sex.* Knight pulled the sheet over Lily's slim shoulder and kissed the base of her neck. "Stay with me."

"Mmm?"

"Nothing. Rest, need to take care of the condom."

Suckling her earlobe, he stayed a few minutes, listening to her mews of complaint. Music to his ears. "Don't go anywhere. We have plans," he mumbled, slowly, dragging himself away from the beauty in his bed.

CHAPTER EIGHTEEN

Daniel had texted her every day since they got back from Wales. Mr Calm, Cool, Collected, took their night together in his stride while Lily was a quivering mess, hoping by a stretch of the imagination his world had rocked the same as hers. She asked Crystal and her answer had been a resounding for sure.

Unfortunately, Pete hadn't left her alone. Guess she should be grateful. Lately, he kept his abuse to messages and not to personal appearances. Fingers crossed, he finally accepted they were finished.

This last week, when she wasn't at the clinic, her days had been busy cleaning Crystal's flat. No time for shopping. Her fridge was bare. Whatever possessed her to invite Daniel to dinner? Growing up, mum in a cute apron teaching her how to cook didn't exist. No family recipe bible with curly pages.

Lily sighed. Hearty minestrone soup would have to do, served with a loaf of crusty bread and too much butter. Pressure off—almost. Could men like Daniel survive without meat? And, right now, she double checked the cupboard, dessert equalled raspberry jelly. *Don't panic.* If she got moving, she had time to run to the shops.

Fresh air would do her good. Her head pounded, thanks to Pete's regular barrage of texts and messages. Tomorrow she'd beg Crystal to give her a dreamy shoulder massage. She grabbed her purse and several string bags and headed for Sainsbury's.

Chaos. People pushing trollies spilled out of the superstore's auto doors, barrelling into commuters standing at the bus stop. A dumb place for a queue, but borough planners neglected to move it when they expanded the store. Someone else in their homes did the shopping. Lily envied them.

She weaved through the maze of shop-and-save aisles. Wine on top of her list. Priceless. The look on Daniel's face when Abrakebabra didn't have a wine list. A glass or two to relax and take his mind off her pathetic cooking. The *Chablis* with the fancy French label should do the trick. That, and the triple-layer chocolate cake with vanilla ice-cream for dessert. Who didn't love that combination?

Meal sorted, Lily headed for the checkout and spent the next ten minutes shuffling her feet, replaying their wonderful night at the hotel, worrying. In the past, giving into physical attraction had landed her with Pete.

"You need a bag, love?" Not waiting for an answer, she pushed the shopping to the end of the counter.

"All good, thanks." She hurried to untangle the knotted string bags before the pile tumbled onto the floor.

After sprinting home, she was thirsty, gagging for a glass of wine, and halfway down the stairs when her blood curdled. Cursing the flickering bulb over the front door, she snatched the piece of paper stuck between the security bars. Even in the dim light, there was no mistaking Pete's scrawl.

"Miss me?"

"No, Plonker," she yelled, her heart skipping a beat at the shuffling under the stairs. An arm circled her waist, another clamped over her mouth. Her locket, caught in the crook of Pete's elbow, dug sharply into her neck. His breath stank of alcohol. *Breathe.* Fighting for her next breath, she fought to stay calm and remember any of the moves Daniel had taught her.

The bastard swung her around to face him.

"Please Pete. You're hurting me." She swallowed hard, her brain fast turning to mush. *Think, Lily. Eyes Open.*

"Don't make me hurt you, Lily. You're coming home. Our home. I've said I'm sorry. That should be enough, you frigid bitch."

Pete spat his fave insult in her face while his hand gripped her chin, making it impossible to tell him to get lost.

"What about us Lily? Don't throw away what we have."

Insane. Ignoring the pain in the back of her neck, she wrestled free. "We have nothing to throw away. How many times do I have to say it? There is no us."

Where had Pete been during their endless late-night chats? Obviously hadn't heard a bloody word. He grinned, the goofy grin that once upon a time she found attractive. Tonight, he reminded her of Chucky.

"I'm willing to give you another chance. Come home. You want a family. Let's make babies."

Last time she checked, that required getting it up, something he had never managed. "No, I can't do this." She sucked in a breath. "I'm sorry." She tried not to vomit. Apology the last thing on her mind, but the 's' word carried Pete power. Enough to stop a punch.

"End it, Lily."

"End what? We're done."

"Don't play games. You're not good at it. Tell me, does Action Man know how unstable you are? How you tried to kill yourself?"

Alarm bells rang in her head. His spiteful tone, his sudden shift of weight, warned her to be careful, to shield herself for the blows to come. "Please, Pete." She was gibbering, her heart thumping, damn sure she would lose her job. Friends, everything. If she couldn't be a nurse? There was nothing else.

"Get rid of your boyfriend, or I will tell. Him, your father, *Afrique Santé.* Those bitches at the clinic."

Pete never made idle threats. How long could she live in this hell? She had to leave London now. In Africa, miles between them, he would forget about her, find someone else. A woman who made him happy.

Pete loosened his grip and released her, but not before he licked the side of her face, the rough edge of his tongue marking her as if she were a stamp on a letter.

"Goodnight, Lily." I'll see you soon.

Lily froze at the knock. Dead on eight o'clock, Daniel arrived. On time. No surprise. Still shaking, she ditched the tea towel and her apron into a drawer under the kitchen bench. Fixing a smile on her face, she took a couple of deep breaths and opened the door. "Hi."

Dressed in denim jeans and a black t-shirt moulded to his impressive pecs, Daniel filled the doorway, wine in hand. The leather jacket she had borrowed more than once completed the perfect picture. Always relaxed and confident, she loved the way his grin crinkled the corner of his eyes.

"Thanks." Concerned he would notice her trembling fingers, she squeezed the neck of the bottle tight.

One eyebrow raised, head cocked to the side, he hung onto it a fraction longer than necessary. The man missed nothing. She admired the label. "Impressive. A cork. One giant leap from the plonk living in my fridge."

"I hope you enjoy it." He shrugged and shuffled his feet. Hard to believe Daniel wasn't used to compliments. "Are you going to invite me in?"

"Sure, but no judging. I haven't finished cleaning." As the door closed, a chill blasted through her. Pete may still be out there, watching. "Have a seat. Dinner's nearly ready." She swept her hand towards the sagging sofa and checked the simmering pan.

"Smells wonderful. Corkscrew?"

"Yes, that drawer there."

She almost dropped the spoon when Daniel's arm swung across her shoulders, pressed a full glass to her lips. It smelled divine, earthy strawberries, if that was even a thing. "Mmm, delicious, thanks."

Astute and funny, the best man she'd ever met sat on the stool opposite, watching her stir soup. His perfect, kissable lips smiled as she played master chef. *End it now.* Pete meant what he said. Lily sniffed. As soon as dinner was over and Daniel left, she'd call Kate and bring her trip forward. She could kick herself for not doing it earlier.

"I hope you like Minestrone. It's simple but tasty. One of Peggy's recipes."

"Peggy? Was that your mother?"

"No. After we lost mum, I mentioned, dad hired Peggy to run the house, our lives. While he built his business, she travelled with us, fed me, made sure I went to bed at a sensible hour. When we were stuck in the middle of nowhere, she stepped in as home schooler."

"I see."

Daniel didn't say any more, even though she could sense lorry load of questions tucked behind his arched brow. She twirled her mother's locket. "I bet you think I'm a spoiled brat. It's true, I grew up not wanting anything, never worked for pocket money."

"Interesting."

"There you go again. I don't believe you sneak up on the enemy. I can hear your brain ticking, working overtime. Making assumptions."

"Apologies. Nothing personal. It's a professional habit, gathering intel. Mind reading's another."

Interrogation time? Great. Her plan to have fun debating the benefits of dark over milk chocolate melted into another uncomfortable moment.

"Come, sit with me for a second. Soup can wait." The deep tone of his voice drew her, boneless, to his side.

"What did you do with your pocket money?" Daniel squeezed the fingers that had found their way into his hand and brought them to his lips.

"Collected stamps. No, don't laugh. We never stayed in one place for more than a few months. They were my anchor. Each small square a reminder of home. Lots of them."

"Just goes to show, money isn't everything." His free arm crept around her shoulder.

Slipping her hand from his, she reached for a pillow and hugged it to her chest. A poor substitute for his body heat. The fire that threatened to consume her.

"I can't lie, family money came in handy, paid for nursing school."

The lump in her throat swelled to boulder size, but she refused to feel sorry for herself.

"You okay, Lily?" Daniel reached for the pillow, but she held on tight.

He didn't insist, simply laid his hand on her knee. Nothing sexual, just so she'd know he was there. His consideration difficult to accept, a foreign sensation, long before Pete came on the scene.

"Yes, I peeled too many bloody onions." She turned her head and swiped at the tear perched in the corner of her eye and allowed him to shift closer.

Had she read too much into his concern? Yes, they'd spent a night together, but she'd been catastrophically wrong about Pete, allowed her libido to lead her places she should never have gone.

She envied Kate and Crystal and their perfect relationships. Daniel would leave again soon. His work took him away any time, day, or night. She had her new flat. A home. It was enough. Besides, if Pete told him what a flake she really was, he'd run all the way back to Wales.

Sod the soup. Confused, her anxiety growing. If she waited, she'd never find the courage to end this, whatever it was. What if he was looking for more? It was unfair to encourage him. She pinched the bridge of her nose and gulped her wine.

"Lily, you're shivering. Are you cold? Headache?" Daniel cupped the sides of her face. His grey eyes turned silver, tugging at her raw emotions.

"Not anymore." *Not since you arrived.* The moon shone through the kitchen window. She wanted him naked and in her arms. Worried Pete may crash through the door, she rested her palm on his chest, resisted when he leaned closer. "What did you do this afternoon? Besides, take a shower?" He smelled great, not too pongy, but all male.

The phone buzzed on the coffee table, shattering the moment. "Sorry." Her least favourite word. One she intended to lose from her vocabulary. "Hello, Lily speaking."

"I warned you, bitch. Get rid of him." Pete's voice snaked into her ear.

Anxious Daniel would hear him, she tried to angle her body, but he caught her chin between his finger and thumb and kept her gaze focussed on his.

"Give it to me." Daniel didn't raise his voice, but there was no mistaking the anger behind his tone.

Tired, unbelievably tired, she didn't have the strength to resist. He caught the phone as it fell from her hand.

"Knight here, arsehole. Lily is with me. Grow a pair muppet, move on. Don't make me tell you again."

A soft click. Call over, but he'd call back soon. "You shouldn't have threatened him. I can handle him."

"You sure about that? You've been jumpier than Peter Rabbit, ever since I arrived. How come he still has your sodding number? Simple, Lily. Change your number and get rid of your fucking SIM. Any kid with access to the internet can track you."

"Seriously?" *Stupid, stupid.* That's how Pete found her. Angry at herself, as well as Pete, she drew in a steadying breath and snatched the phone from his hand. The fingers on her other itched to trace a path over his sweet, caring lips. But one kiss could break her, and she'd lose any chance of doing what she had to. Springing from the sofa, she raised herself to her full height.

"Knight. I think you should leave."

"Hey, easy. Talk to me." His look of disbelief almost changed her mind.

"Please, Knight. What do you want from me?"

"Use my first name for a start. Daniel, remember?" He curved his hand around the back of her head.

"Daniel. I…"

He rubbed the tip of his nose against hers. "I want more time with you, Lily. Smiling, happy to see me, teaching me the finer points of wine."

Pete's threats echoed in her head.

"Hell, I don't know where we are going, Lily. Home-cooked meals, sleeping overnight with you wrapped in my arms, are uncharted waters for me, but let's keep learning."

"No," she choked. The hurt in his eyes crushed her, but she couldn't take the risk.

"Lily, say, if you don't want this. Own it. Tell me you are not interested. I can take it. I'm not your ex."

"Fair enough." Her bottom lip trembled, and her heart felt like it was going to beat out of her chest. "I'm not ready to be with you, with anyone. I hope we can be friends." They both cringed. She added the last bit, hoping to soften the blow. Ending it like this was all kinds of wrong. Dishonest. "Please go, Knight."

"If that's what you want. You have my number. Get me anywhere, anytime. Any more trouble from Pete, you call me. Yes?

He was angry, but more than that, the look of disappointment on his face struck her hard. "I will." Eager to end her humiliation, she stood, stuck to his heels as he strode out of her flat and into the dark. A gust of wind hurled branches over the iron railings and sent them clattering onto the stairs. She slammed the door shut and sank to the ground.

One agonising breath at a time, she fought for control, sucked air through her nose and counted, thought of her new home. *Congratulations, Lily, you have just rented the most expensive storage locker in London.*

CHAPTER NINETEEN

What the fuck just happened? Knight's hand hovered next to the window, wanting to smash it, feel the pain.

He needed his head examined, skipping down Lily's sodding steps, planning candlelight dinners. Exploring unknown territory? Considering more than a one-night stand. Faster than he could blink, his world tilted on its axis.

He couldn't stomach minestrone soup, but he would have drunk a gallon to see her smile. After the last night they spent together, he hoped, get real. He assumed they'd end up in bed where he could show her how much she was beginning to mean to him.

Straight after Arseworthy called, he could tell something was different. The colour of Lily's eyes changed from precious sapphires to polar icicles, and her expression switched from, come here to get lost.

Lily picked the fight, and he swallowed the bait. *Damn it.* He had boundaries for a reason.

Pissed that he let her under his skin, he zeroed in on the numpty driving the Vauxhall ahead, cruising at ten miles an hour in a fifty-mile zone. *Buy British and bugger up the roads.* "Come on, muppet." The heel of his hand hit the horn.

The car's brake lights flashed, and it slithered to a halt. Knight shook his head and unbuckled his seat belt. Road rage wasn't his thing, but a healthy debate on road rules? He could handle that. Out of his car before the other man opened his window, he rested his elbow on the car roof and froze. The man growled at him. Eighty, if he was a day.

"Sorry," Knight mumbled. "My bad." Tables turned again. Not his night. Scrubbing his hand over his head, he returned to his car, held a breath, and willed the old guy not to suffer a bloody heart attack on his way home.

No one robbed him of control. Make that no one, but Lily.

He swerved the MGB hard right. One thing for sure, he knew the bloody way to Maeve's.

Swallowing the bitter taste in his mouth, he marched through her front door and hit the wall. Not even the cloying scent of roses permeating the carpet, and the heavy curtains masked the stale smell of sex. Lots of sex.

Money upfront, Maeve ran a business. She'd hinted more than once he didn't need to pay, but he reached for his wallet and tossed a handful of notes on the gold-plated tray. Him in control, the sensible way of taking care of the itch. No grey areas. No fucking tea lights, chips, or shy, enticing smiles.

He strayed from the plan with Lily. He liked her. It didn't mean he had to enjoy liking her. The sooner he got the hell back to doing what he did best, causing havoc, killing the enemy, the better. Doc and Spanner could use some company in Burkina. As soon as he was back at his place, he'd have Snake schedule him for immediate despatch.

"Come in, Knight. I've been expecting you." The purr in Maeve's voice came naturally. A cat welcoming her prey. "Wine, or do you prefer something stronger?"

"You will do. Get naked."

She placed her glass on the table beside her and tugged on the silk tie of her robe. Her tongue circled her upper lip. A promise of things to come. And his cock stayed soft, oblivious to the tease of cleavage, the plastic grin. Unlike Maeve, Lily's generous smile just kept coming.

Get over it. You're paying for this. Maeve's tits, her mouth getting you off.

Maeve stood and swayed in time to the Latin beat wafting over the built-in speakers.

"Too slow." He kept his hands by his side while his mind and body engaged in a tug-of-war.

He craved Lily, her damn cold feet tugging on the hairs of his inside thigh.

"How much have you had?" He nodded at the half-empty wine glass.

"Just the one. It's been a long night." Maeve's appreciative gaze dipped below his belt.

She hooked her leg around his waist, raised her slender arm, and trailed a sharp fingernail across his chest. Normally, he'd have appreciated the bite. Not tonight.

"A quick shower." He tilted his chin towards the bathroom. Space to get his mind on the job, his body in gear. So what if she wasn't Lily? He wasn't dead.

"You know where everything is. Don't keep me waiting too long, Knight," Maeve mewed.

He picked up two strands of purple ribbon lying beside her empty glass and threw them on the bed. "Get comfortable."

"Yes, master," she teased as her eyes tracked him to her ensuite.

He shuddered at the monochrome sanctuary with its blizzard white walls. Careful to lock the door. No surprise shower sex. He placed his wallet and phone on the marble ledge surrounding the sunken spa bath and stepped into the super-size shower stall.

Steam swirled around him, clouding the mirror. Forearm braced against the glass he took himself in hand, stroked his cock, squeezed his balls, imagined his kisses tracing the line of Lily's delicate collarbone, lingering over her stiff, rosy nipples.

Head bowed, he groaned, relished the blazing torrent pounding his arse. His hips thrust faster into his hand. A final tug and his orgasm roared at the base of his spine and flooded his hand. Lily's name echoing around him, the memory of her sweet smell torturing his nose.

Nowhere near satisfied, he dried off, tossed the wet towel into the basket, and dressed.

In the bedroom. Maeve lay spread eagle on the silk sheets, one wrist secured to the headboard.

"Help me, Knight." She trailed the second strand of ribbon between her legs, moaning at the silk brushing against her skin. Bored before the fun began, he moved in fast, undid the tie, and set her free.

Chin tucked into her chest, false spider-leg eyelashes batting her cheek, she circled her breast with the tip of her finger. "Something different tonight, Captain? I can't wait."

"Sorry, love." Knight pried her fingers from the back of his neck. "Something's come up, gotta go."

"But you paid," Maeve whined.

"Keep it."

Back in the car, he covered his head with his hands. *Shit, shit, shit.* What did he expect, Lily was an intelligent woman more than capable of recognising the darkness in him. For god's sake, he drank beer with dead men, but no matter what happened with him and Lily, he'd never return to Maeve.

He pulled out his phone and dialled Snake. "Tell Spanner to call me tomorrow, zero-eight-hundred, my time. Book me an open ticket to Burkina."

"Sure thing, Boss. What changed your mind?"

In no mood to justify or explain, he cut him off and headed home, happy to break open the bottle of *Laphroaig* he kept for Doc. Once Seckou was out of the way, he'd rethink his options. He could run Sentinel's operation from anywhere in the world. Preferably a spot with lots of rock, forget the green.

CHAPTER TWENTY

Pete called every hour during the night, begging, threatening, making her life hell. She should turn her phone off, but her headache was bad enough without having to deal with a ton of his messages later. It may be a pain, but after she spoke to Kate, she'd organise another SIM and number.

"Camden Women's Clinic. Crystal speaking. How can I help?"

"Hi, Crystal, it's me, Lily. Is Kate there?" She tried to sound cheerful, but lack of sleep killed any chance of a spark in her voice.

"Hi, Lily. Didn't expect to hear from you on your day off. If you were me, you'd be at the spa, enjoying a pongy facial while someone made love to your feet. Not that it's likely to happen. Spanner would never forgive me if I let anyone else do the honours. The man has a thing for toes."

"Crystal, Sorry, I..."

"Okay, too much information. What can I do for you, hun?" The flick of disposable gloves punctuated Crystal's giggle.

"Busy?"

"Really Lily, you have to ask? Anyway, I'm not telling because if I said yes, you'd arrive on the doorstep, sleeves rolled up, ready to work."

"I can come to work if you need help." She'd welcome the distraction.

"Stop. Here's Kate, and you are on strict orders not to put that idea into her head. She's not as generous as me. Roll on the weekend. I'm looking forward to seeing you at *Cereal Killer*. You can catch me up on you and you know who."

Exhausted, Lily flopped on the sofa. On top of everything, she'd forgotten they were meeting for breakfast.

"Hi. Crys is right. Get off the phone. You are not at work." Kate interrupted.

"I will, but I wanted to ask you something. Our trip, is it possible for me to leave earlier?" She could hear rustling in the background. "Kate?"

"Sorry. Patient's waters just broke in the waiting room. That kind of morning. What's up?"

Lily pulled in a long breath and let fly with her prepared speech.

"I can't see a problem. Arriving in Africa early is an excellent idea. There's always plenty to organise before we head out to the rural clinics. You can take over customs paperwork for the Misoprostol. It drives me mad. Anyway, can't talk now. I'll call you when I finish tonight. Mum needs help." Kate's laugh trailed her goodbye.

Lily pinched the bridge of her nose and stared at her long list of stuff still to be done. She opened her locket. Mum's smiling face always lifted her mood.

She arrived early Saturday morning. Seated first, hands clutching a cup of coffee, gave her a sense of control. Back to the wall, nose buried in her book, she waited for her bowl of *Choccopotomus* to arrive. The Cornflakes, smothered in chocolate and ice cream, guaranteed to lift her spirits.

"Morning, Lily."

Her elbowed jerked, sending her books onto the floor. Hearing Daniel had surprised her. It was a stroke of luck that she caught her cup before it joined her book. The low, rich tone of his voice betrayed nothing of their argument. Scrambling to find words, she had never been happier when her friends followed him into the restaurant.

He snatched the book from the floor and placed it on the table. His heated gaze never left her space as he took the seat opposite her. Suddenly, the place felt like a sauna. "Thank you," she mumbled.

Sweat dripped down her back. Wearing the wool jumper was a mistake. It itched. She hadn't planned on seeing Daniel so soon after the other night. Maybe after her trip to Africa. A fresh environment, and hard work, perfect for getting her life on track. She sipped her coffee and hoped he would come around to the idea of them being friends.

Out of habit, Knight stood in the doorway and scanned *Cereal Killer's* interior, sensing Lily before he saw her nose buried in a book. His fingers curled and uncurled, itching to walk through the messy sprawl falling over her shoulders.

The nerve at the corner of Knight's eye twitched. A sure sign he wasn't doing as good as he planned at keeping his cool. He never figured himself a masochist until the blonde who had no clue how to dress for cold weather crossed his path.

No matter how much he wanted to argue, change her mind, he had to respect her wishes, keep his distance. Bothering women who didn't appreciate his attention wasn't his style. This morning he'd come just to make sure she was okay. Let him see a single mark on her and Pete better pray his hand had nothing to do with it.

He waved to the Goth waitress, wedged between two tables, a tray of coffees swaying high above her head, and pointed to Lily's table. "Coffee, black, please."

"Morning. I didn't realise you were coming," Lily blurted. Clearly uneasy, she shifted in her seat.

He collected her book from the floor. *Bradt's Guide to Burkina Faso.*

He bit his tongue and tried to reel in a smirk. Not wanting his size to intimidate, he pulled out a chair and sat, glad to see Lily in a warm coat. "Neither did I. I was at the clinic when you rang Kate. I wanted to see you, apologise for being an idiot. I came on too strong the other night."

"A little."

She smiled, and his cock stirred, remembering his hands, his lips, enjoying every inch of her body.

"But there's no need to apologise. I shouldn't have so sensitive."

"What are you two whispering about? Morning, Lily. Shove over." Crystal, a grin as wide as the Eurostar Tunnel on her face, winced at the creak of her chair legs.

"Morning, folks. Breakfast for everyone?" said their waitress as she tossed more menus at them. "Coffees to start?"

"Fabulous." Crystal looked at him, then winked at Lily.

Kate placed the envelope on the table.

"Here, Lily, before I forget. Your plane tickets for Burkina. I've included a letter to introduce you to Mahmoud, our *Afrique Santé* liaison, and a copy of our itinerary."

He swallowed hard. "When do you leave?"

"Soon." She flicked her wavy hair over her shoulder. Chin up, eyes looking anywhere but at him. "I'm going early to set things up… odds and ends, you know?"

No, he fucking didn't know. Lily was on the run.

"Enough shoptalk. Let's eat," Crystal said.

"Great idea." He dived into the menu. A list of eggs, coffee, and pastries swam in front of his face.

Eat they did, their banter background noise as he kept his gaze on Lily, willing her to lift her head, for a chance to stare into her stunning blue eyes. *Look at me.*

Nervously, she brushed away the crumbs at the side of her mouth. Adorable, messy eater.

"Be still. Here." He handed her a serviette.

"Thanks." At last, she finally looked at him.

The hint of a tear hit him harder than a blow to his gut.

"Ok you two, your faces are long enough to re-carpet my entire flat. What's going on?" Crystal sat back and folded her arms across her chest.

"Nothing. I'm not brilliant company this morning. I was up late packing, didn't get much sleep."

He was half out of his seat ready to chase after Pete, when Lily waved her plane ticket in the air. "Thanks for this. Sorry to eat and run, but I've got last-minute shopping to do."

Liar. She couldn't bear to be around him, and that fucking hurt.

"Safe trip, Lily. Take care of each other over there." Spanner tore himself away from his bacon and egg sandwich and gave Crystal a wink.

"Will do, but I'm sure Kate and Crystal will be the ones looking after me. Bye."

Knight made it all the way out of his seat.

"You going too, Boss?" Spanner said, taking a swig of his coffee.

"Yes." He didn't explain. He tore after Lily, catching her by the elbow as she turned into High Street. "Hey, wait up. Do you need a lift?"

She shrugged out of his grip. Her flapping hands doing a poor job of sheltering her from the thick rainy mist. "No, I can walk. About the other night, I…"

He didn't want to hear it. "Take it. For your head. Please." His baseball cap looked a hell of a lot better on her. He pulled the peak low over her eyes.

"You really have to stop lending me your clothes."

Hell, if she kept smiling, talking, he'd kiss her. Claim her in front of everyone.

"Stop staring at me."

"Why? As far as I can see, there's nothing I'd rather look at." Why lie?

"Here, thanks." Lily snatched his hat off her head and pushed it into his hand. "I have to go, sorry. Let's catch up when I get back from Africa? Lunch."

"Talk to me, Lily. If you must go, fine, but let me take you to the airport." *Desperate much.*

"Okay. Thanks for the offer. I'll call you when I look at my ticket and figure out a time."

And then she ran, leaving him in the fucking rain, his mouth gaping like a sodding fish.

CHAPTER TWENTY-ONE

Lily had no idea how to handle Daniel's blistering intensity. One night with him had caused a seismic shift in her expectations plus she was tired of running from Pete, from herself.

Africa would give her time and space to meet her demons and plan. Hopefully, when she got back to London, she would be free to see if there could be more with Daniel. If he was still interested.

His offer of a lift was probably something he said to fill an awkward moment, and now she'd finally found the courage to cancel, he didn't answer his phone. She'd considered the coward's way, send a text, and turn her phone to silent. Too cold. In a note she could explain.

Half the night she agonised over what to say. At three a.m. she settled on the truth. She had gone to see her friend Sam for a few days and would go to the airport from there. She promised to be in touch when she returned to London.

Now, she had less than an hour to get to the station and catch her train. She kicked the bottom of her case and rolled it to the lift. The doors opened on the ground floor and her heart sank. No Bill. A tall man, with a lot of hair on his head, slid open the glass partition, the one she'd never seen shut.

"Morning, miss."

"Hello, I'm Lily. "Is Bill here?"

"Off sick today. Can I help?"

"Oh, that's not good. Er… yes, thank you. I've just moved in, number eighteen. or at least my belongings have. Bill knows there will be more furniture arriving for me while I'm away and…" Not comfortable sharing too much information with a stranger, she stopped there. Would you mind giving this note to Captain Knight? He's in…"

"Flat nine. No problem. Leave it with me."

"Thanks. Sorry, must rush, my taxi's waiting. Enjoy your day."

Heart pounding, Lily threw open the cab door at Marylebone Station and flew along the platform. Panting heavily, she reached the last carriage of the Oxford train, just before it pulled out of the station.

Passengers spilled into the aisle and around the exits. Resigned to spending the journey sitting on her case, it surprised her when a tall man in a business suit and colourful tie half-stood and offered his seat.

Usually she politely refused, kidding herself she took one for the sisterhood. Not today. Grateful, she mouthed a thank you.

Away from London, cows, goats, and green fields flew past the steamed-up window. Across from her, an older woman chased her ball of wool over the laminated table separating them. Unfortunately, she wasn't doing a great job of ignoring Lily's tears.

Embarrassed, Lily dabbed her nose with a tissue and pulled out the travel guide Crystal gave her. Everything she needed to know about Burkina Faso in two hundred and sixty pages. She flicked to her first stop, Ouagadougou, the country's capital. Kicking Daniel out of her mind, she concentrated on what she had to do over the next few months. She wished he'd call. Tell her he got her note.

"Coffee, baguettes?" A man pushing a service trolley pulled up beside them.

Ugh. The sight of food made her queasy. Must be the malaria medication.

"No, thank you." She patted her lips with another tissue and adjusted the top button of her coat.

After texting Sam her expected arrival time, she settled in for a brief nap, but it was impossible to sleep. Frazzled nerves and nausea, not a good mix. She still hadn't changed her number. Thankfully, there had been nothing from Pete the last few days. Finally giving up, she shuffled her bum into the seat and fished for the mirror in her bag. Paler than usual, feint, grey shadows under her eyes.

A touch of lip gloss should brighten the picture. *Haunted.* Lily smiled at the name on the bottom of the gold case, bought on her last shopping trip with her friends. By the time they finished in Selfridges' cosmetic section, the saleswoman had loaded them with samples, desperate for them to leave.

The tears started again, flowing nonstop. The woman opposite inhaled loudly. *Oh no, here it comes.* Before she could comment, Lily waved the tissue at the window. "Hay Fever."

One eyebrow raised, she took the hint and bit into her *BritRail* sandwich. Egg oozed from the side.

On edge, Lily checked both ends of the carriage, half expecting Pete but lost in a fantasy that Daniel might stride through the connecting door.

Drained, she mumbled goodbye to the woman while the man who had given her his seat lifted her bag from the overhead rack.

"Have a good day," he said, and gave her wrist a gentle squeeze.

"Thank you." Lily wedged her shoulder against the door in time to stop it from closing.

"Over here." Arms waving in the air, Sam rushed along the platform.

"Hey lovely." A scruffy dog yapped at her friend's ankles, tail wagging.

"Hey lovely, yourself." Caught in Sam's famous bearhug, Lily gasped for air.

"Now I know you need a drink. I look like a fucking scarecrow."

Tears swam in Lily's eyes. She'd never been happier to see anyone in her life, except maybe Daniel. "And cheese."

"Come on, truck is over there." She nodded towards an over full carpark. "The cheese is out of the fridge, getting gooey, as we speak."

Fifteen minutes later, Lily clutched her lower back as they bumped off the bitumen onto the dirt road leading to the kennels. Birds sang and tree branches bowed, and some of the stress from the last week lifted. She sighed loud enough for Sam to blow her a kiss.

"Okay, we're here. Hop out, we can get your bags later. No time to waste. Drinks while the sun sets."

Lily laughed. Sounded good.

"That's it. Park your arse right there and spill." She pointed to a wicker chair complete with a floral cushion. Perfect. "And don't waste spit on Pete. I want to hear all about Dan the Man." Sam tickled the ears of the dog who hadn't left her side.

"What's *his* name, Scruffy?" She wasn't ready to talk about Daniel yet. Not sure she could without bursting into tears.

Sam covered the dog's ears. "Be nice. This here is Reginald. Reggie for short. He's off to his new home tomorrow. I think he's nervous. Aren't you sweetheart?"

Reggie panted, a huge dog-smile lighting up his face.

"He is gorgeous. Who's his lucky human?"

"Jack, AKA as Winter. A Vet who doesn't speak. Not that it will be a problem. Reggie here makes enough noise for two. Don't you, boy?"

Reggie agreed. His howl carried into the night.

"Enough dog talk, Lily. Drink up. Dan? Spill."

Lily wrapped her fingers around the tumbler of white wine and smiled. "Don't you have any wine glasses."

"Lily…"

"Okay, okay. Dan. Daniel is not my man. I've only known him a few weeks."

"Oops, I forgot the cheese. Hold that thought." Sam leapt from the swing seat. Reggie sprang to his feet. "It's okay, boy. Stay with Lily."

Glad of the reprieve, Lily let out a breath and watched the sun fall into the horizon and the green fields turned purple.

"Ta Da! Dig in. I've got a mountain of the stuff in the soddin' fridge and I don't want any left when you leave." Sam flopped into the seat and flung her feet onto a small rock positioned perfectly for her boots.

"Mmm, this is delicious." The blob of cheese balanced precariously on the water cracker. A second later and it would have missed Lily's mouth and landed in her lap.

"Delicious? It's fucking orgasmic. Can't say the same for the wine, but I promise Veuve tomorrow night. Now, come on. This man. I can tell by that twinkle in your eye, you are past pizza and a pint."

"I don't drink beer."

"Witch. Come on, it's like old times. Imagine we are in our pyjamas, sitting on our bed in the dorm. Speak." Sam gave the hand command, and the dog barked. "See. Reggie boy agrees."

Listening to Sam huff and puff beside her, Lily took another long swallow of her wine. "He's ex-military, owns a security company, Sentinel, with some of his ex-teammates. Intelligent, knows what he wants."

"Stop. You are killing me. I'll get you to read his c.v. later. Right now, tell me, is he hot?"

"I guess."

"Oh, no. This is not a guessing question. Does he make your toes curl?"

"Well… yes."

"Yip-fucking-ee! That was harder than turning metal to gold. All joking aside, Lily. Does he treat your right? Because you know you deserve nothing less. After Pete, I want you to tell me this guy kneels at your feet."

"Slow down. Yes, he is a perfect gentleman, but…"

"But, what?" Sam reached for the bottle and filled their glasses.

Already feeling a little light-headed, she should stop, but, hell, it tasted fantastic, and all she had to do was stumble a few feet to bed.

"After Pete, I need time. It will be good to be away for a while. If Daniel is still around when I get back and interested. Key word Sam, interested. Maybe we can take it from there."

"Okay, it's your first night here. I won't bug you, but this conversation isn't over Lily. Have another cracker and drink up. There's another bottle in the fridge."

CHAPTER TWENTY-TWO

The moment he left her, Knight suspected, deep in his gut, the likelihood of Lily calling him amounted to zero. Call it a sixth sense, the tell, when her gaze left his as she walked away. Still, he'd given her the benefit of the doubt, hoped she'd be in touch.

Until Tuesday. Sixteen-hundred hours—over and out. A man could tread water for only so long before he drowned. Unlike his mother, in no way, shape or fucking form, was he suicidal. His open ticket to Burkina closed with his flight the next day.

After six hours in a stinking truck, sweat caked to his skin, trucking down another dirt road, they were in position, close to the building where they suspected Seckou had buried his sorry arse. Was today the day he died? He doubted it. Something told him this occasion was the same as the others. A dead end. How many of those were there in the world—in a lifetime?

The fucking story of his life. Walking in circles, staring at gaps in the clouds, so sodding dizzy he wanted to chuck. *Suck it up and move on. Yeah.* He raised his right fist in the air.

Spanner looked at him as if he was crazy, possibly, and kept drumming his fingers on the steering wheel. The thudding was driving Knight insane.

He leaned back against the truck, hoping Lily missed him half as much as he did her. Kate had confirmed she was with them in Africa. It should have been some comfort knowing she was away from Pete. On the same continent. It wasn't. On top of his concern for her safety was the ache, the nagging realisation he may be falling in love with her. His couldn't care less that they'd just met. He had always been quick to decide.

Lily Storm didn't want him. Fine. But no time soon would he forget how stunning she looked lying next to him in bed, how fucking fantastic her mouth felt on him. His cock stirred.

Doc's voice filtered through his headset. "Shit, Knight, you've been cursing ever since we left Ouaga. Change the channel to inside voice. You're giving me a headache."

Itching to release some of the pent up energy running rampant through his body, he went to give McLaren a piece of his mind and remind him who was boss. A screech of brakes stopped him. A beat up Humvee rounded the corner, swung hard right and screeched to a halt on the opposite side of the street.

"Hang tight, going in for a closer look." Spanner said, slipping out of the seat beside him.

Knight lay his combat shotgun across his knee and slipped off the safety. His pulse picked up. With the door opened a crack, he swivelled, ready to move.

Maintaining radio silence, he and Doc tracked Spanner as he circled to the rear of the Humvee. One shoulder butted against the wall of a makeshift garage he eased it open. So far, he'd gone undetected, no movement from the vehicle.

"What the fuck are they waiting for?" Doc hissed.

Knight snorted. Good question. They'd copped to being spotted or were having a last smoke? Whatever. Get on with it. He had plans to visit Aunty at the refugee camp. Check-in with her on any known AQIM threats. Nothing beat on-the-ground intel.

Plus, she'd sent him a letter. Amina's baby had taken her first steps, for Christ's sake. Yeah, time flew when you were having fun. He'd paid for the young mother's schooling. He was due for some R&R.

"Standing by. Movement inside garage," Spanner said.

Yelling came from his direction. Someone not happy. Spanner signalled for them to hang back, stay where they were.

Once again, he pushed Lily to the back of his mind. Her kind of distraction he didn't need. Certainly not in the middle of an op.

"Sitrep, Spanner. What's going on? Copy."

"Not sure. Shit."

"Spanner?" Knight curled his fingers around his gun, shoved his SA80 into the back of his pants and got ready to run.

"Boss. There are women and kids inside. Copy."

Bastards. Loud to surround themselves with human body armour. Didn't matter who it was—strap 'em to you like a rag. "Doc. Good to go?"

"Roger that."

"Two targets on the move." Spanner shifted in his peripheral vision.

A man and a woman, headscarf covering her face, emerged from the Humvee firing in every direction.

"Bollocks!" Spanner hollered.

Knight ran left, Doc to the right, gunfire echoing around them. The man dashed towards where they believed Seckou was holed up while the woman stood her fucking ground. Legs apart, no doubt in his mind, she intended making her last stand.

"Doc, you take the man. Spanner, secure the women and kids inside that garage. I've got the woman."

"Roger." Doc and Spanner said in unison.

"*Pose votre arme!*" he yelled for her to put down her weapon. Even at this distance, he knew. She'd rather die, and he was the damned soul to oblige. "*Laissez tombé.* Drop it." I will shoot you. Knight promised, this time in English, just to be clear.

He raised his gun. Doc came from nowhere, throwing himself through the air and tackling her. *Goddamit.* Her gun fell to the ground. Knight was on it before she could recover it. Swivelling to his right, he pulled the trigger and took out her male companion.

"Spanner. Report. Over."

"Two targets down. A kid in need of medical attention. Doc, you there? Copy."

"On my way. Over. You got this?" Doc said, throwing a chin lift at the woman.

He grabbed the woman's wrists and forced them behind her back. "Fuck, yeah. Piss off, McLaren, before I lose my temper."

He snarled, tired of wrestling with her as she did her best to bite the ever-loving shit out of his hand. "Be still." He pinned her to the ground and tied her hands and feet. "*Seckou. Ou est-il?*" he demanded.

Anger pouring off her, she cranked her head and spat at his face.

Reflexes firing, he turned and avoided her aim. "Seckou. Where is he?"

"*Disparu.*"

Gone. No fucking surprise.

"Boss. It's over. Enough," Spanner said, grabbing his elbow.

He shrugged off Spanner's hand, and without another word, he strode to the truck. Again, Seckou knew they were coming.

Pissed off, Pete paced the manky carpet in his hotel room. His contact in Burkina should have called him two hours ago. Shithead hadn't returned his calls or his messages.

Seconds before he threw his mobile at the tv, it rang. "About fucking time."

"Apologies, I had pressing business to take care of before I gave you an update."

Pete's blood boiled. What could be more important? For the

money he was paying this dickhead, he should be his priority, top of his list. There wasn't a shit terrorist on the planet who wouldn't give his right arm for the prize he had put on the table.

"What's happening? Have you found her?" He curled his hand into a tight fist and beat his forehead, tried to get knock the headache out of his skull.

"Yes. It took my men some time to process your tracking information, but we have her location. She is at a clinic on the Burkina side of the Mali border. My contact confirms there are two other English women with her."

"Yes, yes." Her bitch friends. So far, the man wasn't telling him much he didn't know. "When will you reach her?" Inhaling deeply, he tried to stay calm. "I need to release the shipment, pronto." The cargo was in a safe place, ready to transport as soon as he had Lily's location.

"I understand. A few days."

Pete took a long swallow of his whisky. The bite of the alcohol didn't touch the sides of his anger. The image of soldier boy's paws all over his property seared his brain. Lily belonged to him, and he had plans for his woman.

CHAPTER TWENTY-THREE

"Sorry to leave you there on your own, Lily. We should be back tomorrow, late afternoon. Must go. The man from *Afrique Santé* has finally arrived. Fingers crossed they've got what we need. Take care." Kate waved.

"Drive safely." Lily sighed as her phone screen went blank. Less than a week ago, a steady stream of sick children had drifted into the clinic from nearby villages. Measles.

Kate and Crystal left three days ago. Bloody bureaucracy, but they agreed. They stood a better chance of securing extra vaccine from the hospital in *Ouaga* if they were there in person. She spoke to them every day, but she missed them.

One good thing, no messages from Pete. The chances were slim he'd follow her, but just in case, she made her father promise not to tell him where she was.

Unfortunately, there'd been no word from Daniel, either. Maybe he didn't get her note. Exhausted, her eyes and scalp were itchy. A sixty-second shower would be heaven, but measles outbreaks didn't wear a watch.

Standing at the entrance of the medical tent, her hand fluttered protectively over her tummy. Not wanting them to worry, she hadn't told her friends her news, but the sooner they were back, the better. Yesterday morning the pregnancy test turned pink. Hard to believe she'd done it again just to make sure.

Unfortunately, birth control pills gave her severe migraine, but she had a coil and Daniel wore a condom. She took a long sip of water. Did Daniel want children?

Lily scanned the mats littered with stretchers. Not much air circulated against the thick canvas walls, and the stale, musky scent made her stomach churn. Kids cradled in their mother's arms, many too sick to cry, overflowed onto the tarpaulin floor.

Already feeling guilty, she hated deserting them before the outbreak was under control, but she had to think of her little one, couldn't risk losing her baby. She swallowed hard. When Kate and Crystal returned, she planned on flying home. With or without Daniel, giving it up wasn't an option, she'd be the best mum on the planet.

"Lily." Robes flowing, sandals scraping across the waterproof floor, Mahmoud stumbled towards her.

"For the love of hot chips Mahmoud, what's the matter?" She dodged left, grasped the tent pole, and reached for the packet of rye crackers in her pocket. Any minor upset swiftly elevated to an emergency in the liaison's mind. Another reason she missed Crystal, the only one who could handle him.

Mahmoud scratched his head, puzzled, his shoulders lifted to his ears, and his arms spread wide. Lily rolled her eyes.

"*Il est la.*" Mahmoud's ear-splitting shrill was deafening for this early in the morning.

"*Qui.* Who is here?" Lily kept walking, waving as she passed Sedi, the African nurse who supervised the TBA's. "Over there, bed two, check the I.V." She lowered her voice, not wanting to shout at the local women. Without the help of traditional birthing attendants, her life would be a hell of a lot harder.

"Have our supplies arrived?" Lily faced Mahmoud, half

hoping *Afrique Santé* had paid the bribes demanded by patrolling gangs and freed their long overdue crates. She was running out of options after using whatever scraps of material she could find for makeshift dressings. Sedi's knowledge of Burkina's traditional medicine had been a lifesaver. She made a mental note to call Kate later to see if she could check while she was at the hospital.

Never much help, Mahmoud shook his head. *Damn*. What good was having a liaison? She opened her mouth to say as much when loud noises erupted in the corner of the tent. Simone's sobs commanding everyone's attention. The strain of treating the mass of sick children taking its toll on the youngest of the TBAs. Lily could relate.

She reached for Simone's hand. *"Quel est le problème?"*

"Pardon, pardon. I cannot do this," Simone sobbed.

"Don't be sorry. It's been a long day." Lily cleared her throat. "Take a break. Rest, we can manage."

"Merci. Thank you." Simone sniffed.

"Pas de problème." Lily puffed. Boy, morning sickness didn't make life easy. Anxious about throwing up, she almost choked on the cracker she stuffed in her mouth.

"Lily. He is here," Mahmoud screeched.

"Okay. Take me to this mystery man."

Mahmoud shuffled ahead. "Quickly."

Behind the curtain surrounding her makeshift office, an African, his back to her, flicked through papers on her desk. "Excuse me. Can I help you?"

Not phased the visitor took his time facing her. He was tall, over six-foot, dressed in clothes made from the traditional waxed cotton, a *kufi* covering his head. The corners of his mouth twisted into an overly charming smile.

"Lily Storm? *Enchanté.*" The sound of her name slithered off his tongue.

"Yes, and you are?"

"Please, forgive me. Allow me to introduce myself. Colonel Diarra at your service."

Educated, an affected English accent. Lily shuddered. "Likewise, Colonel." It wasn't unusual for the military to patrol the area. It was odd he didn't wear his uniform, and why was he at the clinic? Did he want supplies for his men? Out of luck, sunshine. *Take a breath, Lily.* Waving palm leaves and rolling out the red carpet. No way, but she should be polite.

"Can we offer you something to drink, tea?"

"No, thank you." Diarra bowed over her hand. Her unease increased the longer he held on to it.

"Forgive me, Colonel. Usually, we are happy to welcome visitors, but there is a measles outbreak. This is not the best time for you to be here. I will have to ask you to leave. I'm sure you understand." Lily smiled and gestured at the exit. Diarra didn't budge.

"Thank you, Miss Storm. I appreciate your concern for my welfare, but I insist on a half-hour of your time."

Insist? Deep in the pockets of her clinical coat, her fingers itched to punch him in the nose. "Colonel Diarra. That is not possible. There are over a hundred sick patients needing my attention." She stepped to the side, opening a path for him to leave.

"Very well. I will stay until tomorrow. We can talk after you finish for the day. Please, join me for dinner?"

A command, not a question. Two not-so-polite words away from telling the colonel to hop it she almost missed him flick a hand at Mahmoud.

"I am sure your liaison can find a suitable home for the supplies in my truck."

"Sorry, I don't understand. Have you brought the Paracetamol, the Vitamin A?" She ran through the list, wondering why *Afrique Santé* hadn't been in contact. "Did you speak with my colleague, Kate McLaren?"

"Yes, in Ouaga, at the hospital, I offered to make sure your supplies arrived safely."

Oddly, Kate hadn't mentioned it, but then they'd been focussed on the vaccine. "Thank you. I am sincerely grateful, but I must attend to my patients. I will see you at dinner. Mahmoud, please show the colonel our store tent and find him a bed for tonight."

"*Merci.*" Before she could stop him, Diarra kissed the back of her hand. "*Ce soir alors.*"

His gaze bored into her. Never-ending darkness in his black eyes. "Yes. This evening." Lily shivered.

Unfortunately, thanks to a mid-afternoon emergency, the day ended long after evening faded. A villager nicked his femoral artery while cutting maize. and it took several hours to repair the damage and stabilise him. If Diarra wasn't waiting, she'd call Kate, then head for her tent and complete her notes.

Instead, one hand on her queasy tummy, she made her way over to a table where Mahmoud entertained him.

"Good evening, gentlemen." Her hand waved over her small plate of food. "*Tigua Dege Na.* My favourite, I'm surprised there's any left. Mahmoud, are the supplies unloaded?"

"Do not worry, Lily. I can call you Lily?" Diarra edged his chair closer to hers.

She nodded, deciding it would only prolong her time with him if she said no.

"We have taken care of everything. How are your patients?" Diarra's arm snaked around the back of her chair, increasing her discomfort. "As well as expected, thanks to you, the supplies will make a significant difference."

"Please, call me Ibrahim. You look extremely tired, Lily. I hope you will rest tonight."

"Hopefully, but as my father is fond of reminding me, you can rest when you're on a pension."

"We can't have you getting sick. Eat your dinner." She flinched at yet another order.

"What time are you leaving tomorrow, colonel? I imagine you will want to get an early start."

"Plenty of time, plenty of time."

Over the next half hour, their conversation deteriorated into a litany of dodged questions. Oblivious, Mahmoud happily filled in the awkward silences with the minutiae of his life.

Finally, eyelids drooping, she was done staying civil. "Please excuse me, colonel."

"Ibrahim."

She nodded. "Goodnight. I'll call my colleague before it gets too late, let her know the supplies have arrived."

"Allow me to accompany you. It's dark."

Torture, spending another minute with him. By the time she reached her tent, she was happy to be rid of him and immediately felt bad. Colonel Diarra gave her the creeps, but he'd done nothing to warrant her mistrust. Some people did that to her, instantly made her suspicious. "This is me. I'm sorry we couldn't have met under better circumstances."

"Indeed. I am sure we will meet again. My business brings me to Soum province often. *A bientôt.*" Mahmoud, hot on his heels, Diara disappeared into the dark.

Pushing open the wooden door to her small bathroom, she fell to her knees and puked into the ecosan toilet. Several shovels of sawdust piled into the hole failed to mask the smell. She stripped and stepped into the outdoor shower. The tepid water cooled her sweaty face. Reaching for her shampoo, she massaged a few precious drops into her hair, looked up at the canopy of stars, and thought of Daniel.

Maybe he'd read her note and decided to wait until she made the first move. What if he didn't want to be a father? But she was getting ahead of herself. She reached for her towel, took her time drying, and wondered what it would be like being a single mother.

Slipping into her sleep t-shirt and shorts, she flipped open her laptop and checked flights to London over the next couple of days. Fifteen minutes later, she rubbed her gritty eyeballs, found her torch, and settled into her book.

CHAPTER TWENTY-FOUR

Damn. She had fallen asleep reading. Beside the camp bed, Lily's torch flickered. One arm flayed in the dimness, searching for her phone. Four-thirty a.m. Bugger the rain and the fact that dawn had still to crack. A walk might clear her head.

Lily pulled on light pants and a cotton t-shirt and slipped into her sandals. Shorts would be more comfortable in the heat, but a woman didn't go bare-legged in Burkina. Not if she wanted to show respect.

Clouds blanketed the rising sun, doing its best to squint through the swaying branches of the coconut trees. Raindrops the size of almonds bounced off the tents. Since Daniel, she hadn't been able to look at rain the same way. He hated it. Understandable, given how he'd found his mother.

Before heading out, she untangled her locket from her hair and tied it in a ponytail. Careful to aim her torch into the mud and not into people's sleeping quarters, she weaved in between tents. She cursed when the bloody thing died just as she came level with the supply tent.

Slapping it against her palm did no good. It refused to spark to life. *Hell.* A sudden flash inside the tent illuminated two figures,

Diarra and Mahmoud. Instinctively, she took a step back and angled her body sideways.

Not the bravest. She sucked in a deep breath and squared her shoulders, prepared to confront anyone trying to steal precious supplies. Footsteps to her left stopped her in her tracks. Cloaked in black, a man with a long, thin bundle under his arm entered the tent. Her heart missed a beat, then another, and one after that.

Pete?

Ridiculous. Pregnancy hormones did strange things to a girl, but hallucinating? Slapping herself for being paranoid, seeing Pete in every shadow, she took her phone out of her pocket and crept over the small rocks. As if sucking in a breath somehow made her invisible, she pried two fingers into the slit in the canvas, hoping to get a better look at the man.

Crumbs. It was Pete. Her blood ran cold as he grabbed Diarra by the front of his shirt and yelled. Over the beating rain, she couldn't be sure what she heard, but there it was again. Guns. Her stomach rolled. Planning to watch the recording in the safety of her tent, Lily tapped her phone's video app. It beeped.

"*C'était quoi, ça?*" Mahmoud's head snapped in her direction.

"*Rien.* Nothing. You 're fucking hearing things." Pete answered. "Stop stalling, Diarra. We had a deal. You get the guns. I get the woman."

Lily clutched her stomach. None of this made any sense.

"*Oui ou non?*" Pete uncovered the bundle under his arm.

No mistake. A gun. A big bloody gun. Her knees felt like jelly, but Lily didn't look back as she retraced her steps. In her tent, she clambered onto the camp bed, released the mosquito net, and ducked under the thin sheet.

The screen of her phone glowed in the darkness as she replayed the video. Her palm rested against her lower belly. *What would daddy do?* Daniel. The expert when it came to bad guys.

Her breath hitched. Outside, she could hear men's voices. Afraid they would see the light from her phone, she tucked it under her pillow.

"Whose tent is this?" asked Diarra.

"The nurse, Lily," Mahmoud replied.

Silence. A beat too long.

"Today, Diarra. It has to be today," Pete commanded.

"*Oui.* I will take care of Miss Storm. My men are here."

She waited until their footsteps disappeared into the night and pressed Kate's number. The thing was dead. *Damn.* The nearest place she could charge it was the medical tent. Rolling off the bed, she crept out of her tent.

Lily hadn't made it fifty yards before four men on motorbikes roared into the village and started shooting at early risers. Caught in the open, there was nowhere to run. Diarra charged, knocking her sideways and taking the wind out of her scream.

Winded, coughing, trying her best to crawl away, Lily lashed out with her heel, but the son of a bitch locked her head under his arm and dragged her to her feet.

A powerful mix of fear and adrenaline charged her blood, and she bit her attacker's hand, digging in, refusing to release him until he let her free.

"*Putain,*" Diarra growled and slapped the top of her head.

Bitch in any language. The words whirled in her head along with the black dots jumping in front of her eyes.

Her teeth lost their hold on the bitter tasting flesh. Diarra dropped her to her feet and wrenched both her hands behind her back.

The zip tie securing her wrists burned and a nagging ache sank deep between her shoulder blades. Determined to protect baby, she cowered over her exposed torso. Invisible walls closed in on her, crushing the sobs between her ribs. *Breathe.* Any chance of escape impossible if she couldn't catch her breath.

"Be still, Lily. Stop struggling, and no one else will get hurt." Diarra snarled.

Her heart smacked against her chest.

Head on a swivel, she searched for Pete. She'd beg, do anything he asked if he didn't hurt her baby. When she didn't see him, her panic turned to blind anger. Whirling around, she aimed her knee at Diarra's crotch. He tightened his grip.

"You want to do this the hard way? *Pas de problème.*" He turned towards the other men and lifted his arm. *"Préparez-vous à tirer."*

"No. Please. Don't shoot."

"Then move, Miss Storm."

"Okay. Just leave them alone."

"Allez." Diarra pulled a black bag over her head. The smell of goat and urine made her gag.

Other than slivers of light bleeding through small holes in the hood, it was impossible to see much. Lily stumbled several times, finally slamming against something hard. Pain shot through her shoulder as the wall gave way. A van—no way. She kicked harder, screamed louder.

Diarra's fist slammed into her face, knocking her to the floor. The salty taste of blood flooded her mouth. She could feel her left cheek swelling, one side of her nose blocked. Panic tore at her insides as the engine revved and they tore away from the village. The gunfire had stopped. At least the villager were safe.

Men inside the van enjoyed taunting her, tapping her with the tip of their boots. Curling into a foetal position, she did her best to stay calm, slow her breathing. It was too early in her pregnancy to feel her baby move, but she had to believe it was alive.

She shook her head, trying to clear her foggy brain. Where were they taking her? Why? *You get the guns. I get the woman.* Her eyes closed. *No. Think, Lily.*

The van screeched to a halt. The sudden jolt threw her against the door just as it gave way. Diarra caught her elbow and hurled her into the dirt. Pain raged through her lower back.

"Get up," he snarled.

Scrambling to keep her feet under her, she tripped up stairs and through a doorway. "What do you want? Pete?" She aimed the question into the air, not sure he was there. Not sure she wanted answers.

"Down, get down. On your knees," Diarra growled beside her ear.

Lily slowed her breathing. One thing she knew, rescue missions for kidnap victims didn't have a high success rate in this part of the world. They would keep her alive only until they got what they wanted.

"Please." Her jaw ached. The bruises on her face made it difficult to speak. Her arm tightened around her waist and she winced at the sharp pull on her hair when the bag was wrenched from her head. Her mother's locket fell into the dirt. She went to grab it. The stabbing pain in her wrists reminded her they were still tied.

Light streamed from a single window, blinding her, making her stomach roll. Slowly, her eyes adjusted. Two men stood on either side of a tripod, a camera pointed straight at her.

"Read this." Diarra pulled her hair and held a piece of paper in front of her.

"What? No. Why are you doing this?" She sucked the blood away from her top lip. Had Pete reneged on the guns?

"You do not get to ask questions, Lily. Read it. Now. Or I will…" Diarra didn't need to finish his sentence. The gun aimed at the middle of her forehead said it all.

CHAPTER TWENTY-FIVE

After the cluster fuck in Burkina, escaping to the Beacons was Knight's last shot at staying sane. Alone, except for Lily haunting his every waking hour. He was getting used to seeing her shape floating in the clouds or dancing in the green at his feet. The bitter wind slammed against his face, reminding him he still had a rock to conquer.

His fingers were numb, and his thighs burned, but thank fuck the rain had stopped. Hanging back in the climbing harness, he scanned the jagged indentations of the cliff face. Technically, any climb had one true route to the top, and he didn't plan on leaving today until he'd nailed this sucker.

Too much to expect that a big open hold or a decent jug might conveniently meet his reach. *Come on.* The toe of his Scarpa found an edge—one more push, a couple of feet to smash this fucker. He blew hot air across his chalked fingertips, leaned for a better angle, gripped the shallow indentation above his left shoulder and aimed his right leg at the hold.

His grip held. A final boost and his torso slammed onto the

narrow ledge. *Yes.* Flat on his back, eyes closed, his lungs gasped for oxygen.

Birds, pissed at his interruption, screeched at the damn phone pinging in his pocket. The sods still found him in the middle of nowhere. "Knight."

"Where are you?" He hadn't expected to hear from Kate. "I've been trying to reach you for hours."

"What's up?" He rose to sitting. Flashes of the last time she'd gotten into trouble in Africa running through his head. They had almost lost Doc as well as Mike.

"It's Lily. She's gone."

"So? I am aware."

"Not in the mood for your particular brand of wit today. I'm bloody serious."

Kate rarely swore, prided herself on having a broader vocabulary than most of his Sentinel team. Correct, if not as colourful.

"Okay, you've got my attention." He rolled onto his knees, then feet, and gathered his rope.

"We have a measles outbreak. I was with Crystal in Ouaga fetching more vaccine. When we got back to the village, the bastards had attacked the camp and taken her." Her voice shook. "Max, her dad, wants to see you. Please, Knight, we, Lily, needs you."

"I'm on my way. Text me Storm's number." He disconnected. Hands wrapped around his rope, he abseiled, headfirst, off the rock. As he jogged the mile to his car, he called Lily's father.

"Thank you for returning my call, Mr Knight. It's my daughter, Liliana. She has got herself into trouble, and I need Sentinel's help. Your help. How soon can you be at my office, or I can come to you if you prefer?"

Knight glanced at his watch. A growing ball of apprehension lodged squarely above his breastbone. "Two p.m. Your place."

"Thank you."

Knight memorised the address Storm reeled off, shoved the car into gear, floored the accelerator and headed for London. The phone on hands-free, he pressed Spanner's speed dial. One positive, he and Doc were still in Burkina and no doubt on their way to the clinic.

Storm's office overlooked the Thames. The top floor of prime real estate on Canary Wharf. The brunette guarding the door twitched her nose as he entered. Less than impressed with his climbing gear or the fact he didn't smell too sweet.

"He's expecting me." Not waiting for permission to enter, he sailed past her. Purely a courtesy call, intel, not a lengthy meeting.

Lily's father was taller than Knight expected. He stood as soon as he entered. "Knight, thank you for coming. Please, take a seat."

Refusing wouldn't get him out of Storm's office quicker. Besides, his clothes were damp, his skin turning cold. The leather seat by the window welcomed his stiffening bones. Sniffing in a short inhale, he crossed one ankle over his opposite knee and fixed his gaze on the photo of Lily sitting on Storm's desk. *What the hell have you got yourself into, Princess?*

Storm opened the art deco drinks behind his desk. "Can I offer you a drink, Captain?" From his Armani suit to his Gucci loafers, the man was used to having his way, but his hands shook as he struggled to keep a grip on the neck of his whisky decanter.

"Knight will do fine. And no, thank you."

"You don't mind if I do?" Storm tilted his glass in his direction.

Knight shook his head. "Your daughter, Storm, what do you know about her disappearance." Playing social with Storm didn't get him any closer to Lily. "Who has her, and how did they contact you?"

"Straight to the point. A man of few words. I appreciate that. Do you remember Lily, Knight?"

Sweat trickled along Knight's spine. Unbelievable. Either Storm had nerves of sodding steal, or Lily was right about her father's indifference. Anyone who ever met Lily had her indelibly printed on their soul. Knight unfolded his legs and sat forward in his seat.

"I remember your daughter well." Despite every step he'd taken to erase her from his memory. Getting over her one fuck at a time.

That tactic proved an epic failure. Awake or asleep, Lily Storm wreaked havoc on his universe.

"Sorry, I wasn't sure how aware you were of her recent activities."

In half a mind to accept Storm's offer of a stiff drink, Knight released the tension in his hands. "Yes. I met your daughter before she left for Africa."

Storm took a swig of his whisky and swilled the contents. Knight stood. If Lily's old man wanted to play silly buggers—let him. On his own time. "Spanner will be in touch."

"Please, Mr Knight, I'm sorry. I'm having trouble coming to grips with the possibilities. Much against my wishes, Lily went to Sikire, a small village in the Sahel."

Storm's prattling faded into the ether. He knew she was in Africa but hadn't quizzed Kate for her exact location. Sikire was less than fifty klicks from where Seckou had kidnapped her last year. What was it with *Afrique Santé*? They did a shit job of looking after their people.

Think. Damn it. Knight rose to his full height and faced the window.

Storm shifted behind him.

"Get to the fucking point, Storm. You don't need my professional opinion to know you are wasting time."

"I made inquiries, but no one has seen Lily since gunmen raided the clinic compound several days ago. I understand her work colleagues had left her alone."

Fuck. Knight closed his eyes, willing this to be over before it began. "Have you contacted the local authorities, the gendarmes?" The sensible move. Then again, with this arse, who knew?

"Yes. Nothing. My contacts tell me you, Sentinel, are the best."

Yeah, yeah, stop stroking it. "Any ransom demands?" The usual scenario.

Before he got his answer, the brunette burst into Storm's office, strode to his desk, and swivelled his laptop to face him. "Sir. I'm sorry to interrupt, but you must see this."

"I'm sure it can wait, Laura."

Shit. Every fibre in Knight's body dismissed that idea. He curled his fingers into fists and stepped closer to the nervous PA. "Go ahead, Laura. What is it?" He softened his tone, but his blood shot through the ceiling knowing Lily was in danger.

"This just came through on Mr Storm's email." Laura waved her hand at the screen.

"Show me." Laura hit enter.

Nothing could have prepared him for the sight of Lily on her knees in the dark hut. Two men twice her size towered over her, gripping her upper arms.

"Laje n." A man off-camera yelled in Bambara for Lily to look at him.

As if Lily sensed him there, her eyes half hidden behind a curtain of matted hair met his. Two words shot front and centre of Knight's mind—*dead men.*

Protective instincts in overdrive, his fingers desperate to soothe her swollen face, he lunged at the screen. Flecks of dried blood caked around her nose. *Hang on, Lily.* Search and rescue ops were Sentinel's bread and butter.

"Read now, whore," the man on screen shouted. This time in almost perfect English.

"No. I..." Lily sniffed and raised her chin.

Gutsy. His heart soared with pride even as he silently begged her to keep quiet.

"Do it now or die."

Another man stepped from the shadows and slammed the side of her head with his rifle. Coughing, she sagged in the grip of her captors. These fuckers were serious.

"Last chance, *putain.*"

Do it, Lily. Say whatever the fuck he wants. Stay alive. Knight growled and poured every ounce of his strength into the screen. "I'm coming, Lily," he said out loud.

"I, Lily Storm, am a prisoner of AQIM. They hold in contempt all those who defile the will of Allah and demand two million US dollars for my release. If the money is not received in forty-eight hours, my life will be sacrificed," Lily choked. "God is great. Glory to Islam."

"How long ago did this arrive?" he shouted at Laura.

"I'm not sure." She burst into tears.

"How long." His voice ricocheted off the walls. *Shit.* "Sorry, here, sit. Storm, a glass of water." Aware every second counted, he forced himself to wait while she took a sip.

"An hour. I think. No more."

"Okay. Thank you." Knight drew his phone from his pocket and called Snake.

"Boss?" Snake answered.

If anyone could find Lily, it was Sentinel's comms man. He didn't get his codename for nothing. His skills had improved in the years since leaving the military and he ranked A grade then.

"Listen up. I'm sending you a video. Find out everything you can. Check on Doc and Spanner's whereabouts and meet me at my place in half an hour."

"Roger that."

Knight ignored Storm's 'money is no object' shit and strode out of his office. Thanks to a short, but very influential list of regular clients, Sentinel's bank balance was more than healthy.

"I'll be in touch." He threw the words over his shoulder as the solid brass door thudded closed.

CHAPTER TWENTY-SIX

Several hours later, Knight and Snake stood at the private airstrip just outside of London, waiting while their bags cleared security. Time was fast running out for Lily, and they still had no fucking idea where AQIM held her prisoner. The Islamic jihadist group commanded loyalty in North and West Africa, willing or not. She could be anywhere.

Despite the memory of Lily's tears searing his brain, he had to focus or kiss the deadline goodbye, along with her head. His phone buzzed. Something. Anything.

"Boss, switching to speaker. Go ahead, Crystal."

"Hi, Knight. Thanks for helping Lily. I know her dad's a complete dick."

No argument.

"Aunty called. The attack on the clinic is all over the news. She says she knows where they may have taken her."

Thank Christ. Nothing beat good on-the-ground intel and Aunty had come through for them. "Where?" Knight urged.

"She gave me an address in Déou, says it's an AQIM safe house."

"Did she say how she got the address?" Knight asked, thankful

Lily may still be in Burkina and not across the border in Mali.

"No. Do you think she's right?"

A good question. But they had no choice but to act on her lead.

"Location, Crystal?" Snake scribbled as she spoke. "Thanks. Keep your head down."

Knight scanned the map on his phone and located the house square in the middle of the known terrorist stronghold.

"Snake, alert the Burkina authorities. Make sure they know we'll be in country."

"On it, Boss. We're cleared for take-off as soon as Storm arrives with the ransom. On cue, a Rolls Phantom rumbled to a slow halt several feet from the hangar.

Knight glanced at his watch, impressed with the speed Lily's father pulled together the cash. Lily mentioned she'd never wanted for a thing. *But money isn't everything, is it, Lily?* He strode to meet Storm, not expecting to see the short bald bloke who exited the vehicle.

"Are you Captain Knight?" the man asked, his eyes fixed on a spot above his shoulder.

"Knight, yeah, where's Storm?"

"He sends his apologies. Unexpected business meeting. I have the money."

On the man's signal, Snake opened the boot, pulled out the case and opened it. Two million dollars in crisp US bills. Contingency, in case the exfil went tits up.

Last time they spoke with the kidnappers, Knight insisted Lily's father demand proof of life. Standard procedure. He'd seen and heard it all, dated footage, supposedly live audio, but there were no guarantees. Ever since leaving Storm's office, he had survived on a cocktail of dread and anger.

"Thanks for coming." He braced against the wind gusting across the tarmac, cleared his throat and refused to believe Lily was dead. If Sentinel—if he failed, he had no reason to come home.

What he wouldn't give for a second chance to hear her soft

moans, the ones she hummed inside his mouth when her orgasm took hold. Perhaps for the first time in his shitty life Knight prayed. After this was over, if Lily still wanted nothing to do with him, at least he'd have gazed one last time into the warmth of her blue eyes. Bathed in the smile that pulverised his resolve and ripped open his fucking ordinary life.

"Time to go, Boss." Snake slapped him on the shoulder, setting the world right. The steel bar in his pants softened. Good thing. Risky parachute jumps, along with bumpy landings, were a hell of a lot safer without an erection.

Knight snatched up the Bergan loaded with the ransom and fell in step with Snake. Head in the game, George trotted beside them, sniffing the night air.

On the plane, strapped in for take-off, the familiar vibration of the engine rumbled inside his boots. He breathed out through his nose, braced against the metal backrest, closed his eyes, and ran the plan. Every tiny detail seared into his reflexes. Starting with the satellite images of where they believed Lily was being held. In the middle of arse-fuck nowhere.

Confirmed. Doc was at the clinic with Kate and Crystal, helping them with the casualties. Whoever took Lily had wounded ten people, some seriously. A miracle none were killed. In Ouaga, he and Snake would rendezvous with Spanner and Oumar, leader of the Burkina team.

Sentinel's best men on the job. Locked into a narrow time frame that left no margin for error. If they didn't bring Lily home, no one could. A quick in and out. Grab Lily and head for the extraction point. A helicopter would take them to Ouaga, then a plane to London.

Hours later, Snake tapped his watch. Seven minutes to thirty-five thousand feet where they'd exit the plane, free fall to just around eight hundred before deploying their chutes. At night, HALO jumps were tricky, always a chance someone spotted you before your boots hit the ground. Shot you out of the sky.

George's wet nose nudged his hand. "Okay, mate, we've gone over this a thousand times."

"Easy, boy." Snake placed the harness over the dog's head and strapped him to his torso.

Time. They lined up by the open door. The roar of wind silencing further conversation. Arms braced on either side of the exit, he watched as Snake and George jumped into the night.

"Go." A tap from the co-pilot signalled his turn.

A gale barked over his head. Frigid enough to shrink his balls. At one thousand feet, he pulled the cord and his chute roared open. Hitting the ground running, he rapidly gathered the chute to his chest and unhooked the rifle from his shoulder. No enemy in sight, but experience warned not to be complacent. Shit loved to hit the fan when you least expected.

To his right, Spanner and Oumar emerged from the shadows.

"Boss." Spanner said. No wordy greeting.

Knight nodded and offered the same to the man standing beside Snake. "Oumar, how are you brother?"

"*Très bien,* Knight. You?"

"Getting there." Knight pulled his night goggles over his eyes. On alert for a sniper picking them off from the trees, he gave the hand signal to move. "Stay alert."

"Stay frosty," Spanner added. Chuckling, he pumped his fist in the air.

Fuck's sake. He'd missed the comedian. After watching one too many Yank shows while holed up on a stakeout, they had adopted the term. Knight imagined an army of snowmen, complete with top hats and carrots for a nose, surrounding the enemy.

So far, undetected, they made it to where they believed the terrorists held Lily and fanned in a wide arc around the building. Through the green glow of his goggles, he could make out a small group of men spread out beside the hut. Surely there were more. "Spanner you see them?"

"Sure do, Boss. Set up like fucking skittles. Over."

"You and Oumar take the two at your three o'clock. Snake, handle the others. Copy?"

"Roger that." The team answered as one.

Simultaneous shots rang into the night, each one finding their target. Men down. *Where the fuck are the others?* The nagging voice in his head grew louder. No time. He honed his focus on Lily and ordered Snake to track him, cover his six.

Too easy. Knight kicked open the door. The interior was bare except for the tripod and camera. Heart hammering in his chest, he choked on the breath lodged in his windpipe.

Lily sat on a chair in the middle of the hut, dressed in filthy clothes and a fucking suicide vest.

Snake and Spanner were behind him. George straining on his leash, eager to get to Lily.

"Go. Leave. Get the hell out of here." Knight spat the words.

"No way." Spanner argued.

"That's an order. Now."

A brief shuffle of feet while they weighed up whether to push their luck. "No sweat, Boss. We'll be outside. Don't take too long. The helo won't wait." Spanner, ever optimistic.

The left side of her face was red and swollen, covered in bruises. Her weak smile had to hurt like hell. Typical. They were in hell, a ticking clock threatening to send them both to ash. And his first thought was to secure her in his arms and swear she was safe.

"Daniel? What are you doing here?"

"Nice seeing you again too, Lily." Silently, he cursed the tremor in his voice. Strong, she needed him strong.

"It's a bomb. There is nothing you can do. Please leave, I don't want any of you to get hurt."

Now that pissed him off. Martyrdom. AQIM's most successful weapon. He'd be fucked if they'd recruited Lily.

"Be quiet. There's no way I'm leaving."

Her chin rose, no tears, but her heart beat fast. Too damn fast.

"Sorry, sorry, give me a minute, Lily. Let me think." But they didn't have a fucking minute.

"Please, Daniel, get out of here." Lily shuffled in her seat, digging her heels into the dirt, trying to get closer to him.

Worried she might trigger the bomb, he dropped to his knees in front of her and begged. "Stay still. Don't move."

He scanned the device. "It's going to be okay. I do this all the time." He forced a chuckle, amazed when she joined him. He circled her delicate fingers with his big, hairy hand, gave it a reassuring squeeze and ran the checks.

An overhead vest secured to Lily's torso by shoulder straps. Canisters filled with ball bearings, probably screws, nuts, any shit bits of metal sewn into outside pockets. Loaded to secure maximum damage. Take her head clean off.

"What have we got, Boss?" Spanner asked over the headset.

Knight swivelled his mic closer to his mouth. "The usual variation on a Claymore." A device like the IED that had blown Mike to smithereens. He let go of Lily's hand and drew his knife from its ankle sheath.

"Okay, Lily, you ready?"

She nodded and jerked her face to the ceiling. Not before he saw the tears glistening in her eyes. When her chest heaved with sobs, he returned to being scared shitless.

"Easy. Look at me. I need you to stay still. Tell me you can."

Lily bit her lip.

"I need to hear you say it, Princess."

"I can do it."

"Good. I'll have this off in a minute." Knight slowed his breathing. Salty sweat poured from his forehead into his eyes. He sliced into the straps around her waist and prayed they hadn't missed any stray fucker out there with his finger on a remote detonator.

"Now, gently, Lily, raise your arms. That's it. Almost there."

Inch by agonising inch, he eased the vest over her head and

lowered it carefully to the ground. "You did great. Time to go. Give me your hand." It was icy. After a wobbly start, she stood.

Keeping her as close to his body as he could without carrying her, they made their way to the safety of a group of trees. Once clear of the hut, he turned and locked his arms around her. Relief, strong enough to make him unsteady, sailed through him. Safe and vibrant in his arms, it took a sec to realise Lily was talking. Drawing in a breath, he stepped back and forced himself to listen.

"Daniel, it's okay, I'm okay. Breathe."

The brush of her lips over his cheeks quietened the thunder in his ears. A slow burn started in his gut and blazed throughout his entire body. He turned and blocked her view of the dead guys. After what she'd been through, she didn't need to see them. "Can you walk?"

"Yes. I'm a bit battered, but not helpless."

"Okay. Stay behind me." He daren't risk looking at her in case he changed his mind and carried her to the helicopter.

Snake and Spanner flanked them. George barked, the bloody empath straining on his leash. Knight could relate. He wanted to glue Lily to him until they were well clear of danger.

One night in her arms and she had him by the balls. Not so long ago, he wondered if Lily might change him forever, but she left him long before he could work her out of his system.

Move on. Lily had.

"Sorry, Boss. Change of plans." Snake slackened George's lead.

"What the fuck now?" Knight snarled.

"Short of it. The helo's out of commission. We'll have to make our way to Djibo by alternate means. Oumar scored us a truck."

"Good man." Not the first time the Burkinabe had saved their arse.

George whined. Snake tossed his head at Lily. "She okay?"

"I'm fine, and I haven't lost my hearing," Lily answered.

"Must be." Knight held Snake's gaze.

"You Boss?" Spanner said.

"All good," he lied.

CHAPTER TWENTY-SEVEN

Dressed to his neck in full camouflage, rifle slung over his shoulder, handgun holstered at his waist, a knife strapped to his knee, Daniel carried enough ammunition to kill a hundred people. A frown knitting his brow, the growl rumbling under his breath, completed the picture of a hardened warrior.

Heart in her mouth, Lily asked him again. "Why are you here?"

"Fantastic morning for working on the tan. Thought I'd pop in–catch up over breakfast. Offer you a lift out of here."

The hairs on the back of her neck bristled. He was doing it again, deflecting with schoolboy sarcasm. Why couldn't he just answer the damn question?

His right hand steadied her, the other ran the length of her body, checking for injury, but it still felt intimate. Waiting for him to finish, she smoothed her hair. Her eyes flashed to the bodies splayed in front of the hut. Blood, lots of it. Her head spun into orbit.

"Easy, Lily. They're dead. Can't hurt you. We are here to take you home."

We. He made it clear, but the edge in his voice didn't hide the underlying softness. Warmth radiated through his clothes, knocking the chill from her bones.

Oumar jogged with them to meet the men in uniform spilling from an army lorry. Head spinning, Lily fought to keep her feet moving.

"Okay. We're out of here. Oumar, you liaise with the locals. Call me if you run into any trouble," Daniel ordered, pulling her to his side.

"*Oui*."

Daniel handed her into the back of the lorry before she realised her feet had left the ground. The jolt made her already queasy stomach lurch.

"Spanner, you drive," he said as he jumped in beside her.

Snake sat on the other side of her and grinned. "Cheer up, Lily. Almost home. Right George?"

The dog barked, tongue hanging out, a smile on his face. She winced at the pain shooting through her cheek as she tried to do the same. Daniel's whole body stiffened. She rested her hand lightly on his knee and tried to get him to look at her. "I'm okay."

Knight whirled on her. "You shouldn't be here. Don't you girls talk? Last year, Kate almost got killed playing Florence Nightingale."

Her cheeks flushed. "But it didn't. From what I heard, she saved Doc's backside. Even if you think I am an idiot, *Afrique Santé* takes every precaution."

Daniel huffed. Exasperated, she tried to shift away from him, but Snake didn't budge. "For Christ's sake. Putting four-thousand miles and flying to another continent should have been enough. How was I supposed to know Pete would stalk me to Africa?"

She gasped, not prepared for the speed Daniel moved. He grasped her shoulders and shook her. "What the fuck are you talking about? How did Pete get here?"

This time Snake took pity on her, rocked his weight sideways, so she could shrug from Daniel's hold. George growled.

"I have no idea, but I swear. I saw him. At the clinic talking to Diarra just before they kidnapped me."

She hugged her waist, her bottom lip trembled as she prayed baby was okay. How long before the image of Diarra strapping her into the suicide vest faded? Suddenly freezing again, she fought to keep her eyes open. She could sleep for a week. "Forget I mentioned it. I'm exhausted."

"Not possible, Princess. We will sort this out. That's a promise. For now, sleep. There is a long way to go before we're out of this hell hole."

First sensible thing Daniel had said all day. Her head banged against the side of the lorry. The last thing she remembered was Snake pulling it to his shoulder. The next thing a hand was shaking her awake.

"Wake up, Sleeping Beauty."

Instinctively, she reached for Daniel. Deserted, her hand trembled over the empty seat.

"Just me, Lily. Relax. The Boss is outside, mulling over the intel you sprang on him."

"Are we there?" Not that she had a clue where there was, or how far they had come.

"Not yet, a spot of engine trouble. Spanner's taking care of it." Snake jumped from the van, causing it to rock and groan.

Daniel stood a few feet away, back to her, one hand on his weapon, staring at the road behind them. The side of her face throbbed from Diarra's punches, but she needed air. Gingerly, she shuffled forward. When Daniel's hands spanned her waist and lifted her to the ground, her breath hitched, and her stomach rolled. *Please, don't let me be sick.*

"Thanks." His familiar warmth flowed through her body. Short-lived. His hands dropped from her body, and she stumbled in the inky darkness. Surrounded by people, feeling alone, she hugged herself and thought of their baby. "About before..."

"I haven't forgotten. We'll talk. First, let's get you out of here."

"Okay, in the meantime, take this." She fished in her pocket for her phone. Miraculously, Diarra hadn't taken it. "It's proof. Pete with Diarra."

Daniel took it. She didn't wait for a response. "Sorry, I need to pee."

"Snake. Go with Lily. Those trees over there."

"No problem, Boss. Come on." Snake whistled softly, and George followed.

When they returned, Spanner's head and shoulders were deep under the bonnet of the lorry. A cloud of steam billowed around him. "You holding up okay, Lily?" Small lines creased the side of his eyes as he offered a grin.

A tear rolled over her cheek. "All good."

"Yeah, right?" Snake handed her a rag from his pocket. "Spanner, you're taking your effin' sweet time fixing this pile of junk."

"Only one pair of hands, smart arse." Spanner rubbed his oily palms together and winked. "Don't worry, Lily. Grumpy guts over there has a plan." He lifted his chin at Daniel. "You will be on a plane home soon."

Stuck in the middle of nowhere, they were both bending over backwards to cheer her up. Pretending terrorists weren't chasing them. "Me, worried?" Lily swayed, gulping for air.

"Thought so." Snake grabbed her forearm and steadied her. "Sit, rest for a sec, catch your breath." He reached for his canteen and lowered her gently to the ground. George licked her hand.

In three strides, Daniel stood next to her. His expression could have cracked concrete. Shivers ran the length of her spine. Tall, fierce and oh so bloody capable. It had been months since she'd left him the note—the longest of her life. Why hadn't he called? Vowing not to cry, she thanked Snake for his help.

"Cosy," Daniel sneered. "Spanner. Tell me we are ready to roll."

"Not yet, Boss. 'Fraid we might be on foot."

Daniel cursed. "Snake fan out. Check ahead. Eyes peeled. Spanner, keep working."

Lily took another swallow of water from Snake's canteen and met Daniel's gaze. Even sitting, she felt dizzy. "Don't wait here on my account. Lead the way, Boss. I'm okay to walk."

"Damn it, Lily. If we are on foot, I'll throw you over my shoulder, like the fucking gorilla I am, and carry you." He tried to hide it, but she heard the concern in his voice. Knowing she'd caused it made her want to reach out and apologise, but his torso remained rigid, angled defensively away from her.

A solid brick of panic sat in the centre of her chest, blocking full breaths, but she didn't plan on dying. Not here. "How far?"

"Too far. Dammit." With a tug, he pulled her to her feet and against his chest. "Breathe, Princess."

Palms etched with calluses cradled her bruised face. His mouth hovered over hers, sending her heart slamming against her ribs. His eyes gleamed with an emotion that reverberated through every cell in her body. *Kiss me.*

Stuck in the middle of nowhere, chased by terrorists, she wanted him, ached to be sitting somewhere normal, having a coffee, forgetting he'd been too busy to call. Did he want to be a father? The question paralysed the tears threatening to fall from her eyes.

He tucked a knuckle under her chin and brought his mouth to her ear. *Yes, kiss me.*

"Shh, someone's coming." Daniel released her face, grabbed both her wrists, and pulled her behind him.

Engine noise carried on the night breeze. She searched the blackness. Nothing. Then a series of pops split the air.

"Bloody hell. We're taking fire." Spanner sprang from the front of the lorry and tore into the night.

"No, shit." Daniel placed a hand on her back, pressed her to the ground, and reached for his gun.

An agonised cry shattered the darkness.

Lily's heart leapt towards him, even as the warmth of his body left her.

"Fuck," Spanner yelled in the distance. "Snake's hit."

"Coming to you." Daniel replied. "Wait here, Lily. Stay down, I'll be back."

"No way. Snake's hurt. I'm a nurse. I can help."

"Jesus. Okay. Stay behind me. Don't let go of my belt."

She hooked her fingers over the leather and did her best to keep up with his pace. Bullets whizzed over their heads as more gunfire cracked into the night.

CHAPTER TWENTY-EIGHT

"Lie still, moron!" Violence burned in the Englishman's dark irises, gleaming with a rage that chilled Diarra's bone marrow.

Frantically, he lashed out with his fist at his face, kicked furiously with his feet. Already weak from the beating, he could do nothing to dislodge the man straddling him.

Pete was too heavy to budge. He pinned him to the floor and hit him with the butt of his pistol. His nose cracked and the salty taste of blood filled his mouth. A small part of Diarra thanked Allah he didn't shoot him, even as his forearm pressed against his throat, squeezed the air from his windpipe.

Mercifully, Pete eased his hold, and the air rushed into his lungs. Within spitting distance, Pete's face hovered over him. *Yes, yes, come close enough to bite.* Diarra swirled the phlegm in his mouth. Did he dare?

He took too long to decide, and Pete's fist slammed into the side of his head, spraying blood and spit everywhere. Above the ringing in his ears, Diarra heard him growl. Not wanting to believe death was near, he shook his head, opened his mouth to scream.

No sound came out. Swallowing hard, he tried to get rid of the dryness in his throat. Laughing, Pete increased the pressure on his throat and black dots skipped across his vision.

"You stupid son of a bitch." Pete slapped him again. "We made a deal. I kept my end of the bargain, brought you the guns. Bring me what's mine. All you had to do. But, no, you greedy fuck, you held the slut for ransom and her soldier boyfriend came running."

What could he say? Denying the truth wouldn't save him. Pete would enjoy killing him. Terror seized his guts, loosened his bowel. Urine leaked from his crotch and trickled the length of his inside leg.

"Hah! Call yourself a Colonel, Diarra? You are a disgusting pig. A big girl. Bet you wish you'd taken the guns and run now. Handed the woman to me as agreed." Pete chuckled and poked his finger in his eye.

Diarra wept, pleaded with the maniac. *"S'il vous plait, je suis désolé."*

"Sorry? Too late, fuckhead. Pete's elbow pressed on his windpipe.

True, it was a lame excuse for wanting more. No escape. Paralyzed, he prayed death came swiftly.

His eyes locked on the glint of Pete's knife.

"No. Please," he whispered, expecting pain, feeling only numbness creeping over him.

"Go to hell, you fucked waste of space." Pete plunged the blade into his chest.

Diarra watched in horror as he yanked the blade out of his chest and stabbed him again.

He opened his mouth, sucking in what must be his last precious moment of oxygen. Pissed off, he prayed for the last twenty-four hours to start again. But life had other ideas.

Cold, drowning in the pool of blood spreading around his body, seeping into the dirt underneath him, Diarra struggled for one more breath. Now the pain began.

Pete scrambled to his feet and kicked him in the ribs, over and over, until his heart stopped beating.

Watching Diarra beg for his life hadn't been half as much fun as Pete thought it would be. He stood over him waiting for a twitch, any movement that said he was still alive, any excuse to kick the arsehole again. Diarra had ruined everything. Death was too good for him. For a second, Pete considered chopping him into tiny pieces. He sighed, regretting he didn't have more time. Bending over, he wiped the knife clean on Diarra's trousers. His next victim deserved a pristine blade.

He kicked Diarra's body. "Some fucking hideout, dickhead." If he hadn't gone to the outside bog for a shit, G.I. Joe and his men would have splattered his brains along with the others. He had to walk three miles back to where Diarra waited. No wonder he was in such a filthy mood.

Pete checked his phone. If he hurried, there was enough time to get to the airport and catch his plane. "I'm coming, Lily. I have plans." Plans that included… He chuckled. Time for that later.

Just for luck, he kicked Diarra in the head and took pleasure breaking each of the dead man's fingers, one fat, greedy digit at a time.

He couldn't wait to catch up with Lily and make her pay for her part in this mess. For a few hours he'd have to comfort himself, kick back on the plane, savour a gin and tonic, large, maybe two, and plot her exquisite death. A suffering, death. Suffering—the word had an exquisite ring to it.

CHAPTER TWENTY-NINE

Knight crouched beside Lily and brushed the top of her head with the side of his hand. Staying close, he shielded her with his body as she ripped open the buttons on Snake's shirt. Her fierce intensity in sharp contrast to the delicate, vulnerable woman he'd first met. The woman he loved.

Shit. He reminded himself it was impossible. The heart banging against his chest strongly disagreed. The seed had been sewn when she emerged from the rain at Kate's party. A body blow that left an indelible mark.

A round of bullets pinged off the rock next to them. Lily cringed. George pawed her forearm and whined. Under her breath, she urged Snake to hang on. She had it covered. Knight didn't doubt it.

"It's okay, boy, Snake's going to be fine."

Knight grabbed George's collar and brought the dog to his side. "You're doing fine, Lily." More gunfire ripped over their heads. He turned his head to his mic. "Spanner. Stop pissing around and kill that fucker."

His fear for Lily at fever pitch Knight's heart hammered in his chest. Determined his massive frame would catch any stray bullets before they hit her, he swivelled his head and searched for Spanner.

Three shots, one after the other, bombarded the night.

"Mission accomplished," Spanner hollered and chuckled.

"Get your arse back here," Knight ordered, turning his attention to Snake just as his eyes rolled in his head and he heard the unmistakable hiss of a sucking chest wound.

Lily patted her sides and dug her hands in her pockets "Plastic, I need plastic." Her voice was cool as spring water. He admired that.

Knight grabbed the pack from his shoulder and pulled out the medical kit and an MRE. "How about this?" Covered in plastic, the ready to eat meals were inedible unless you were starving.

"Perfect. Thanks." Lily snatched it from his hand and tore it open with her teeth.

Strictly business, hands steady, she skilfully taped the improvised patch to Snake's chest. He held the roll while she tore off the strips and taped the plastic in place on three sides. Seconds ticked by before the hissing stopped.

They both sighed with release. Knight squeezed her shoulder. "Great job, Nurse Storm."

"Thanks. It's only temporary. We need to get him to a hospital."

"Let's get the fuck out of here." Spanner joined them, echoing Lily's statement.

She nodded. "I can finish dressing the wound in the lorry."

"Okay, let's get him in the vehicle." Spanner grasped Snake's ankles while he crossed Snake's arms over his chest and took hold under his armpits.

"On my count," Lily said. "Three, two, one. Lift."

"Any more shooters," Knight asked as they carried Snake.

"A single gunman? What are the odds, Boss?" Spanner asked.

"Fuck knows. He may be a scout, but we're sure as hell not hanging around to find out." Out there, single gunmen didn't exist.

After making sure Lily and Snake were comfortable in the back of the lorry, he joined Spanner up front. "Are we operational?"

"Almost there, Boss. The engine overheated. Give me a sec. I'll ration enough water for us and use the rest to finish her cooldown."

Knight pressed his tongue to the roof of his mouth and sucked. He returned to Lily and knelt beside her. Blue eyes met his filled with a mix of tears and glassy intensity and something else impossible to name. It sucked the air right out of him.

A foot shorter than him stood the bravest person he had ever met, the dark shadow around her black eye now a deep shade of purple. Lily didn't belong here anymore than Kate, Doc's wife.

Unable to speak in case he lost control, his mind had blanked when she mentioned Pete's involvement in her kidnapping.

Lily may not want him, but he'd never stop protecting her. He wanted to take her in his arms, protect her from any evil fuck lurking on the road, but when they'd made love, his size and weight had frightened her.

"Lily, I'll be up front with Spanner. You okay here with Snake?"

"Yes. Don't worry about me. Taking care of people is what we do."

George barked and licked her hand. "Yes, I haven't forgotten you, boy. We've got this." Her hand dropped to her stomach.

"You sure you're okay?" She'd been through more than most these last few days. He'd never forgive himself if he'd missed something.

"Yes." She didn't say anymore.

A true professional, she returned her focus to her patient. His heart swelled. "Bang on the wall if you need us. Lily, I…" The rumble of the truck's engine stopped him from saying anything stupid.

"Ready to roll, Boss." Spanner called.

"Remember. Anything you need."

"I'll… we'll… be fine."

"I know." Because he'd die before he let anything happen to her. He wrenched away from her and joined Spanner, knowing if he stayed any longer, he'd never leave. "Take the R6 into Dori. Exposed, but it's the fastest."

"Roger that, Boss."

Not wanting to risk stopping, they drove the best part of two hours without a break. No word from Lily. Hopefully, a sign Snake still had fight left in him. Spoke too soon. The sharp rap on the metal wall behind his head made the hairs on the back of his neck bristle. "Pull over."

Spanner checked his wing mirror and drove to the side of the road. So much for staying put, Lily appeared at his window.

"How much further?"

"Couple of miles. Plane's waiting, ready to go. How's Snake?"

"Stable, but I have to pee. Sorry."

She was a bit too pale, but alert. He let it pass, opened his door, and jumped onto the side of the road. Her tongue swept her bottom lip and his balls tightened.

"Over there. Stay where I can see you and be quick."

Not wanting to take his eyes off her he watched as she trudged to the edge of the trees.

"Oh, here I forgot. Found this outside the hut. Judging by the photo inside, it belongs to Lily." Spanner said behind him.

Knight turned to see Lily's locket dangling from his fingers. "Thanks." He took her locket, shoved it in his pocket, and returned his focus to the trees.

"Another thing, Boss. This was inside. I'd have missed it, but when it fell, the thing came loose from behind the photo."

"Son of a bitch." Knight stared at the small tracker Spanner placed in the palm of his hand.

CHAPTER THIRTY

"Thanks." Lily felt guilty for stopping, but the constant swaying of the truck made her want to vomit. Morning, make that any time of the day, sickness. Few escaped the pregnancy nightmare. Luckily, it usually ended after three months.

"No problem. Let's get moving." With one elbow resting on the open window, Daniel barely looked at her.

Overwhelmed, she stared at her hands. Anywhere but the cold, hard lines pulling at the corners of Daniel's mouth. She shivered. Blood didn't faze her, just the sight of it caked to her skin.

Daniel frowned. "You're cold?"

"A bit, which is impossible given it's a hundred degrees in the shade."

"I've got a pair of socks in my pack."

If she hadn't looked up then, she'd have missed the wry smile Daniel fought to hide. No such luck with his gravelly, concerned voice. She grinned. Less than a day together and they were sharing clothes. "No. Thanks."

Daniel excelled at the death stare, the seeing into her heart, daring her to make the next move. Heat pooled low in her stomach. Not unpleasant, perfect. Like the night he pleasured her until her head couldn't lift from the pillow. "Sorry, I didn't mean to be ungrateful. I'd better get back to Snake."

His door opened and Daniel jumped down from his seat. His boots crunching in the dirt, his hand resting on her lower back, he guided her to the back of the lorry.

"Sodding hell, Lily. Stop with the bloody apologies. Forget I mentioned the bloody socks."

"All right." Salty tears stung her eyes.

"Dammit, Lily. Why did you leave without a word? Did Pete bother you? You had my card, why didn't you call me."

"I left a note with Bill."

"Funny. I never got it."

The bottom literally dropped out of her world. Could it be that simple? A lost note.

"Look, I can't lie. Not hearing from you pissed me off for a long time. It, you, me. I had never felt connected to anyone like I did to you. I wanted more. But I'm over it. Over you."

He didn't believe her. He pulled away before she could explain Bill hadn't been there, that she left the note with the temp. "I never meant to hurt you. I'm pre…"

"You didn't. In you get, we need to move." He pulled the canvas aside and lifted her into the lorry.

Less than an hour later, they arrived at a small airport. Lily sighed with relief when several men rushed to help Daniel load Snake inside the plane. She thanked them, hooked up the saline drip and checked her patient's pulse. Thready, but still there.

Okay, baby, we're almost home. She rubbed her tummy, tried to unscramble her brain, and calm her racing heart.

"Wheels up in five, Boss. How's Snake, Lily?" Spanner stood in the doorway next to another man. The pilot, she guessed.

"He's not out of the woods yet, but he's stable. Ready to go home." Bleeding was under control. That was the main thing.

"Aren't we all?" Spanner tipped her a half-salute and continued speaking with the pilot.

As they took off, the walls of the plane vibrated. Her stomach dropped as the nose of the plane lifted and soared out of Africa.

When the seatbelt sign went off, Lily stroked the silky hair behind George's ears, trying, failing, not to replay Daniel's words. *Over you.* "You might be my only friend in the world, boy." Snuggling her nose into the dog's fur she almost believed it, but for the sake of the little one inside her, Daniel wasn't getting out of her life easily. He had to give her a chance to explain.

With a barely audible whine that made her heart flip, George shifted and rested his head on Snake's legs. "It's okay, lovely boy. He will be fine. I promise." She hoped she'd done enough, and his lung didn't collapse before they landed in London.

Her hands trembled in her lap. Staring out the window, the night sky offered no distraction. Too dark to lose herself in misshaped rabbits hidden in tree clouds.

She wasn't game to look in a mirror, but her bruises didn't ache as much. Being so close to Daniel brought the real agony. Head resting on the small pillow pressed against the window, she counted the days, weeks. One night, when nothing seemed impossible.

More than great sex, it was the being able to talk, to connect to someone who listened to her opinion and made her feel special. Not that she needed a man to do that, but it didn't hurt.

The naming angels got it right. Daniel Knight, warrior. Saviour. Pity he didn't need her. Fine. Ever since her mother died, she'd taken care of herself. No reason to stop now. Being a single mother was never in her plans, but she would be a great mum.

First, Daniel had a right to know he was a father. All she needed was the right moment to tell him. George's ears twitched at the click of her safety belt. Leaning forward, she checked Snake's vitals. "Keep your eye on him for me, boy. Need to go to the loo." Lily raised her eyes to the ceiling and slipped off her seat.

Spanner's eyes stayed shut as she nudged past him. Most likely not asleep. None of them would rest until they were on the ground, and Snake in hospital.

After taking care of her bladder, she turned to close the door of the loo.

"Why aren't you resting?" Daniel's growl made her jump. For a big man, he was light on his feet.

"Probably for the same reason you aren't." She pointed at the loo.

Daniel's solid body filled the gangway. Her arms longed to wrap around him. Better they stayed plastered to her sides. Disagreeing, her fingers twitched, eager to run through the stubble on his chin before she kissed him.

"I have a job to do," he grumbled.

Blood rose to her cheeks, a nervous laugh bubbling under the surface. "And I don't?" She bit her lip, not proud of picking a fight, but she wanted to shake him, demand he give her a chance to explain about the note. Okay, not her bravest move, but she hadn't ghosted him.

"Point taken." His brow furrowed.

Close, out of her reach, an invisible wall between them. If only she could wrap her arms around him, reassure him, show him how she appreciated him coming for her, that she was alive. "How long before we land?"

"A few hours. Doc is standing by with transport. Go back to your seat. Sleep. I'll sit with you and keep my eye on Snake. I'll wake you if there's any change."

"Thanks. I've never seen anyone shot. I did a trauma rotation during my residency, but what if it's not enough? Her chest tightened, taking a deep breath impossible. The plane ran into unexpected turbulence and dropped. She stumbled.

Daniel steadied her, drew her closer to his solid frame. "You did great, Lily. Doc couldn't have done better."

"Wow. I'm sure that's not true. I missed you, Daniel." The words sailed towards him before she swallowed the lump in her throat.

"You were the one that ran, Lily."

"I told you. I left a note with the porter. A fill-in because Bill was sick." She curled her hands into tight fists. "Things between us were moving fast, and I needed time to think, before I went to Africa." She left out the bit about Pete's threats. It seemed redundant now. True, they didn't know where he was, but she wouldn't go there. Her mind had to be clear, focussed on Snake.

"I get it. We should have talked, gone slower. After Pete, I wasn't worth taking the risk."

His words sliced deep. The pain in his eyes unbearable. In front of her stood the little boy whose mother killed herself rather than stay with him.

Did he honestly believe she didn't trust him, that she thought he was anything like her ex? She choked back her tears, turned, and stared out of the small window. Burnt orange slashed across the sky. Almost dawn.

"I never got the note," he repeated. His eyebrows narrowed over his dove grey eyes. "Like I said, it makes no difference." Furious, and the saddest, sexiest man she had ever met.

Her heart ached. *Be careful.* Dangerously close to blurting it out, telling him she was pregnant, thinking if she told him, maybe they'd have a life together. Crazy. She'd been alone for a long time. Inhaling deeply, she swallowed the words, willed herself not to let one tear leave her eye. "Daniel, can I ask you a something?"

"Depends."

She took a breath. "Kiss me."

CHAPTER THIRTY-ONE

Serious or not, note or not, Knight didn't give Lily a chance to change her mind. He grasped the tip of her chin and lifted her face. If they did this, she sure as hell was going to look at him.

Her long blonde hair, caked with dried blood, hung in knots over her shoulders. Gently, he threaded his fingers through the tangled curls and cradled her head in his massive hands. His Lily. An odd mix of frailty and fixed strength. She would never lose the power to slay him.

Angry for wanting her, needing her, desperate to pull her close until she disappeared inside his skin, safe from the fucking chaos surrounding them. Lily didn't belong in danger zones where psychopaths blew innocent people apart.

Killing fields were for zombies like him. Men who said goodbye to their souls a long time ago. His blood ran cold, thinking of how he almost lost her. Now he had found her, he wouldn't survive without her warmth defrosting frost-bitten, fucked-up life.

"I understand if you don't want to kiss me. I shouldn't have asked."

"Fuck, Lily, do you have any idea what you do to me?" he said, knowing full well that she did. Her eyes sparkled with passion, glinted with the same need as his to have their mouths sealed together. A pre-requisite for sanity. He pulled her into his arms and matched her shudder.

Part of him said push her away, end the torture. The lunatic part cupped the back of her head and lost itself in fantasies of relationships being more than a single, satisfying fuck. A long night of mutual lustful gratification.

Spinning towards begging, pleading with Lily not to leave him again, he brushed her lips with the tip of his tongue. His balls hardened as her head tilted to give him easier access to the pulse beating fast at the side of her neck.

Her eyes welled with tears. Gathering his shattering control, he moulded her to his chest and absorbed the silent sobs rocking her body.

"Daniel. I can't stop shaking." Her hands clutched his shirt.

"It's okay. You're safe, Lily. You'll be home soon." These last hours she had shown more grit than many people under his command. Pride wasn't enough to express how he felt about her courage.

"Snake?"

"Don't you worry about him. He's tough, he'll make it. Who'd look after George. Mangy mutt isn't coming home with me."

Lily half-smiled, the palm of his cheek pressed into his cheek. The soft pads of her finger traced the side of his mouth, sending shivers from his skull to the base of his spine. "Damn it, Lily, you shouldn't have run. I was happy to kiss you, keep on kissing you, until they carried me away in a box."

She took a tiny step and widened the gap between them. He should have left it there, not smash his lips against hers. His tongue begging entry into her wet, warm mouth. "Please, Lily." His turn to beg.

Her hands slipped over his shoulder blades. His inner demon roared at his fucked up desire to own her as she owned him. Their tongues played in a hot, sensual dance of give and take. The scent of oranges filled his nostrils. The same sweet smell that never left him haunted every bed he slept in, screwed with his head, beat the hell out of his heart.

She'd kill him before this was through. He held her in his arms and tried not to go down a path littered with anchors and lifelines.

"Daniel, there is something you should know." Her skin paled, her sharp intake of breath was making him very nervous.

Keeping hold of her wrists, he unwrapped her arms from his neck and brought them to her side. If she planned on another goodbye, he didn't want to hear it. He gazed into her pretty blue eyes, shrugged, and set her free. Yeah, if they weren't flying in a tin can thousands of feet off the ground, she'd sprint for the nearest exit.

He shifted his weight, gave her space. "Shh. No sweat, Lily. We both know this, us, can't work. I'm not content stealing kisses. When you touch me, I want more."

Snake moaned.

"Let me pass." Lily pushed past him.

Chest heaving, Knight returned to his seat next to Spanner.

"Need something, Boss?" Spanner yawned and stretched.

"Yeah. The return of my bloody mind." As if scratching his head could bring back his brain, he dug his nails into his scalp until it hurt.

His mate tossed him a shit-eating grin. "Where did you last see it, Boss?"

Knob'ed. He stared across the aisle at Lily. "She shouldn't be here."

Spanner shrugged. "Bollocks. And you know it. Have you considered finding your mind might not be your major problem? When you retrieve it, I suggest getting it fucking examined."

Totally uncalled for, he lied to himself and waited. Sure enough, Spanner hadn't finished.

"You and Doc go round in circles—bloody broken records. It's a wonder you don't spin into orbit. Lily, Crys, Kate, they were born to care. Service ingrained in their DNA. Surprised you don't recognise it? No questions, no mind fuck. We should be on our knees, thanking the sodding universe they chose our sorry arses to hang with."

Tell me what you really think. Knight gripped the armrest. Spanner was more than a genius cook. Not just a pretty face. He had an uncanny knack of cutting straight through the bullshit. "Thanks," he said, head screwed in place.

"You're welcome, Boss. Step into my office any time." He crossed his arms and pulled his cap over his eyes. "Now, fuck off, and let me get back to my dreams. Crys doesn't like to be kept waiting." Spanner's elbow digging in his ribs signalled end of consultation.

Knight shoved his hands in his pockets and went to where Lily checked Snake's vitals.

When she saw him coming, she rubbed her cheek. "Hi. Anything wrong?"

Still swollen, her face had to hurt. When he found Pete, and he would, soon, death may be the fucker's easy way out. "Nothing's wrong. How's Snake?"

"Slight temperature. I'm worried there's an infection. No shortness of breath so the seal's still in place, but we'll both breathe easier when we land and he's in proper care."

"Come here." Knight had to touch her again. With one finger, he tilted her chin until their noses rubbed together.

"Don't be mad at me. We do need to talk," she whispered, her soft breath brushing his lips.

"For what it's worth, I missed you too." His voice hitched.

"Thank you for coming for me. I'm sorry Snake got shot."

He reached for her hand, intertwined their fingers, and squeezed. "God, Lily. None of this is your fault. No matter what, I will always come for you."

Their gazes locked. Could she be on board with any part of what he planned? Tongues entwined. Their naked bodies rocking to the rhythm of his cock inside her.

Lily grabbed Daniel, bunching his camo shirt between her fingers. Pressed against his chest, her nipples hardened. Their lips touched. *Heaven.* A lifetime suspended in his kiss would be too short.

Cupping his jaw in both hands, she took the lead, kissing him, pouring every fear, hope into him. He retreated, ran his thumb over her lower lip, and blinked. A slow open and close, like the shutter of a camera. Memories, the first of many? Perhaps.

"When we get home, I plan to spend the rest of my fucking life convincing you never to run from me again." Daniel's gaze lingered on her breasts.

She quivered. "No argument from me."

Daniel squeezed the tops of her arms. "This time, Lily. Be sure it's what you want."

Snake's moan interrupted them. A sharp reminder her patient needed care.

"Be sure," Daniel repeated.

She placed her palm on Snake's head and checked his temperature. Too warm.

"Buckle up everyone. We have begun our descent. Landing in approximately twenty minutes." The pilot's voice echoed through the aircraft cabin.

One last check of Snake's pulse, thready but strong, and she settled into her seat. Pleased Daniel chose to sit next to her, she let out a long breath. His arm snaked around her neck and drew him to her. Ear against his shoulder, Lily listened to the even thump of his heart. Strong, sure. Hugging her waist tight, she dared to breathe in a future. She hugged her waist. *This might work out, little one.*

Once they landed, Lily adjusted Snake's canula and IV and waited for the door to open. Red lights flashed in the dark. Doc ran towards the plane. Two paramedics jogging behind him with a stretcher. The tension in her hands lessened. The muscles in the back of her neck stayed stubbornly tight.

"How are you going, Lily?" Doc greeted her at the top of the stairs, and she nearly lost it.

No. Not now. "I've been better, and I'm very glad you are here." She welcomed Doc's half smile.

"Looks like you've done a great job. Talk to me, Lily. When was Snake last conscious?" Doc's voice edged behind the fog of insecurity building behind her eyeballs.

Had she done enough? Expecting to see Daniel, she looked for him by the door, but he'd gone. Her heart sank. "Er... last conscious at..." Voice shaky, she glanced at her watch. *Don't lose it now.* "Three hours ago."

"Good. You're doing great, Lily. You're with me. We are *en route* to the military unit at John Radcliffe. Okay?"

"Yes. Yes." She knew it well. They'd brought Sam to the Oxford hospital after her injury.

Doc squeezed her hand and issued orders for the paramedics to transport.

Daniel re-appeared just as they exited the terminal. No longer armed, but the familiar scowl still fixed on his face. Doc urged her to keep walking.

Ready to climb in beside Snake, she had one foot on the stair of the ambulance when Daniel grabbed her arm. "Lily."

"Two minutes." Doc hopped into the ambulance, leaving her staring into the smoky grey of Daniel's eyes.

"Let me tie up ends here, then I'll find you. We'll have that talk."

She nodded, but the blare from the siren killed the chance to say more. The ambulance doors slammed shut.

CHAPTER THIRTY-TWO

Time alone after a mission. Knight usually welcomed it, an opportunity to retrieve his head from mission mayhem—re-orientate to civilian life.

His mind on Lily, he secured his weapons in the gun safe and shuffled paperwork. Sentinel did occasional black work for the government. All his team were licensed to carry, but unlike the US, no handguns were permitted in the UK. Not without authorisation against a confirmed threat.

Usually, once a mission was over, his body didn't have a problem dispersing the adrenaline, but right here, he sucked in air that didn't make it past his chest. His fist thumped the desk. Where the hell was Pete?

After he left Lily, he put feelers out for him. No luck. So far, the bastard had found a black hole to bury himself in, nowhere to be fucking found. Snake was the best at finding the lost, but Sentinel's 'B' team had its comm stars, and they were on the job.

Lily was in expert hands with Doc, still every nerve ending in his body twitched. A quick shower to clear his head. She should be back in London, and he had a pretty good idea where to find her.

No matter how vigorously he scrubbed, the smell of Snake's blood clung to his skin. Thinking of Lily, he lathered up a third time and resisted the urge to take himself in hand. More than wanting to scratch his sexual itch, he craved her soft grace. Had he missed her? Shit yeah. He'd kill to hold her hand.

An hour later, still wired, Knight leaned against the barstool at The Lark, Sentinel's preferred pub when they were home, and scanned the crowd of locals and happy-hour groupies. It didn't take long to spot Alpha team in a corner booth. Talking, reclaiming normal. Lily's laugh soar over the crowd. Eager to be closer, he elbowed his way to her side.

"Miss me?" he nuzzled her ear. The fresh scent of citrus teased his nostrils.

"Daniel. Of course, I missed you. Ask Spanner. He had to hold me back. I was a second away from landing on your doorstep, dragging you away from your paperwork. Sit, sit. Move over, Spanner." Lily patted the seat next to her.

Knight ignored the urge to swipe the smug smirk off Spanner's face and curled his arm round Lily's neck. He loved excitement at seeing him. He hated the tiredness dimming the sparkle in her eyes.

Bed. Sleep, he silently promised. Soon, he'd take her in his arms and prove how much she meant to him? In the meantime, he ravished her mouth with a throat-deep kiss. Her breathy moan urged him on. Not wanting to embarrass her, he reluctantly separated from her soft lips and parked his shoulders against the back of his seat. "Sorry."

Lily wriggled her backside closer. "No need to be sorry. I am relieved you're here, that everyone's here. Safe. Doc is making sure Snake is getting the best care. So, drinks on me."

"Sod, Doc, no offence mate. You did us proud, Lily." Spanner said, before shooting him a look. Crystal squeezed his bicep and blew Lily a kiss. Kate laughed.

His last conversation with Spanner in mind, Knight gave him a single nod. They were lucky to have these women as part of Alpha team, including Lily. "The round is on me." He rose from the table. "Same again everyone?"

Content to sit with his fingers intertwined with Lily's, for the next half-hour they kicked back, but his attention was never far away from his phone and Pete.

"Turn around." He pulled Lily's locket from his pocket and placed it around her neck.

Her hand flew to her neck. "Thank you. Where did you find it?" she squealed.

"Easy. I didn't. Thank Spanner. He found it outside the safe house, but I forgot to give it to you." Telling her about the tracker would only add to her stress. Best not to tell her, not yet. Later, when he had her wrapped in his arms.

The brush of Daniel's fingers against her skin sent tingles running up and down her spine. Pity they were in the middle of a crowded bar. She longed to touch every inch of him. Slow and tortuous, as she convinced him just how much she'd missed him and shared their baby news.

It wasn't fair they knew before Daniel, but Crystal guessed as soon as she saw her. Professional sixth sense.

Now or never, Lily. She leaned over and pecked Daniel's cheek. Nothing like the face smash he'd given her, but he didn't seem to mind as he nuzzled against her lips. "Let's go," she whispered.

His eyebrows wiggled. "Thought you'd never ask."

Laughter came easily as she grabbed his hand and they shuffled out of the booth.

"Hey. Where are you two going?" Spanner asked.

"Relax, hun." Crystal linked his arm with hers.

"I won't expect you at the clinic for a couple of days, Lily." Kate winked and waved.

The crisp night air nipped her cheeks and nose as they hurried to

Daniel's MG. Under the windshield wiper, a piece of white paper fluttered in the wind. Expecting Pete to jump out of nowhere, her stomach rolled.

"Bloody parking ticket. Not something I love about London." Daniel screwed up the fine and tucked it into his pocket. "Hey, you okay?"

"Yes. Fine." She snatched the ticket from his hand. "Your lucky night."

"You bet." He took her in his arms and placed her head on his chest. "Don't worry about Pete. We'll have him soon."

She nodded.

"Okay Princess, you dragged me out here, and I'm not complaining. Where do you want to go?"

"Take me home."

"Sure. Home it is." Something odd flashed across his face.

No. Nothing was going to spoil this evening. She hadn't unpacked all her boxes, and they'd have to sit on the floor, but she wanted to be on her territory when she told him about their baby.

When they arrived, Daniel pulled up outside the front, leaned across the console and kissed her. Not one of his long, toe curling best, but she wasn't complaining.

"Go on inside and get warm. I'll be there in a sec."

It was at least ten degrees cooler in the underground garage. She appreciated his thoughtfulness, plus she could check if Bill had her note tucked away somewhere.

Five minutes later she was still standing outside, staring up at the chequer board of window lights.

"Why are you standing there? Come on, inside." Disappointed she'd dressed for the weather, she tugged on his flapping coat. She missed the warmth of his borrowed clothes.

"Your place, or mine."

"Come to mine. Kate and Crys gave me a house-warming present. Wine. Not sure if it's up to your standard, but…"

"You will never let me forget our first date." He smiled.

"Never."

"Okay." Daniel nibbled her ear. "Pour me a glass and I'll cast my vote." The rumble of his laughter chased them through the door.

Unfortunately, no Bill.

Inside the lift, Lily rested her head against Daniel's broad chest. His lips played in her hair, tugging, and pulling as his hand stroked her lower spine. Knowing he wanted her made her heart soar. How long could she resist him? Half an hour before they were naked? *First things first, Lily.* This shouldn't be hard. She broke news to patients, good and bad, all the time.

The tip of his index finger hooked over the top of her jeans. His breath hitched as the palm of his hand slid into her underwear and cupped her mound. "What's this?"

Her insides tightened, the foreplay left her breathless. If it wasn't for the ping of doors opening, she might take the risk and reach for the hardness pressing against her pelvis. "Daniel, I…"

"Hold that thought." He tapped her forehead and pulled her behind him to her flat.

The door slammed, and the breath whooshed from her lungs. Backed against the wall, right where she wanted to be, in his arms— no difficult conversation. No tears. Her soft gasp of surprise, the space he needed to slip his tongue into her smiling mouth.

Panting harder, the trail of butterfly kisses he planted along her collarbone had her on her toes straining for more. In response to her moan, he thrust his leg between her thighs, spreading her wider.

Damn, the man could kiss. Her head flopped onto Daniel's shoulder, seeking the curve of his neck, the spot where his pulse beat. Too easy to get lost in the moment. Struggling to keep it together, she eased herself away. "How about that drink?"

"If we must." Daniel flicked the light switch and frowned.

"Yes. No electricity. Tomorrow. If I'm lucky. There are candles somewhere. Are you stopping?" She tugged at his coat sleeve.

"Oh, that door has closed, Lily." He sat on the sofa, one ankle resting on his other knee, his eyes feasting on her body. Doing her best to ignore him, she found the candles and lit them.

"Have you called your friend Sam? How are her dogs?" He cleared his throat and patted the spot beside him.

Thanks to the candles, a warm glow crept across the walls and ceiling. She loved how he remembered, showed interest in her friend. "Sam's doing well," she said, joining him. "The bank gave her a loan to fund a new venture. She wants the veterans who have taken her dogs to help her work with kids. I don't know the details, but she sees it as a win-win for both groups. I can't wait to find out more."

"When Snake's recovered, we'll introduce him and George to Sam." Knight cleared his throat. "I'm thinking, common interests and he has contacts."

"Ah, it's not what you know, but who you know? Or are Kate's matchmaking skills rubbing off on you?" She snuggled into his side.

The candlelight caught the blue streaks in his grey eyes. Reaching up, she cupped the back of his neck and blew gently on his full lower lip. "Open for me, Daniel." Her breath caught at the glint in his eyes.

"What are we doing, Lily?" Daniel chuckled, stroked the spot between her shoulder blades.

"I haven't decided." *Procrastinating.* She pressed her lips together, rolled her guilt into a thin, hard line.

"Let me help you make up your mind." Daniel brought her wrist to his lips and trailed kisses over the pulse point.

"Good idea." She trailed her palm down the buttons of his shirt and stopped just above the button on his jeans.

CHAPTER THIRTY-THREE

Knight's head fell back onto the sofa, lost in the warmth of Lily's touch, the smell of her shampoo. Happy with whatever she had in mind. If that meant going no further than kissing on the couch, okay, but it just might kill him.

She surrendered to his kiss, her tongue playing with his, her familiar taste intoxicating. Every whimper, each gasp, made him harder as he feasted on her wet mouth. Lily's soft moan echoed inside him. He lifted the edge of her soft, blue jumper, loving the way the colour brought out the best in her eyes. "You, okay with this?"

"Yes." She grinned.

He lowered his mouth in line with her breasts. Rounder, fuller than he remembered. Was there a word for more perfect? If not, they'd better fucking invent one. His breath hitched at the glorious sight of her nipples straining against the soft silk of her bra. A low groan rumbled in his chest. He wanted to make love to her, tattoo permanent laugh lines to the corner of her eyes.

Lily blushed. Not giving a shit if she read his mind, recognised the need raging through him, he lowered his head and suckled her.

He froze at her soft gasp. *Why didn't you learn your damn lesson?* "Do you want me to stop?"

"No. Don't you dare. Sensitive that's all."

Must be that time of the month when women's breasts were extra delicate. "You're sure."

"Yes. Like before. Slow."

"Whatever you need." It killed him, but he took his time undressing her, kept his eyes on hers for any sign she had changed her mind.

After her ordeal, he should make her comfortable, take her to bed, but damn, he couldn't wait that long to sink inside her. The scent of her arousal matched his own. "I want to taste you." He trailed two fingers to the juncture of her thighs. "Here."

"Please."

Knight sucked in another ragged breath, slipped off the sofa and knelt at her feet, awed by the courage of the woman above him. Heart thudding against his chest, he leaned forward, inhaled her musky heat. Sweet hell. If his dick got any bigger, he'd explode.

He counted to three before sucking her clit, teased, and stroked her with his tongue, praying she liked it. The memory of her taste, moans, and the catch of her breath were imprinted forever on his soul.

"Ah, more." Caught on a gasp, her whisper was the green light his lust had been waiting to hear.

More than physical, an unspoken truth drove his hands, mouth, and cock to show her how much she meant to him, how her surrender made him feel as though he could conquer the world. If he questioned it before, now there was no doubt in his mind. He loved this beautiful woman. Unsure where they went from here, he hoped she'd be by his side.

Eyes still pinned on her face, he slid a finger inside her, and stroked until her eyes closed and she moaned again. He added a second and then a third, curled them until they hit her sweet spot.

"Oh, my…"

"You like that?"

"Hhhate it."

Knight laughed, loving this playful side of Lily. He uncurled his fingers.

"No!" Her hands fisted in his hair, and she shuddered. "Daniel."

As much as he enjoyed taking his time, bringing her to the edge, then backing off, his own arousal strained against his pants, ached, painfully, to bury his cock inside her.

Lily arched her back. A wave of moans and groans swam around him, urging him on, begging for more until her orgasm caught her breath and her inner muscles pulsed around his fingers. He stroked her pleasure, watched her drift away, just like she had that first time, and the lines of tension on her face finally faded.

Rising from the floor, he sat on the sofa. Head slumped against his chest; Lily felt good in his arms. "Come back to me, Princess. Look at me."

Lily's eyes fluttered open, and her gaze locked with his. Sex had never been like this, intimate. Not even his Sentinel brothers guessed what he'd shared with Lily. Or maybe they had?

Sitting here with her, hearts beating as one, her face glowing from the light of those bloody candles she loved so much, a peace fell over him. He'd never stop searching for Seckou but knowing there was a possibility Lily would be there when he came home could make all the difference to his ongoing sanity.

"Time for bed." He nuzzled her ear before blowing out the candles and lifted her off the sofa. Ignoring her squeals, he stumbled through the dark, climbed the stairs to the mezzanine, and fell onto the bed, careful not to land on top of her.

Knight kissed her forehead. "Sleep."

"G'nite." A lopsided grin and her eyes drifted shut.

Still dressed, on and off through the night, he soothed away Lily's nightmares. As he finally drifted off, Kate's words rang in his ears. *There's a woman out there for you Knight and when you least expect it, she'll come waltzing around the corner and knock you for six.*

"Morning," he said, enjoying the smile that teased Lily's lips. "You okay?"

"Yes, thank you. Best night in a long time." The grey smudge under her eyes told the truth of it.

"You?"

"Same." He took hold of her hand and pulled her closer.

His lips brushed against hers, and her face flushed. "I want to kiss you." His fingers trailed across the front of her neck to a spot above her left breast. "Here?" He teased, "Or here?" He cupped the space between her thighs.

Just a nod was all it took. He dipped his head and kissed her. Her lips were warm, wet, firm against his as he explored her lips, plunging deeper, their tongues lost in a delicious dance. Blood pounded in his veins. Her delicate hand clasped him tightly around his neck.

Mad to have make love to her, he skimmed his mouth over her throat, along her breastbone, and blew gently across her nipple. He didn't feel the push on his shoulders until he heard her hoarse whisper.

"You need a shower." Her smile didn't make it to her eyes. "Coffee?"

"Sure. You have coffee?" He inhaled deeply.

She nodded and ran her hand through her hair. "Yes, and cereal."

Lily slid from the bed and put on a fluffy dressing gown covered in cats. *Ugh.* He hated fucking cats. One day soon, they were going shopping for more suitable nightwear.

One shower later, breakfast made, Lily hadn't said a word.

"Anything wrong, Lily. You worried about Pete?" According to Oumar, local authorities confirmed he left Burkina. No confirmation, but the odds he was heading back to London were strong. Airports were on alert. Only a matter of time before he was in custody.

"Partly." Both hands wrapped around the cup, she nosedived into the rising steam.

"You're safe with me, Lily. I'm not leaving you alone until we know authorities have him. My place or yours. It's up to you."

"Thanks, but who knows how long it will take? You can't stay here forever."

"Trust me. Forever is not an option, but I'm here until he's caught." He regretted his harsh tone, but she had to understand he had no intention of leaving. "At the moment, nothing's more important than keeping you safe."

"Thanks. Daniel, there's something I need to tell you." The hitch in her voice worried him.

"What is it, Lily? Tell me."

"I'm pregnant." The words fell from her mouth. Not as loudly as she intended.

"Fuck's sake, Lily?" Daniel's gaze bored into her, and he didn't look happy. "Whose is it? No, wait, don't answer that, it's no skin off my back." Daniel leapt to his feet and slammed his cup on the counter. Hands on his hips, he paced in front of her, wearing spots off her rug.

"It's your baby Daniel." Lily folded her legs up to her chin. Perched on the kitchen seat, she wrapped her arms around her trembling knees, praying he'd listen. Stay, and believe her. "I'm sorry I blurted it out. I've wanted to tell you since Africa, but I kept waiting for the perfect moment."

Eyes the colour of clouds bursting with rain peered at her from a hard-edged mask, a face she couldn't read. Lily swallowed her tears. She'd cried enough the past few weeks and didn't need Daniel's pity.

"Well, that takes the cake. What makes you so sure the kid's mine?"

"What?" Terror mixed with mind-splitting anger brought her to her feet. "That's the first thing that comes into your head. How do I know the baby is yours? Of course, it's yours. Why would I lie?"

"No brainer, Lily. You ran. How do I know who you've been with?"

Lily leapt to her feet, joining him wearing holes in the floor. "You didn't just call me a slut?"

"No, of course not."

Crumbs if she didn't know better, she'd swear he blushed.

"How far along are you?"

"Not long. I'd thought you'd be able to tell. An experienced lover like you." Pent-up grief, anger, and loss exploded in her skull. "You've spent the night with your hands all over me." Her hand landed with a loud crack on his cheek. Furious, she went to do it again.

Daniel caught her wrist. "Not again, sweetheart."

"Let go of me. Get out of my flat, my life. Stay away from me."

"With pleasure. But you stay right here, Lily, until I get someone to watch your door."

"Fuck you!" Lily screamed.

CHAPTER THIRTY-FOUR

Fuck me! Really? Head pounding with a million places he would love to take that thought, Knight bypassed the lift, preferring to free fall, three stairs at a time, out of the fucking building. Momentum at his back, he didn't see Bill until he barrelled into the lobby and almost knocked the man for six.

"Whoa! Morning Captain."

"Sorry, mate, can't stop."

"No problem. But I've been meaning to give this to you. Ships that pass in the night, and all that. I missed it, hidden under the mess that muppet fill-in left me. Lazy bugger. Still, that'll teach me to get sick. Remember last year when I…"

"Thanks, mate." In no mood for a chat, Knight stuffed the piece of paper into his pocket, pulled up his collar and sailed into the rain. Tossed sideways by the wind, hail bit into his face. He felt guilty about leaving Bill hanging, but he'd make it up to him later.

Shit. A hand braced on the roof of his car, he sucked in the bitter air. Of all the ways he'd imagined last night panning out, Lily being pregnant hadn't figured. Fucking impossible. *Clearly not,* but he'd worn a condom and Lily said she used protection. *Sex Ed 101 knob'ed.* Nothing was one hundred percent conception proof.

Knight slammed the door of the MG and shoved his keys in his pocket. Given he wanted to tear up the motorway at a hundred and fifty miles an hour, driving wasn't a great idea. He hailed a passing cab, settled into the back seat, and headed for Doc's. If anyone had an explanation for this mess, he guessed it might be Kate.

"Where to, mate? How's your day been so far?" the cabbie asked.

Fuck awful. Knight gave him the address and slid the glass partition closed with a soft thud. Twenty minutes later, he pounded on Doc's door.

"Hi, Knight. What are you doing here? I imagined you'd be busy," Kate greeted him.

"Funny." He ignored her raised eyebrow, angled sideways, and brushed past her.

"Is Snake okay?" She called after him as he marched into their living room.

"Did Lily tell you she was pregnant?" Straight to the point. No use fucking around.

Doc frowned and cocked his head to one side. "Good to see you, Knight. Sit. Can I get you a beer? Whisky?"

Not a fucking answer. Tempting, the offer of a Laphroaig, Doc's favourite poison. He couldn't refuse. "Sure, whisky's good. Kate? Did Lily tell you?" he asked again. His eyes searched her face for confirmation he wasn't the only stupid prat in the dark.

Doc wound his arm around Kate's shoulder. "Easy, mate."

He got the message, Doc's not-so-subtle body language. Anger simmered in his belly. He sat at the table, breathing deep, trying his best to lower his rising blood pressure. Elbows on knees, he sucked in a breath and waited while Kate took her sweet time answering.

"Yes, she told me and Crystal." Kate brought Doc's hand to her chest and smiled. "If it helps, we guessed. And before you ask, I'm not sorry I didn't tell you. Why would we? It's not our news to share."

"When did she tell you?" He shoved his hands in his pockets and held on as his world spiralled.

"After you deserted her at the airport."

His fist flew from his pants and thumped the table. "What the hell are you talking about? Lily didn't need me. She saved Snake's life and boulder face here had it covered." He lifted his chin at Doc, who stuck to Kate like blue to sky and chucked him the death stare. "As operational lead, I dealt with Storm and the authorities."

Justified. Fighting back the conflicting emotions roaring through him, Knight knocked back the whisky Doc poured for him. Over-fucking-whelmed, his permanent state with Lily Storm. Fucked if he had the faintest idea how to handle it.

Coming through the door of the safe house, finding her shrouded in a suicide vest, knowing Pete was the cause, blew his mind.

"No Knight, own it. You ran. What was it, Luke?" She turned to Doc, who was busy pouring them both another drink. "Paperwork to catch up on. Please. After what Lily had been through? You know, I think of you as my grumpy older brother and I love, we love, your overbearing arse, but honestly now Lily's told you, if a baby scares you this much, run and don't stop. She is better off without you."

Kate didn't have a clue. His father's son. Men who destroyed women. "A father? It can't be."

"You shooting blanks? Now that's a turn up," Doc snarled.

Knight gritted his teeth and ignored the voice in his head, begging him to leave it there, keep his mouth shut. "Lily disappeared, said she left a note, but what the hell. She could have been with anyone." The poison in his gut finally spewed. Love didn't hang around for him. It ran, died before it lived. *Fuck.*

Kate shrugged Doc's arm from her shoulder and leapt from the sofa. Hands on the table, elbows locked straight, she came an inch from his nose. Impressive, a cobra poised to strike.

"Honestly, Knight? Do you believe the words coming out of your mouth? I'm not sure exactly what happened before Lily asked to go to Africa earlier than planned, only that Pete wouldn't leave her alone. No bloody secret."

"You were there when I gave her the ticket. She spent a few weeks with her friend Sam until she flew out of London. And, for the record, Lily is no liar, and you'd admit it if you weren't hell bent on shirking responsibility. If Lily says she left you a note, she did." Kate threw her hands in the air. "I expected more of you, Knight."

Knight didn't move, willed his world to swing three-hundred-and-sixty degrees and right itself. "Bullshit."

"No. Not bullshit. Or any other shit-shit."

"Easy, sweetheart," Doc said.

"No, Luke, don't sweetheart me. Thick head needs to hear this. Believe me, Knight, Lily is having your child. Congratulations." Kate grabbed his shoulder. "No shit." Her soft tone raised a lump in his throat.

Knight cradled his head in his hands, tried to squeeze sense into the space between his ears. "Fuck."

"Yes. No doubt that had a lot to do with it." Kate chuckled.

"And you, Doc? Got anything to add?" Ashamed, he stared at a point past his shoulder, not able to look his friend in the eye.

"No."

"Hard to believe."

"And I don't give a fuck. If you are happy to implode, destroy the best thing that ever happened to you, have at it."

"Yeah, cheers to you too." Knight skolled the shot of whisky in front of him and, with Kate hot on his tail, made for the door.

"Knight, wait."

"Let him go," Doc said.

Knight stood outside, staring at the muddy Thames, his fingers grasping the piece of paper Bill had given him. Lily hadn't lied. Kate, the whole sodding world, everyone but he knew it.

He raised his face to the pummelling rain and swallowed his tears. His head swivelled left and right, half hoping to see Lily. Blue dress, no coat, shivering, so he could hold her tight, and beg, yeah, beg her forgiveness.

He'd shared the best night of his life with her, come with a force that permanently altered his reality. Watching her fall apart in his arms, buried to the hilt in her wet heat, he felt like a million quid.

A baby. His baby. Everything good. His heart swelled. Corroded by his own nightmares, he had stormed out of her flat. Left her alone and vulnerable with that son of a bitch Pete still on the fucking loose.

Imprinted on his eyeballs was Lily's disbelief when she told him. Sure, he was angry, but there was no excuse for the words he regretted as soon as they left his mouth. Words could cause more damage than fists.

His father never laid a finger on his mother, but the verbal scars he left etched into her heart until she no longer wanted to live, not even for her son. Remembering her smile sent the blood rushing from his brain. His knees buckled. *What have I done?*

He loved Lily, and he had ruined the best damn thing ever to come into his sorry life. Kate was right, Lily and the baby were better off without him. She shouldn't give him a second… third chance… hell, he'd lost count, but he would camp at her door until she agreed to see him. Beg her for the honour of spending the rest of his life making it up to her, of being the best husband and father a woman could ask for. Lily deserved nothing less.

CHAPTER THIRTY-FIVE

How could any man be that pig-headed? Lily shuddered. Served her right for believing she might mean something to Daniel. Not everyone jumped at the idea of being a parent. She understood that, but when he questioned if the baby was his, the tendons attached to her heart snapped. Fine. They didn't need him.

Stuck in the apartment. The walls closed in on her. What she needed was air, space, a drive round the block. As she was rostered to open the clinic this week, Crystal had lent her the work car, so she didn't have to get up early. Lily snatched the keys from the hall table and headed out the door.

As usual, there was no one else in the concrete garage. Cold, empty. The place was always creepy. She lifted her chin and focussed on where she'd parked the car and glanced at the exit ramp, expecting to see Daniel striding towards her, livid because she'd left the flat. Not his problem. *Work. Damn it.* She pressed the remote a third time and swiped away her tears.

Lost in thought, she missed the shuffle behind her. Heard nothing until Pete slammed her against the car door.

Pain ripped across her hips and stomach. Determined not to

scream, she bit her tongue and tried to escape the hands groping her chest. "Get your hands off me." Digging her nails deep into her palms, she lashed out with her foot, aiming for Pete's shin, failing to hit her mark.

"Nice one, stumpy legs. Pity you're such a short arse," Pete snarled, grabbed her chin in one hand and twisted her face to look at him. "Look at me."

She closed her eyes. The pathetic act of defiance earned her more pain. Pete forced her arm behind her back and tightened his grip on her wrist. Jabs of fire shot across her shoulders.

"Get off me." Mind reeling, she sucked in a breath. *Think. Think.*

"Please, Lily. Pretty please. You know it turns me on when you beg." Spit slid from the corner of his mouth onto his chin.

Her stomach heaved, the acid taste of bile burning the back of her throat. "What do you want?" Pete pinched her cheeks together and silenced her.

"You bitch, Lily. But nothing I ever did was enough. Never satisfied, always whining, wanting more."

Her knees trembled. "I'm sorry." No way did she mean it, but it gave her time to think. Survive.

"Even when your friends told lies, and stole you from me, Lily, I never stopped loving you. You didn't think I could find you, but I did, and if Diarra hadn't been fucking greedy, we'd be together."

"Pete. You won't get away with this. The police know you kidnapped me. Let me go, please, don't make matters worse. Run while you have a chance," she pleaded, happy to fall on her knees to protect her baby.

"It's too late, Lily. You ruined everything when you fucked soldier boy."

Her body stiffened. If Pete guessed she was pregnant, he'd kill them for sure. If it were just her, she'd die rather than live a single moment more in this hell, but baby needed its mother.

For a second, the sound of the garage door opening, and the screech of tyres as another tenant exited the building, gave her courage. "Help." The words hadn't left her mouth before the back of Pete's hand slammed against her cheek.

"Not a word, Lily. Come with me or I will kill you right here."

"No." Dazed, she swallowed blood and watched the car disappear.

"Nooo?" Pete mocked. "You have no choice. If I can't have you, no one else will. Your choice. Say it. Say you love me."

"I never stopped," she stuttered. Bile lodged in her throat, but he'd never hear the word love from her lips.

"Lying will make me angry, Lily." His fingernail scraped the side of her neck, digging deeper until she felt the warm trickle of blood dribbling towards her chin.

Angrier than she'd ever been, she raised her chin and pulled on his jacket. He wanted close, she'd give it to him, knee him in the balls and... Another slap across her face knocked the idea out of her head.

"Say it, Lily. Say you love me."

Palms sweating, unable to take a full breath, her fear mounted. "You deaf? I never stopped." She gulped, the sobs threatening to choke her.

The back of Pete's hand hovered close to her jaw. "Careful, Lily liar. Get in."

Pete snatched her keys. Before she could run, he opened the driver's door, shoved her across into the passenger seat, climbed in behind her. Driving like a maniac, he tore out of the garage onto the busy main road.

Lily swiped at the blood dripping from the side of her mouth and eased the seat belt away from her waist. "Slow down. You'll kill us."

Pete swerved towards the pavement, slammed on his brakes, flung open the door and leapt from the vehicle. Lily's seatbelt locked, pinning her in place.

"You want to drive?"

Bloody hell. Air gushed into her lungs as the belt released. Ignoring the flashing lights from passing cars, Pete stood in the path of oncoming traffic, his arms spread wide. Eyes pinned on the keys dangling in the ignition, Lily shifted in her seat.

"Try it, Lily," he taunted.

She froze.

"Fucking idiot. You got a death wish or something?" A van driver swerved and shot Pete the finger.

Lily pressed her hand against the door, fighting to keep it from slamming. "Pete. Please, get inside before you get killed." As if she cared if he ended up as roadkill. Too dizzy from the slaps to her face, if she ran, she risked a car hitting her. She weighed up the odds and waited for a better opportunity.

"Don't want to drive?" Pete sneered.

"No. Let's go to my place." Fearing another back hander, she forced a smile and edged closer to her side of the vehicle. "We can talk."

Pete got back into the car and turned up the car stereo. "Okay, your place will work. You don't deserve it, but I'm willing to forgive you. We can plan a trip. Somewhere warm," Pete cooed.

Bloody certifiable. "Okay. Okay." Anything to calm him.

Pete swung the car into a screeching U-turn and headed to her building. If she could keep it together, they'd make it past Bill. She'd never be able to live with herself if Pete hurt him. He would. She saw it in his eyes. Violence poured off him.

Not wanting to risk antagonising him further, aware the least little thing could flip him completely, she stayed silent until they parked. She opened the door to the lobby, and her heart sank. Bill looked up from behind his desk. Quickly she pulled her scarf over her face, hoping to hide evidence of Pete's punches, and kept walking.

"Morning, Miss. Bit nippy out there."

"Yes. Make sure you stay in there and keep warm."

"Will do. Your tv arrived. Maybe your friend could help take it to your place?" He nodded at Pete, whose fingers bit into her elbow, urging her to not to stop.

"Thanks, we'll come back for it later."

"Right you are, Lily. I'll keep my eye on it."

They made it to her front door before Pete's foot slammed into her lower back, hurling her inside her home. Tadpoles of light swam in front of her eyes, but she had to keep it together. If she passed out, she may never wake up again. "How about I make us some coffee?" The thought made her sick.

"That's better, Lily liar, but first I want you to do something for me."

She screeched at the sharp tug on her hair as Pete pulled her to the ground and dragged her to the coffee table. Pinned between his thighs, the jute fibres of the carpet dug into the skin on her legs. Hands placed either side of her head, he ranted. "Why are you so cruel? Can't you see how much I love you."

Lily wiggled her jaw, wincing at the pain, but it wasn't broken. She swirled the tip of her tongue across her teeth, claimed a miracle when none were missing. The semi-darkness heightened her senses, every move playing out in slow motion.

Her gaze fell to the ultrasound photo on the coffee table, the one she had wanted to show Daniel. Swallowing the lump in her throat, she prayed their baby was okay.

"Eyes on me, bitch."

She fought past the nausea and pushed onto her elbows, did her best to block Pete's view of the photo. Too late. A spiteful grin twisted the lines on his face as he grabbed the photo.

"What's this, Lily?" Pete snarled.

"I don't know. It must have fallen out of a patient's file."

"Lily, liar. Who is it?"

"Please, don't hurt my baby," she sobbed and dug her nails deep into his forearms. If he murdered her, she'd make damn sure she saturated him with her DNA.

Pete undid his belt and sniffed the side of her neck as though she were the Sunday roast.

"You bitch. You fucked him. It's his."

"No, I…"

"Not another word, Lily. I am going to kill you and the kid. Then I will find action man. Take my time. Make him suffer for daring to put his paws on what's mine. Then I will kill him, too. Slowly. Or maybe I'll do you first. Make him watch."

"No," Lily screamed, and tried to gouge his eyes, but his weight fell on top of her, suffocating her. Head spinning, she kicked, but he held her thighs with his knees and dragged her skirt to her waist. The heel of his hand ground into the tender spot between her legs. *God, no. Please, no.* "Get. Off. Of. Me."

"If you had come back to me, I might have forgiven you, Lily. You ruined everything."

For the baby's sake, she willed her heart rate to slow. "We can still be together, Pete. Like you said. I'd love that drink. How about that G&T?" In her heart she knew it would never happen.

The son of a bitch smiled. Her terror turned him on, drove the sick fantasies percolating in his warped brain. He pulled on the hair wound tightly around his fingers and heaved her onto her knees, pushed her cheek into the carpet. Now she couldn't see her precious photo, she tried desperately to hang on to her courage.

"Look at me," he screamed, as he wrenched her head back, opened the zipper of his jeans, and frantically pulled on his limp penis.

If she never laid eyes on another man's dangly bits again, it would be too soon.

"Suck, baby." Pete kept one hand on the scruff of her neck and forced the tip of his penis to her lips.

Why. It never works. "No. I can't."

"You deaf and fucking stupid? Suck. Tell me how much you love it, Lily."

She closed her eyes and fled to the space in her heart, to Daniel and their baby.

"Pay attention, Lily. Do it right, and I might let you keep your nose."

The tip of a small knife stroked her lips. *Where the hell did he get that?*

Out of the corner of her eye, she spotted the African pot on the coffee table, a present from Aunty. Rage like she'd never felt took over every fibre of her body.

Doing her best not to gag, she lifted her head and traced the tip of her tongue around Pete's flaccid cock. His hips responded, thrusting in an awkward rhythm. His grunts grew louder, the corded muscles in his neck pulling tighter. She sucked harder, but nothing happened.

"Bitch. Suppose you'll say this is my fault. Why do I waste my fucking time with your pathetic mouth? I deserve so much more." Pete shoved her hard and pressed the knife to her throat.

A pinch and then a slow trickle of blood. If he cut her throat, it was over. Yelling, she grabbed the vase and smashed it against the side of his head. Panting hard, Pete fell to one side. Faster than she ever moved before, she scrambled to her feet, raised the vase high above her head ready to hit him again if he blinked. Pete didn't move.

Hands trembling, Lily fumbled with her phone and punched 999.

"Hello, emergency. Which service do you require? Fire, police or ambulance?"

"Ambulance… police. He threatened me with a knife. I killed him."

"Connecting you now. Stay on the line caller." The operator's voice faded away.

Terrified Pete might regain consciousness, Lily didn't move, her eyes fixed on his lifeless body until sirens blared in the street.

Bill stood in her doorway with two paramedics. "Lily. What happened, love?"

One paramedic grabbed her arm and walked her to the sofa.

"I hit him. He's been unconscious for…" Hell, how long? The paramedic checked his vitals and nodded at his partner. Lily sobbed.

"What's your name?" The paramedic reached for her wrist.

"Lily. Lily Storm. Is he dead?" Her head bowed in shame. The paramedic shook his head and relief fast turned to dread. The son of a bitch was alive.

"Relax Lily. Let them help you. I'll call the captain," Bill said, taking her arm.

His voice drifted away before she could tell him not to bother.

"Oh, oh, too late. Looks like we'll need another stretcher." Lily struggled to hang onto the paramedic's words, losing the fight as her world turned black.

CHAPTER THIRTY-SIX

Through half-opened eyes, Lily squinted at the stranger palpating her stomach. No windows, only the overhead fluorescent reflecting off his face. No clock to tell the time. She swallowed twice, trying to ease her dry throat, and flinched at the icy sting of his steel stethoscope.

Parked beside the bed were several machines. No wires attached to her body. Thank God. His Lily was tough. She had belted Pete over the head, left him bleeding and unconsciousness.

Her cheek throbbed from where Pete had punched her face. Lifting her head from the pillow, she strained to see over the shoulder of the man prodding her chest.

"Hello, I am Dr Khatri. You are in the A & E at UCH. Please, take another deep breath."

"Daniel?" Lily rasped. Her hand reaching for her sore cheek.

"Yes. Your husband is here."

Her stomach clenched. "I'm not married."

Uninterested in details, Dr Khatri grabbed the clipboard from the end of the bed. "You've had a nasty knock on your face. Any headache, dizziness…" His voice trailed away.

"Slight headache. A little dizzy, but I'm fine, I need to leave." One arm swept the sheet off her legs, the other clenched her stomach. The contents swam into her mouth.

"Please. Take it easy, Ms Storm." Emphasis on Ms. On a better day, she might have taken issue with his tone.

Beaten, body and soul, she tried not to heave the last thing she ate.

"You have a slight concussion, so your headache is to be expected. I suggest we keep you overnight for observation. Your husband says..."

Lily raised her eyebrow. Not this again. Despite the stabbing pain in her jaw, she opened her mouth to speak louder and thought better of it. She couldn't risk Dr Khatari asking Pete to join them. She folded her hands over the sheet. "When can I go home?"

"Will your husband, er, partner, stay with you?"

Not if I can help it. Lily reassured him she wouldn't be alone. She planned on calling Kate as soon as he left.

"Very well. I am sure I don't need to tell you but return to casualty if you experience any nausea or loss of consciousness."

"Dr Khatari. My baby. Is she okay?" For the first time, Lily felt as though she finally owned the tiny person growing inside her.

"Your baby is fine, Ms Storm, but you need rest."

Her head fell against the pillow. Tears welled behind her eyeballs.

"I'll write the discharge order. Take Paracetamol for the pain. I'd rather not prescribe anything stronger."

"Of course, thank you, Doctor Khatri. What time is it?"

He nodded at the clock she'd missed, just visible over the top of the curtain rail. "A little after 3 p.m. Take care, Ms Storm. Goodbye."

Gingerly, she swung her legs off the bed and put her feet on the ground. So far, so good. Until the room spun a full revolution. A long breath through her nose steadied her long enough to slip on her shoes before pulling back the curtain.

Unfortunately, any chance of avoiding Pete and sneaking out of the hospital disappeared. He stood next to a male and female police officer at the nurses' station wearing a turban of white bandage. The only sign of injury.

Her heart beat faster. Positive the police were there to arrest her she sucked a long breath in through her nose and wrapped her arm around her waist. *Okay, mummy can do this.*

Pete grinned at her as she approached. A young nurse stood beside him, smiling. Fresh out of college, judging by the colour of her uniform. The female police officer pointed at an office behind the counter. "Ms Storm? If we could have a word?"

"Yes, certainly." Sweat dripped down the back of her neck.

"You too, Mr Holdsworthy."

"Of course, officer."

Pete kept his back to the police, pushed past her, and flopped in a seat at the head of a small table. Backs to the wall, the police stood in separate corners. Lily chose a chair closest to the door. Easier for a quick exit.

Occasionally scribbling in their notebooks, everyone listened to Pete turn on the Holdsworthy charm. His list didn't stop. Forgive Lily, clumsy Lily with the over-active imagination. No, no knife. He even managed a tear for his pathetic wife.

The policewoman thanked him for his cooperation—cheers to the sisterhood. Shaking with mounting panic, words stayed locked in her throat. At least they weren't arresting her.

"Is that it, officers? It's late. I'd like to take my wife home." Pete's arm landed heavily on her shoulder.

"Yes. Unless there is anything else you wish to tell us?" The male officer stared straight at her.

Lily shook her head. No point. Too many times, she tried to tell them, but it only made things worse. The cops flicked their notebooks closed, convinced the call-out was a waste of their time. Another trivial domestic.

Lily bit her tongue, sucked in a breath, and clutched her mother's locket. Not enough air. *I can't breathe.*

"Time to go home, darling." Pete reached for the discharge papers sitting on the counter.

Her head swam with the effort to beat him to it and failed. Her hand fell limply to her side. "Can I have a minute? I need to use the loo."

"Okay, make it quick," Pete sneered, and the nurse frowned. He nudged the nurse's elbow and winked. "Time to take my poor wife home, put her to bed."

"Thanks." Lily hurried to the loo and fished her phone from her pocket. *Breathe, take your time.* Too slow. The thumping on the door made her jump.

"Need help, wifey dear?"

"No, I'll only be a minute. Dr Khatri said he'd leave me a prescription, but I must have forgotten to pick it up at the desk. Can you ask the nurse for it, please?" Her teeth ached at the saccharine sweetness in her voice.

Head splitting, she vowed to stay conscious long enough to escape. She listened until Pete's footsteps faded and called Kate.

"Hi Lily. I thought you were opening this morning. Where are you?" Kate asked.

"I'm at UCH Emergency." Lily braced a hand on the wall.

"What? Are you okay? Is Knight with you?"

"No. I tripped on the stairs. Not used to the mezzanine. Bumped my head, but I'm fine, next time I'll turn the light on when I go to the loo. I'm going home to sleep. Sorry, but I won't be in for a couple of days."

A pause, then Kate's voice broke the awkward silence. "Lily, how are you? Knight was at ours last night. He told us what happened."

"Oh." Exhausted, her head hurt. She didn't have the energy to deal with this hell. "It's Pete, he found me. I almost killed him."

"Almost? Shame you didn't. Call Knight."

"No." Lily lowered her voice.

"Do it, Lily. He will help you."

"I can't do that. He made it clear he wants nothing to do with me, us." Tears ran down her cheeks. "He thinks I lied."

"Don't worry. I put him straight."

"It changes nothing. I don't want to see him."

"Lily, Knight can be, is, an arrogant idiot, but he would never abandon you or his child. Hang up and I'll call him. Doc's here, we're all coming to help you."

"Time to go, Lily liar." Pete's voice rang through the door.

"No, Kate. I'll call you later." Lily hung up and moved too quickly. Before she could steady herself, her hand slid across the wall and landed on the floor beside her head.

"My wife. Someone help me." The bathroom door crashed open, and Pete knelt beside her.

"I am not your wife, arsehole," Lily hissed.

CHAPTER THIRTY-SEVEN

Knight skidded round the corner into Beaumont Palace and jerked to a halt outside UCH. "Where are you?" he yelled into his phone as he crashed through the entrance. No sodding parking, nothing new. They could tow the damn thing for all he cared.

"Inside, Boss." Spanner replied.

He kept moving, hoping they'd be by his side before he faced Pete, but it didn't much matter. Luckily, he'd been half-way to Lily's when Kate called. A quick turn and he'd made it to the hospital in no time. It didn't excuse the fact he should never have left her. Unprotected. Alone. He'd never forgive himself.

Sure enough, inside, Doc and Spanner were waiting for him.

"Where Kate? Okay, got it. Call you back, take it easy." Phone pressed to his ear; Doc kept pace with him as he bulldozed a path through the crowded foyer.

"Acute Medical Unit." Doc confirmed.

"This way. First floor," Spanner called out, halfway to the exit door.

Knight took the lead, cursing the fact he had no gun. Not that it mattered. His, any of his team's bare hands, were lethal weapons. Pete was a dead man.

"Lily Storm. Which room?" Knight slammed his fist on the counter at the nurse's station and shrugged Doc's hand from his shoulder. "Yeah. Sorry. Please. This is urgent."

"Seven-twenty-two, but patients are only allowed one visitor at a time, and she has someone with her."

Knight's blood ran cold. *That fucker,* he cursed under his breath. "Call the police," he shouted at the nurse. He nodded at Doc and Spanner, giving them the hand signal to position either side of her door.

Outside Lily's room, he wiped the sweat from his brow. "Stay here," he mouthed. He was going in alone. Gradually, he increased the pressure on the handle and slipped inside to face his worst nightmare.

Pete had Lily in a headlock, the tip of a knife pressed to her throat. Terror glistening in her tears, Lily smiled at him from Pete's headlock. *Bastard.* Any sudden move on his part could see the knife sink deeper into Lily's neck.

"Hey Pete. Put that down. Let's talk." *Until I can get my hands around your fucking neck.* Keeping his voice even, he stretched his arms wide. Back plastered against the wall, he edged to the left.

"Don't fucking move, soldier body. One more step and I'll cut Lily Liar's throat."

"And you'll never be able to close your eyes again. I'll be right there, mother fucker." Rage, bone-deep fear, burned like acid into his heart, when Lily lurched to the side and lashed out with her elbow, smacking Pete in the face.

"You bitch," Pete howled, shoved Lily to the ground, and kicked her once, twice, then held the knife above his head.

"No." Knight hurled himself at Pete, the force of his bodyweight sending them crashing to the floor. "You Fucker."

Lily screamed, instinctively covering her head and pulling her arms tight to her torso. In a blur, Daniel landed on top of Pete, his fists pounding his face. Blood and spit flew from Pete's mouth. His pathetic whimper echoed off the walls.

Terrified he might kill him, Lily grabbed Daniel's shirt and tried to pull him away, but he kept punching. "Stop. You'll kill him."

Spanner crashed through the doorway. "Boss. Enough." Together, he and Doc pulled him off Pete and kicked the knife out of his reach. Unmoving, Pete lay bashed and bleeding on the floor.

"He fucking kicked her." Daniel slumped against the wall, heaving, tears pouring from unseeing eyes. "Lily?"

"Here. I'm here." She crawled to him, cupped his face in her hands, forcing him to look at her.

"The baby. God, Lily, what have I done?"

She cradled his head against her chest and stroked his hair. "I'm okay," she wanted to reassure him, but her head was pounding and despite swallowing hard, she struggled to draw in her next breath.

"Doc," Daniel yelled.

"Thank you for coming for us," she croaked.

He gathered her close and tucked her face into the broad expanse of his chest. "You did a pretty good job on your own."

If Daniel left again, at least she'd have his smell imprinted on her memory. "I had a great, bossy, teacher. Sorry," she whispered as her eyes closed.

"See to Lily, Doc, I've got this son of a bitch." Spanner dragged the half-conscious Pete out of the room.

"Okay. Easy," Doc said. "Knight. Let me look at her, make sure she's okay. Lily, up here for me."

She leaned into Daniel as he helped her onto the bed. Holding her breath, Lily ran checks of her own, any wetness. Was she bleeding?

"Any pain, Lily?" Doc gently palpated her abdomen.

"Not much." She couldn't hide the wince. Pete's boot had hit a few old bruises.

"Doc?" Her hand crushed in his, Daniel stood on the other side of the bed, pleading for Doc's reassurance.

"Honestly, Daniel, I'm fine, just a little winded."

"Give her room, Knight. Maybe step outside a sec while I examine her."

"I'm not going anywhere. Ever again."

Her heart swelled. She knew before he spoke what his answer would be. Hands by his side, Daniel still touched that part of her she struggled to understand, the part that belonged only to him since they first met. How easy it had been at Abrakebabra. She wanted that again.

Despite what happened earlier, she didn't have the heart or the will to push him away. "Sit there, Daniel," she whispered, pointing to a chair by the window.

Without argument, he sat, but his eyes never left her. With the light streaming over his face, he reminded her of a little kid, adorable and sad. When Doc finished and left them alone, she wanted him close, where he belonged, for as long as he wanted to stay. "Come here."

Two strides and his mouth lowered over hers, peppering light kisses across her nose and top lip. When he sucked gently on her bottom lip her arms clasped the back of his neck, Ignoring the ache all over her body, she did her best to leverage him closer, take the kiss deeper, wrapping her arms tight around him as if she'd never let him go, knowing she probably must.

He blew out a breath. "Shit, Lily, I made a right bollocks of this. If I could start again, I'd do it. But I don't know how you can forgive me."

Mouth open, she stared at him. For a smart man, he was incredibly dim sometimes.

Daniel frowned. "I'm sorry. I'll say it as many times as you want. Better still, I won't stop showing you until you believe me." The corners of his mouth drooped.

Suddenly, the last few hours caught up with her. "I'm tired." She placed Daniel's hands on her belly.

"Okay. That's it. Talking can wait. Everything's changed, Lily. I never fell for a woman before I met you. My life was my job. I liked it that way."

Her eyelids weighed heavier than blackout curtains.

"Lily?"

"Mmm."

"It's okay. Sleep. Rest."

Barely lifting her head off the pillow, she looked around the room. "I can't."

"Why not? Doc says the baby's okay. You're tired. Get some rest." The hitch in his voice almost broke her heart. She cupped his face and stroked the stubble on his chin with her thumb.

"I'm scared."

"No need. Pete's gone. I'm here."

"I know, but I don't want to be in the dark. Need to stay awake and watch." It was getting harder to shove the words past the lump in the back of her throat.

"You have a few months before baby's here," he chuckled. "Even warrior princesses need to sleep."

"I can't," she sobbed, ashamed of how weak she felt.

"How about this? I'll stay right here, awake and watching. When you wake up, you'll do the same for me. Watch while I sleep. Deal?"

The concern, the gentleness in his usual gruff voice made it impossible to say no. "Deal."

Daniel turned his head sideways and laid his cheek next to her hand resting on the sheet. "I love you, Lily."

"I love you too," she said, not sure she heard him correctly, only certain she needed to tell him.

"Sleep. I'll take care of you both. Not that our kid needs me, with such a kick arse mother."

Lily shuddered. "Pete?"

"Gone for good."

"Okay. Wake me when it's your turn."

"Promise."

A smile spread across his face as she slipped deep inside with their little girl. Her heart finally able to beat.

CHAPTER THIRTY-EIGHT
SIX MONTHS LATER

Lily breathed in the sweet perfume of freshly cut grass, the top of her head nestled underneath of Daniel's chin, as they waited in line at the entrance of Regent's Park's open-air theatre. Convicted and locked up for a long time, there was no chance of Pete leaping out of the bushes. Finally, she could relax and enjoy getting to know Daniel better.

He told her he loved her a thousand times a day. Close to the end of her pregnancy, she was the size of Sam's barn, but he insisted she was the sexiest woman he had ever met. *Love is blind.*

The best part was watching him rub her tummy, telling her how much he looked forward to being a family and the long-slow love-making that inevitably followed. When she told him she suspected they were having a girl, he'd visibly paled and joked about already having a full-time job.

She could see him standing at the door, tapping his foot, trying not to look anxious as he waited for his daughter to come home from a date. The morning sickness, niggling headaches, and overwhelming tiredness had stopped, replaced by fat ankles. Very attractive. A month to her due date. To say she was looking forward to a glass of wine and dried crackers with creamy blue cheese was an understatement.

The breeze swirled around her shoulders, and she shivered.

"Cold?" One arm around her, Daniel's front pressed to her back, they swayed to the music drifting over the outdoor speakers.

"A little." Technically, the calendar said summer, but the evenings were chilly when the sun disappeared. Above them, a canvas of purple and pink clouds dashed across the evening sky.

Daniel's clean, manly scent excited her senses. "You smell nice, tonight." She rose onto her toes and kissed his cheek to reward herself with the salty taste of him.

"You always smell good." Daniel breathed the words into her hair.

Lily stared at his corded forearms. His muscular body oozed power from his calves to the thick muscles of his neck, but when he touched her, it was always with a gentleness that soothed her.

"I'm glad you didn't run a mile when I showed you the tickets." His nose nuzzled the side of her neck.

"Why would I?"

"Not everyone appreciates Shakespeare." He kissed her nose, a flash of uncertainty in his grey eyes.

"What? Who?" Lily tilted her head. "You did well." The tip of her finger grazed his bottom lip.

Daniel tensed, and the hardness of his erection pressed against her lower back. "As long as it doesn't bloody rain," he grinned.

"Don't worry, I'll shelter you. No melting men on my watch." She did her best to growl and offered a salute. "Oops, sorry wrong hand."

Daniel grabbed her hand and brought her fingers to his lips. "Insubordinate. I need to punish you with kisses. Wet kisses."

Transfixed by the gorgeous woman in his arms, Knight exhaled. The same need pulsing in his veins reflected in her eyes. A foot shorter than him, he loved her growing body.

"Punish me, please." Lily's words reached him on a hot breath, and he wished they were home in bed.

Bending slightly, he lowered the picnic basket and freed both hands. "Mmm. You must know what you do to me to Lily." Not a question, but despite initiating the lip-lock, Lily wasn't an exhibitionist. She wouldn't appreciate being ravished on the lawn. He chuckled. "Hup."

The line shuffled forward, and Lily wobbled. Steadying her with one hand, he grasped the basket with the other and led her down the steep steps to their seats.

"Front seats? Who did you have to shoot to get these?" Lily's gaze danced over the curved wooden stage.

"No blood spilt. An honest swap for cup final tickets."

"No, I don't believe it. You didn't?"

"Believe it, Princess."

"Thank you, it's beautiful." Lily's fragile fingers, certain and strong, circled his wrist.

He had to admit, bathed in warm pre-performance lights, the Midsummer Night's Dream set screamed magical. Perfect for what he had in mind. He tapped his pocket, made sure the ring was where he put it.

"Fancy a soft drink before the show begins?" he asked.

"Not unless you do. I'm happy sitting here. This is my idea of fun, people watching."

He didn't do nervous, but sitting in Oberon's fairy fucking kingdom, it hit him with the force of a tank. He would never survive if he lost Lily. So why he had to spoil the moment was a mystery. "Did you see anyone, Lily?" Head forward, eyes focussed on the empty stage, he waited for an answer.

Lily turned to face him. "You're joking? When?"

"Before, when we weren't together."

"No, Daniel. I haven't been with anyone else, not since the first time we made love."

Knight caught the tear trickling across her cheek and his heart dropped to his boots. He didn't think he'd ever understand how someone as perfect as Lily, could want a man like him.

Lily squeezed his hand, and God help him, he squeezed back. Grasped the only thing that made sense in his sorry life. He kissed her, every sweep of his tongue an apology. "Sure, you want to stay?" his words echoed in her mouth.

'... O, methinks, how slow this old moon wanes! She lingers my desires...'

"Shh, Daniel, it's started." Her palm pushed against his chest, not enough of her to shift him, but he did as she wanted, and turned his gaze to the King and Queen of fairies fighting it out on stage.

No way was she going to let his question ruin a perfect evening. How could she? If she was honest, she'd wondered the same thing. From now on, there'd be no one else for either of them. She knew that in every molecule of her being, but insecurities built over a lifetime didn't disappear overnight and she'd tell him at Intermission.

The minute the lights went up, a sudden, sharp pain radiated across her back and around her waist. Another wave followed by another robbed her of breath. Lily gripped her abdomen as another cramp tore through her.

"You okay, what's happening?" Daniel grabbed her elbow and steadied her.

"Baby's happening. I think it's time."

"Shit. It's too early."

"Tell that to your daughter." Lily grabbed Daniel's hand.

"Yes, right. Sorry. What do you want me to do?"

Pain ripped through her lower back. They must have rehearsed this moment a thousand times. "Hospital," she gasped. Luckily, she had packed her hospital bag weeks ago and placed it in the boot.

"Okay, okay. I'm here. Should I call an ambulance?"

Even as another cramp robbed her of breath, she smiled. Her big, bad warrior was white as a sheet. "No. Just get us to the car. I know women give birth in a field, but I don't want her to be born in a park if I can help it."

"Do you need me to carry you?"

"I must weigh a ton. Hell yes." She laughed, trying to make him lighten up.

"Er... breathe, Lily. Deep breaths, right?" Panting like a steam train, he swept her into his arms.

"Doing my best, hero."

"Crikey." Lily closed her eyes as another cramp ripped through her.

"Hold on, Princess, I've got you.

The night sky swam above her. Sucking in shallow breaths, she plunged headlong into oblivion.

EPILOGUE

"Show us your scar," Crystal said, her face beaming.

"Bloodthirsty, much? Leave the poor woman alone." Kate pried the edge of her nightdress from Crystal's hand.

"Okay, okay," Lily lifted the sheet and rolled up her nightdress to show the cut just above her pubic line from the emergency caesarean.

When the nurse came to take their daughter for more tests, Daniel had insisted she stay and rest while he went with their daughter. "They've been gone awhile. Do you think everything's okay?"

"Of course. Don't worry, it's only been half-an-hour. You know it's just routine for a preemie," Kate reassured her.

Her heart swelled, thankful to have such good friends surrounding her. After giving her such a fright in the park, baby decided coming into the world may not be such a great idea after all. Hours later, her blood pressure had shot through the roof, and they'd whisked them up to theatre.

"Mind if I have one of these, hun?" Crystal pointed at the box of chocolates Sam had sent her.

"Have at it." Lily laughed and checked the clock again. She missed them.

Except for leaving to shower and change, Daniel hadn't left their side. Her father had popped his head in briefly, wished them all well. The offer of his blank cheque book left her cold, but she thanked him, determined not to take a penny of his money ever again. She felt a little guilty. After all, if he hadn't called Daniel, she may never have left Africa alive.

"There you two are. Lily's been fretting We thought Spanner had found you and whisked you off for a meal." Crystal stood as Daniel strode back into the room.

Lily studied his face, looking for any sign things hadn't gone well. Wow, she loved this man. Sensing her worry, he kissed her on the cheek and placed their daughter in her arms.

"She's perfect," he said and kissed her again.

"Okay, we're going. Come on Crystal, let's leave this family in peace," Kate said.

Family. Lily's eyes met Daniel's. He slowly nodded.

"If I must, hun, but I'll be back later for a proper cuddle." Crystal called over her shoulder as Kate dragged her out of the room.

"Everything okay? They haven't worn you out?" Daniel perched his hip beside her on the bed.

"No." She looked at her daughter's scrunched-up face. It would be time for a feed soon.

"We will have to find a name for her soon, Lily."

"Yes, I've been thinking."

A frown creased his brow.

"Ozenda. Do you like that?" She couldn't resist teasing him. The look on his face? Priceless.

Fuck no, Lily couldn't be serious. He'd give her his life, but Ozenda. A step too far. Knight slid his arm around Lily's shoulder and stroked the side of his daughter's cheek. He loved the way she nestled against his finger. Hell, his hand swamped her head. His stomach rolled and his breath locked in his chest. If Lily found out how petrified he was that he might drop his precious girl, she'd never let him hold her again.

As she cradled Ozenda in her arms, *please no*, the neck of Lily's nightdress slipped over her slim shoulder, baring her delicate, pale skin. He bent and kissed the side of her neck, and almost caved at the love buried deep in her blue eyes. Eyes stinging with tears, he fixed his gaze on the sheet, not wanting to speak in case he destroyed the moment.

He didn't deserve Lily, and he'd never get enough of his family, but... "Lily, you know I love you. Are you locked on the idea of calling our daughter Ozenda?"

"No, darling, I'm not."

"Thank you." He let go of the breath he'd been holding.

"What was your mum's name?"

"Mary. But..." She brought two fingers to his lips, and he sank his cheek into the warmth of her palm.

"No more buts. Our daughter's name is Mary, and we love you."

He gasped. "Thank you, Princess." He pulled out the box that had been burning a hole there for days, waiting for the perfect moment. "Marry me, Lily?" He flipped open the lid and watched as her eyes took in the sapphire and diamond ring. The colour of the stone matched her eyes perfectly. No one had helped him buy this. "Say yes, Lily."

"Yes. Mary and I thought you'd never ask."

JUSTICE
SENTINEL SECURITY BOOK 3

Thanks for reading. If you enjoyed Saviour you can pre-order Justice (Sentinel Security Book 3) now.

https://books2read.com/u/47ODrE

A Man on a mission. A woman who walks alone. Two paths. One destiny.

John (Snake) Cole, the newest member of Sentinel Security, is working hard to prove he belongs with the team, determined to avenge his predecessor's death. With their enemy within reach, now is not the best time to meet the sexy woman who claims more than his attention.

Samantha Leigh lived her nightmare. Two tours in Afghanistan and she's done. Craving as much alone time as possible, she trains assistance dogs for military vets living with PTSD.

Snake and Sam didn't expect to find each other. When Sam's demons re-surface, and a child goes missing. Snake must decide who comes first, Sentinel or the woman who just might be his soul mate.

AUTHOR'S NOTE

Sign up for my newsletter at www.elizarenton.com to keep up to date with all news excerpts and freebies.

Or find me at

facebook.com/elizarenton

or

twitter.com/renton_eliza

How can you help authors if you liked their books? Tell your friends and family.

Consider leaving a review at your favourite online book retailer.

Thank you and happy reading,

Eliza

www.ingramcontent.com/pod-product-compliance
Lightning Source LLC
Chambersburg PA
CBHW020405120726
47904CB00002B/712